UNTAMED

REJECTED MATE ACADEMY
BOOK ONE

By
E. M. MOORE

Manufactured in the United States of America
First Edition April 2021

PA's: Affinity Author Services (Bibiane Lybaek & Ashton Reid)

Cover by 2nd Life Designs

Edited by Chinah Mercer, The Editor & The Quill

At the Buzzer

Rockstars of Hollywood Hill

Rock On

Spring Hill Blue Series

Free Fall

Catch Me

Ravana Clan Vampires Series

Chosen By Darkness

Into the Darkness

Falling For Darkness

Surrender To Darkness

Ravana Clan Legacy Series

A New Genesis

Tracking Fate

Cursed Gift

Veiled History

Fractured Vision

Chosen Destiny

Rogue

The Adams' Witch Series

Bound In Blood

Cursed In Love

Witchy Librarian Cozy Mystery Series

Wicked Witchcraft

One Wicked Sister

Wicked Cool

Wicked Wiccans

*S*orrow surrounds me like an unwanted hug.

I breathe in slowly, trying to temper the chaos of feelings brimming under my skin. Two Lunar Pack elders sit in the front seats of the most expensive car I've ever ridden in, and I just know their holier-than-thou asses are attuned to my wolf's emotions. Fucking pack bond. I would sooner sever it than have them read my pain. I focus outside the vehicle's window to hold it all in. Acres of moonlit grass lead to Greystone Academy's two stone turrets peeking above the centuries-old trees in the distance. Lunar Pack is incapable of flying under the radar. Glad to see that's true even for the place they keep their unwanted.

Rejected Mate Academy.

From the first moment I learned of its existence in

fourth grade Pack Civics class, I knew I would end up here. The note Bitch Queen Laura threw on my desk that day only solidified those thoughts. *Welcome to your future hell, bitch* was a lot harsher than the caption in my textbook: *Greystone Academy takes in ill-mannered pups for reform.*

That's me. Ill-mannered, and in need of reform.

Above those bland words was a black and white picture of the same sprawling structure looming in front of me now. What they don't describe in detail when you're in fourth grade is that when you arrive at Rejected Mate Academy, you'll be grief-stricken from a broken heart you never wanted. So, in essence, I guess Laura was right all along.

This *is* my new hell.

My wolf whines, and I bear down my jaw. I swear the Council elder sitting in the front seat gets a whiff of my suffering and enjoys it. His nose twitches before his lip quirks at the corners, and he drives even slower up the long, desolate road toward my new home as if to draw out my agony.

It's cool. I'm used to my own pack taking pleasure in my misery. Bunch of pretentious, know-it-all asshats if you ask me. But the elder taking me to this hellhole should be above the bullying and teasing, right?

Wrong. Because this ride of shame proves what everyone's been saying about me since I was a young pup.

I'm unwanted. Unloved. *Untamed*.

The blacktop road turns to gravel as the car inches past an ornate gate. Stone columns give way to an arch of iron flourishes that reads *Greystone*.

The name is well-known in my pack, supplying us with a long line of strong alphas. Greystone Academy was Silas' brainchild—the third leader from that superior bloodline who made most of our current laws, and in his tenure, built this enormous school while writing mandates that secured its use. Currently, Lunar Pack is on our tenth Greystone alpha. When I was little, I pretended I was the daughter of that strong line. After all, Greystone wolves don't get tormented every day of their lives. They're revered.

My mind drifts too close to the topic I would do anything to forget right now. My wolf perks up, but I shut that shit down with as much force as I can muster. My wolf and I have been at odds with most things. Hell, I'm not even sure we like each other, mainly because I've been avoiding her thoughts and feelings since she started to awaken. Ignoring shit is my coping mechanism. It's worked wonders for a very long time.

Today of all days, though, we might be the closest

3

to syncing. Still, she wants to think of *him*. She wants to relive the pain.

I'd rather die.

I smirk when my wolf gives me the cold shoulder. Have you ever given yourself a brush off? It's pretty freaking weird.

The height of the building as it comes into view draws me closer to the window. The stone turrets I spied before are impossibly tall and large, even from the ground. The gothic structure spans thousands and thousands of square feet. It's what happens beyond the exterior that scares me the most though. I can only recite the facts I learned from that textbook years ago. Inside these walls, rejected mates learn civility, obedience, pack mentality, more education or less education, basically anything a wolf needs to assimilate back into their own pack on the arm of the mate who rejected them in the first place.

I'm already calling bullshit.

The car slows, coming to a stop in front of an arched wooden door at the top of gradually inclining steps. The sparse evening light casts the medieval structure in shadows, reinforcing the gothic look the builders were apparently desperately trying to achieve.

Between the two turrets, the moon shines bright, and despite myself, the hair on my arms pricks, and my wolf gets restless. Electricity courses through the interior of the car. The moon coupled with this time of night is when our wolves are most alive. New shifters like me aren't expected to control their shifts. However, I've been disagreeing with my wolf for so long, we don't have that problem. Plus, she's sulking.

The pack elder in the passenger seat pushes his door wide. With a deep breath, I wrap my fingers around the strap of my book bag lying next to me on the seat. The door to my right opens, but before I can step out, the yellow wolf eyes of the driver catch on mine through the rearview mirror. Turquoise blue flares from his pupils, ending in a starburst of sunlit gold. His cruel smirk has me exiting the fancy ride quickly, and when I straighten, I stare up at the seemingly never-ending structure. *Just...wow.*

The main academy itself consists of four floors of gray stone. The steeples and turrets rise up from there like they're trying to touch the moon itself. Before tonight, the biggest house I'd ever seen was the alpha's. His, too, is rock built and large, but this massive structure dwarfs the biggest house in Lunar by far.

"This way," the gruff voice next to me orders. He takes off without bothering to see if I'm following and has already ascended the steps before I can make my feet move. I hike my book bag up my shoulder and march forward, quickly catching up so that when he yanks the huge, wooden door open, I'm only a few paces behind.

Our footsteps echo through the cavernous, stone halls. Every doorway that splinters off from this main artery arches high above us. A mixture of primitive and modern style meshes together with iron chandeliers and sconces for a design that is both impressive and classic. Voices drift down the corridor, but we're alone as we traverse the building that's half stuck in time. My wolf peeks her head up to admire our surroundings. It doesn't last; she settles back down with a whimper almost immediately.

I straighten my shoulders and do what I always do: put on a brave face.

"Ms. Ebon is your advisor," the Lunar Pack Council elder rattles off. "You'll be meeting with her to acclimate you into Greystone Academy."

A hundred questions burn my brain. Is this Ms. Ebon from Lunar? I've never met a wolf from another pack before. Was she rejected, too? Is that why she dares work with ill-tempered shifters like me?

For all the academy horror stories passed down, no tale went beyond its reason for existing. It was nightmarish enough that wolves were sent here, so there was no talk of what it was actually like once they stepped beyond the doors. Now that I have to call this place my new home, I'd like to understand more about it. Considering I had to leave my parents, my home, and my life—as pathetic as it was—against my will, I deserve some sort of guidance.

Attendance at Rejected Mate Academy is mandatory once you've been, you know, rejected.

A wave of fresh heartache pinches my chest. I mentally wall it behind a locked door to unpack later. If anything, I'm going to be the first student at Greystone that isn't wallowing in my own self-misery. I'll make sure of it.

The council elder stops at a door to our right, rapping on the wood, and a few moments later, a woman with long, raven hair stands before us. She pays my escort no attention, keeping her dark gaze fixed on me. "Kinsey Walker?"

"Yes, ma'am," the council member interrupts my own confirmation. "Lunar Pack," he grunts as if I'm a disgrace to his very being.

I guess, in actuality, I kind of am. *I'm* the reject—the wolf shifter the pack basically shunned. And to put the chocolate sauce on the turdburger, I'm also unwanted by the wolf I'm supposed to be fated to. My partner—my *mate*.

My wolf really whines now. The guard next to me

shudders involuntarily, but Ms. Ebon doesn't blink. She must have built up an immunity to newly-shifted, despair-ridden pups. If she's worked here for any length of time, she no doubt had to.

"Thank you, sir," she says stiffly. "I'll take over from here."

He retreats, his footsteps waning. I turn my head to watch him go. From when we're pups, we're taught pack above all else. We're taught pack before family even. The greater good. As the elder turns the corner, I don't know when I'll see someone from Lunar again. It doesn't matter that I disgusted him, my instincts warn me that this is wrong.

"You're going to be fine, dear," Ms. Ebon states. Her voice is sharp yet even. She has naturally thin lips with large eyes. Her straight hair is silky smooth, parted down the middle in long sheets like cascading water.

I watch her, my naturally suspicious nature rising to the surface. I've never been at home in my own pack, but I'm not sure I can trust this woman either.

She tugs the neck of her buttoned shirt down, revealing her brand, and my lips part in recognition. I have the same exact black, quarter moon mark on my clavicle. However, while hers is aged, mine sits stark in comparison. For most of my life, I hated the damn birthmark. Loathed it to my very core. Yet today, it's oddly comforting.

"I'm the Lunar students' advisor because I'm from Lunar Pack. The seven other advisors at Greystone represent their own packs as well." Stepping back, she gestures toward her office. It's a large space, filled to the brim with bookshelves and a huge, wooden desk. "Do sit in the chair just there."

Two eggplant upholstered chairs with high backs face each other. Pintucks gather fabric together under glassy, circle ornaments. It looks too nice to sit in but I do as I'm told anyway.

She takes a seat in the fancy chair opposite mine, her discerning gaze traveling down the length of me. I place my hands on the arm rests, attempting casual when this day has been anything but. In fact, it's arguably the worst day of my entire life. I just happen to be truly gifted at separating my emotions from my actions. A lesson taught to me at a very young age by my wolfpeers.

Her brow wrinkles. "You are an odd one, aren't you?"

I blink. "Excuse me?"

"My new students are usually crying by now."

I scoff. "Because one self-absorbed asshole goes against his basic instinct and rejects the one thing that's supposed to be fated in our entire lives? Gee, I can't imagine why."

The corners of her mouth quirk. "Yes, that about sums it up nicely. Most pups take it harder than you."

I relax back into the chair. "If you're expecting waterworks, save your tissues. I learned long ago that tears don't solve anything." I pretend like I'm not studying her, but I am. When I'm around another wolf in my pack, I'll usually recognize them as such—an inherent sixth sense that everyone in Lunar is born with. With Ms. Ebon, I don't get anything, and a piece of me wonders if it's because I've already separated myself from Lunar? Have I pushed my wolf so deep down that I can't feel my pack anymore? I wish the elder was still here so I could reach out to see if I'm going crazy.

"Excellent," Ms. Ebon notes. "Consoling is my least favorite part of the job. Perhaps we'll get right down to the business part then, shall we?"

A wave of trepidation hits me. Knowing I'd most likely end up here did nothing to prepare me. Wolf reform is about as vague of a descriptor as you can get. And in all honesty, Jonah—

My wolf lets out a howl of anguish. I moan, my fingers curling into the arm of the chair. I'd forgotten to curb my thoughts, and the despair drives into me so quickly I double over.

The truth is, I'd never felt anything like it before. The true bliss of shifting for the first time coupled with the overwhelming call of nature. The sense of family with my pack. Then, the hint of the most delectable smell on the wind. Pawing through the grass as fast as I could until I spotted *him*. A deep russet, shaggy coat. His ears alerted, and the most overpowering warmth cocooned me in acceptance and love. A feeling so foreign that it buckled all four of my legs, bringing me to the forest floor.

All rational thought left. Everything I'd told myself not to do. *Don't track. Don't look. Don't let your guard down.* My wolf had taken over, and she found him. Her mate. Her fate.

His rebuff will mark the lowest point of my life ten times over. A hundred times over.

I am nothing without him.

Ms. Ebon arches a brow. "You were saying?"

2

*H*ave you ever wanted to hit an authority figure? I have. Many, many times.

I stuff that urge—along with the growing grief—back into a small ball. My wolf bares her teeth, growling as if Jonah rejecting us is all my fault. I breathe out in a rasp once I've forced her to retreat, and when I glance up, Ms. Ebon holds a glass of water in front of my face. Grasping it, I give her a small "thank you."

She takes her seat across from me again, staring more curiously. When I meet her gaze with my own, she pulls a file into her lap and starts flipping through its contents. I instantly straighten, peering over, trying to catch a glimpse. It must be about me. What else could my advisor be doing during our first meeting?

When I spot the quarter moon in the center of a few of the papers, it dawns on me that it must be Pack Council letterhead. That, right there, is communication about me from my own pack.

I take another drink, gulping down half the glass before placing the cup on the side table. I wish I'd had more time with Mom and Dad before I left. We were too shocked for proper goodbyes. Mom didn't even start crying until I was forced in the back of the Pack car with no reassurance of when I would return.

Actually, that's a fantastic question. I clear my throat and peer at Ms. Ebon. "How long do I have to stay here for?"

She glances over the file. "Until you're reformed."

"That sounds vague. When will that be?"

"When you move through your appropriate classes and your mate"—she checks the paperwork again—"decides that he'll accept you."

I scoff. I don't mean to. It just comes out. Why the hell would I care if he wanted to accept me? What about what I want? Maybe I don't want to accept him.

"If you fail to do so, you'll be cast out of Lunar Pack, the other packs will shun you, and you will live Feral."

Oh right. Fuck. Sometimes I'm too stubborn for my

own good. I'll unpack my feelings about him later. This is much more serious.

My wolf barely reacts, so either I've majorly pissed her off or she's not listening anymore. While she pouts, real fear slices through me. If Greystone Academy was the cautionary tale of wolf society, Feral was the scary story told around campfires. No one who went Feral ever lived to talk about it.

Ms. Ebon still studies me, so I tap my fingers against the arm of the chair and nod toward the paperwork. "Is that about me?"

She flips the folder closed and offers me the entire file. "It is. It's communication from both the Lunar Pack Council and Jonah Livestrong."

My stare immediately tracks to her, questioning as she waits for me to take the folder. It doesn't seem likely that she would let me read what everyone has to say about me. Unless I'm missing something...

She shakes the manila folder. "Go ahead. I don't believe in keeping things from my students. You have a fight in front of you, young one."

I take the file from her, spying my name in elegant handwriting on the tab. My stomach squeezes. I try to stifle my nerves, but when I open the folder on my lap, my hand quivers. I have no doubt Ms. Ebon sees my reaction. She's been watching me like a hawk since I got here, and I'm suddenly well aware that she's most likely assessing me at this very moment. Maybe her opinion matters in this whole scheme of things—in my "reform."

I sit up straighter as I scan the first document. Mate Rejection Slip is typed on the top. I almost shut the fucking file right there. *Mate Rejection Slip.* Taking those words in makes me nauseous. Why would anyone reject their mate? Their true love? Isn't doing so like a huge slap in the face of our pack dynamics?

When you think about it, it doesn't make sense that I'm the one in here and he's out there. A growl crawls up my throat. It sounds like my wolf and I can find something to agree on. We might—well, *she* might crave him on some sort of instinctual level, but that doesn't mean we have to like him right now.

He's the reason we're here, and I'm not sure I can get over that.

If only fate had skipped me. I would've been happy as an unmated wolf. Fuck all this love and politics shit.

"Why don't you go ahead and read why your mate rejected you. It's in the big box at the bottom." My gaze tracks down the page. Curiosity brims at the surface, but I know anything he says is going to be the biggest bunch of bullshit. He doesn't like me because no one likes me. Because I'm different. Because they got it in their heads when we were pups that I wasn't like them. "Aloud, please," she instructs.

I snap my jaw shut. Apparently she wants my humiliation to be spoken instead of just internalized. I'd thought she was pretty cool, but I'm rescinding that assessment.

I clear my throat. "Kinsey Walker has never tried to become part of Lunar Pack. Due to my future position under the alpha, I don't believe she and I will be the perfect mating pair." My jaw practically dislodges. "I've never tried to become part of Lunar Pack?" I screech and then laugh. "He's kidding, right?"

She leans back, crossing her legs at the ankles. She looks so regal sitting there with her long, black hair against the purple chair that I calm my tone a bit as she narrows her eyes. "I don't imagine he is. He lodged the complaint with the Council, and he's aware what that would have done to him as well."

I glare at her. I really want to tell her that Jonah can go fuck himself. He's the one who brought this on both of us. In fact, I know a way he could've avoided this all together.

A trickle of unease rolls through me at that. You can't force mated pairs. It's the ultimate F-U to the universe. Hence the reason for Greystone Academy's existence.

What I don't understand is why it's always me that has to suffer.

"Why don't you tell me about Jonah's position in the pack?"

I blink down at the summary box. He's literally only written those two lines as if he wanted to give me nothing to go on. "Is it in here somewhere?"

"It is. I'd like to hear it in your own words, though."

I smile smugly. If I never tried to join the pack, how would I know anything about them? Living amongst the wolves who hated and feared me gave me a lot of time to watch, listen, and learn. "His family is third from the alpha. They've taken over alpha security, sometimes whole pack security and Council security, too."

My advisor presses her lips together, frowning. "A political position."

I roll my eyes. "Very."

"I understand his concern, then."

The bite of her words puts me back in my place. I keep forgetting where I am and what I'm supposed to be doing. Despite everything riding on this, I can't find a reason to fight for my fated pairing. I don't know how anyone who gets stuck here does.

Feral, my wolf reminds me.

Fuck. That's right. I shiver. Living solo means no

chance of survival. Lone wolves aren't equipped to sustain themselves. We persevere in packs. The shifter race has a long history—and a dwindling population—that proves this very thing. The solution to our problem? Fated mates. It's the only coupling that will breed healthy wolves. They're so important to our society that we do anything to protect them.

"No comment?" Ms. Ebon probes.

I eye her, still unable to figure her out. Is she on my side? Or theirs?

Hell, who am I kidding? I've never had anyone on my side.

Time to play the part like I've been attempting my whole life. "Yes, I can see that," I tell her. "His mate will have to be involved in alpha and pack business."

"Kind of hard to do that with a wolf who hasn't tried to be a part of the pack. The alpha's family has to trust you."

I stifle the eyeroll that threatens, but I don't quite curtail my tongue. "Why couldn't Jonah have mated with someone who they could trust, then?"

She tilts her head to the side. "You don't want a mate?"

I backtrack quickly. "No. No, I do," I lie. Well, it's not totally a lie. I never wanted a pairing from Lunar

Pack. Give me one from any of the other seven packs, and I would have been happy. I think.

She doesn't seem as if she believes me, and that's a problem. Saying I don't want a mate is like saying I deserve to be here, among other things. Like fucked-up, living feral things.

I clear my throat. "I was just wondering aloud that if fated pairings are essential to pack life, how come fate didn't pick someone who would've been a perfect match for Jonah? Why pick me when he was going to reject me?"

Ms. Ebon's brow furrows. She regards me for a long while before answering. "Your question is like asking why the moon dictates the tides. It just is."

Will I get smited if I think fate was wrong in this case? Because...hello, the proof is in the Mate Rejection Slip.

My wolf yips at me. Looks like there's one being in this body that doesn't think the universe played the wrong hand. Even so, the advisor's reasoning sounds like one of those "there, there" shoulder-rubbing scenarios, as if she's trying to talk down to me while also not having the real answer herself.

Or maybe I'm really not cut out for pack dynamics. My whole life I've been watching from the perimeter. I'm not sure if I was born that way or circumstances dictated that I put up a barrier between me and my pack, but from my position, I've been an outsider since I was too little to comprehend what the word meant.

"Why don't you turn to the Lunar Pack Council form?"

"The Council?" I hesitate, losing some of my nerve.

"Yes, every mate pairing gets a write-up. Most of the time, their forms are blank, but in your case, Kinsey, they have concerns about the pairing as well."

I tamp down a growl that threatens to burst free. I've never met anyone on the Pack Council, but I already know what this is going to be about. And if it is—

My stomach clenches.

Was everyone else right? All those times I fought against the lie, what if it was true?

I flip to the next page. The Lunar Pack quarter moon rests in the top center. This form is much like the one Jonah filled out, except for the letterhead, distinguishing the importance.

"Out loud," Ms. Ebon demands again.

I push my shoulders back and trudge on. I won't let anyone see me weak. When I scan the page for the box, it holds less information than Jonah's. The single statement says everything, though.

"Concerns about Miss Walker's lineage."

My wolf scratches to come out. This is the one thing she and I have always agreed on. A buzz starts at the surface of my skin. It turns into a prickling, as if I'm being tattooed over every inch all at once. I breathe through my nose, trying to calm myself as fur ripples down my arms and my back arches against the chair.

Ms. Ebon's authoritative voice rings out. "Calm yourself, pup."

The thing is, since my first shift was mere hours ago, it's hard for me to control her. I stand, the contents of the file spilling onto the floor, and my advisor gets to her feet with me, reaching out a steady hand.

I'm too far gone, though. I turn, running toward her office door and whipping it open so I don't wreck her room. I'm sure I'll already be written up if I shift within the very first hour of being here, but the punishment will probably be worse if I also destroy academy property in the process.

My ragged breaths deepen as I step beyond the threshold. I no longer hear voices in the halls, which is perfect because I don't need to look like a freak in front of my new wolfpeers.

My back arches again, bones cracking in place. When we were told transforming into our wolf hurt, they weren't fucking kidding. I yell, my human voice giving way to a long howl as claws slice through my fingertips. My body throws itself on all fours, and for a split second, I'm still fully human before my wolf takes over.

She shakes her head, copper fur billowing like a halo around her neck. Ms. Ebon yells, but my wolf is entranced by the most familiar scent filling her nostrils. Her head perks, ears driving up and forward. It's as if she's been acquainted with this aroma her whole life, could roll and play in it—

She takes off, claws digging into the slippery floor, skidding before regaining her balance. Her focus homes in on the figure rounding the corner ahead.

Mate.

Jonah's deep brown eyes widen as she careens toward him. Her keen wolf vision glimpses the emerald greens sparking through his irises. She sniffs the air. Instead of the beautiful scent she chased after, potent fear fills the air. She put the brakes on and careens across the floor, scrambling to stop her momentum.

Recognition flashes in Jonah's eyes and disappointment and anger teem to the surface, muddying his beautiful features. The look on his face is like getting rejected all over again.

My wolf throws her head back and howls her pain while trying to recover her balance. The hulking, disapproving figure grabs her by the nape as she slides toward him. The brief pleasure of being touched by her fated match is squashed when he spins her to her back and places a huge forearm over her throat, pinning her to the floor.

Gazes locked, her copper paws move to his shoulder, but he leans forward, cutting off her breath. She whines, the sound emanating from deep inside. From the point of all my hurt and pain. From the place where I piled every rejection, big or small. It comes alive and sours the air between us.

"Know your place," he growls.

3

*J*onah's features soften for a fraction of a second, and he eases the pressure. Even in my wolf form, he's stronger—bleeding authority and strength. My wolf tangles her paws around his arm as if she's giving him a giant hug, then licks his exposed bicep.

Instead of responding in kind, Jonah bares his teeth and growls. "Shift."

His commanding words rip me back into reality. My pained wolf retreats in spectacularly fast fashion, once again rejected by the person who is supposed to love her unconditionally.

My back arches, bones re-breaking before I've had the chance to forget about the last shift pain. Skin and limbs take over until Jonah hovers over my human form. "Back the fuck off," I pant, pushing at the arm that's over my throat.

He backs away, moving to a standing position and glaring down at me with cold, brown eyes. With my human vision, I don't notice the emerald in his irises as much. All I see is hatred and disappointment.

I get to my feet, only realizing then that I'm naked, a trail of tattered clothes in my wake. "For fuck's sake," he mutters, yanking his shirt off and offering it to me. He avoids my stare while I stand with hands on my hips, not backing down. "Take it, Kinsey. Christ."

With a huff, I tug on his shirt. It falls to my thighs, dwarfing me. Cocooned in my mate's smell, I feel at home, and I have to fight the smile that threatens to betray my inner emotions. My wolf, on the other hand, nuzzles against my chest as if she's trying to cuddle the shirt.

That's when I break. Surely him showing up at Greystone Academy is cruel and unusual punishment. "What are you doing here?"

Jonah's gaze sharpens. Wolf yellow irises rise to the surface before he controls himself. His wide torso and bulging muscles that are now on display prove why the Livestrong's were sought after to become alpha security. They're huge. Jonah's father is one of the biggest shifters—and subsequently humans—I've ever seen.

Jonah has his genetics, for sure. He's looked ages older than the rest of our wolfpeers since we were pups. He's broader, stronger, and taller. Next to him, I feel small which makes my flight or fight kick in.

"What am *I* doing here?" he hisses. "Why in the hell are you wolfing out in the middle of Greystone Academy?" The severe look on his face tells me all I need to know. He's disgusted. He doesn't care about my reasonings. He only cares how my actions will make him look to everyone else, and it's clear he thinks I can't control my wolf—or myself.

Ms. Ebon's high heels click on the floor behind me. "I see you have a shirt arranged. I thought we'd have to call the guards to retrieve our newest student."

"I'm very sorry for the inconvenience," Jonah offers her with a pointed glare toward me.

My advisor hands me a pair of Greystone Academy sweats, and I pull them on right there in the middle of the hallway. I don't mimic his apology. I'm not sorry. I've never understood the reasoning behind my ridicule. If the rumor behind my lineage is true, it's not as if it's my fault. Yet, I'm the one who takes the brunt of everyone's hurtful comments and actions. Like being here, for instance.

"I can't say I've ever had a student wolf out on me during our first meeting."

"I wasn't going to hurt you," I mutter.

"Oh, I'm well aware, Miss Walker. You just want to hurt everyone else."

Her words attempt to drown me in shame, but honestly, she's not wrong, so I brush them off. Why wouldn't I want to hurt everyone else? They've hurt me.

She nods at my mate. At least she gives him the same blunt treatment she's been giving me. Her heels click again, retreating. I turn, giving Jonah my back, and walk away, trying to get how freaking handsome he is out of my head. I told myself not to ogle his muscles, and I did a good job considering, but that doesn't mean his pecs aren't currently burned into my brain. Fucking damn him.

"I'll expect my shirt returned," Jonah calls out.

"I'll give it back right now."

He growls, the sound low in his throat. It makes me stop, the hair on the back of my neck rising.

"No mate of mine will be walking around topless."

I pull my shoulders back. "You rejected me, remember? I am no mate of yours."

My wolf bares her teeth again, but I'm on a roll now, so I ignore her. If I also didn't think walking around topless was a horrible idea, I'd whip the shirt off right here in this hallway to prove my point. I still have to continue my talk with Ms. Ebon, though. What a way to finish a meeting that started awkward. I'd be upping that factor by a few hundred notches if I went in tits out.

He doesn't respond as I turn into her office, closing the door behind me with a little more force than necessary. She's sitting in the same chair, waiting for me. I plop down opposite her. After a bit of time passes, she drops her gaze to the floor where the file and its contents are strewn everywhere and then back at me. I sigh, bending to pick it up before putting it all together on my lap again.

"Judging by your response, I'm going to assume what the Council wrote is a trigger for you." I grimace, and Ms. Ebon quickly responds with, "We don't have to discuss it today as you're not mature enough to control your wolf." Her eyes turn sad for the first time since I've been here. She leans closer, frowning. "Miss Walker, you are in a very dire situation. If you are found to have an unnatural lineage, you will not be able to mate with Jonah even if he should accept you. You will have to leave Lunar Pack immediately."

I blink at her, dread knotting in my stomach. "And go where?"

"Feral," she tells me, brows pinching. "You will not

be allowed in any of the packs. You will be shunned. For good."

I breathe in deeply, letting the air out slowly. Her words shouldn't scare me like they do. "It won't be a problem," I assure Ms. Ebon. "My parents told me I'm the product of their pairing." They've been telling me that my whole life, but it still hasn't stopped the rumors from flying—my mother's a whore; my mother had sex with another man after she mated with my father.

In the human world, cheating causes whispered rumors and catty remarks. In the wolf world, she may as well have signed my death certificate and my family's displacement from society. I can't tell you how many times I've stared at family pictures, trying to talk myself into the fact that I look like my father. *Dear God, let me look like my father.*

"Very well," Ms. Ebon says simply. "Your whole family will be under inspection from this very moment. For your sake, I hope they can prove your lineage."

I swallow the lump building in my throat. Mating with Jonah has pulled my parents into this mess again. The same mess that occurred right around the time I was born. "What's going to happen?"

Ms. Ebon leans back in her chair. "Pack Council business, I imagine. But I need you focused on your studies here. Since you're the product of the mated pairing, there is nothing to worry about except gaining favor with your mate."

Her words don't exactly help any. Once again, I want to scream. If only I'd gone without pairing. Why couldn't the universe have kept me unbonded? It would've saved everyone a lot of trouble. Now, my parents' personal affairs are going to be picked apart at length. Jonah will be ridiculed. And me? No one will ever think of me and the hell I'm going through here.

My advisor points to a spiral notebook I'd placed back in the file. "Those are the rules of Greystone Academy, Miss Walker. I expect you to know them before you start your classes."

"What classes?" I ask. According to the textbook all those years ago, I'll need some sort of lessons to ready myself for a fated mate pairing, and I'm not sure that's exactly doable.

"I will come up with your schedule, taking the recommendations from Jonah and the Lunar Pack Council into account."

I shake my head. Human history should tell us shifters that this sort of control is bad for the population. Nothing good ever came from it. "You're going to decide what I do here? So, as my other wolfpeers are going to school for real education toward occupations, I'm going to suffer through, what? Etiquette classes?"

"If you need them, yes," Ms. Ebon remarks. "Among other things. Every wolf who comes here is different. Many times, we don't have a particular set schedule that every wolf takes. We still have general education courses, by the way. It's all in that manual. Remember that the sooner you leave here, the sooner you can assimilate back into regular wolf society and go to the University your wolfpeers are attending."

On second thought, I'm not so sure I want to go to the University with all those assholes. It might be nice here with a little bit of freedom from everyone. And new people. I've never met anyone who didn't know everything about me.

"We have a fair graduation rate," Ms. Ebon continues. "Seventy-five percent of wolves are accepted by their mate within the first year."

At this moment, that favorable figure doesn't help. I can't imagine Jonah ever accepting me. In fact, my back still aches from his body slam. "How many wolves are cast out?" I refrain from using the word *Feral* as it always makes an icy sliver of fear cut down my spine. The idea of living that way has always taunted me since I was a pup.

"Twelve percent, Miss Walker. My personal number is much lower than that, and I'm not going to let you ruin my statistics. I expect you to conform. I expect you to try. I expect you to do everything in your power to get Jonah Livestrong to listen to his internal feelings instead of his brain. Do you understand?"

My lips thin. Everything in me says it's wrong that I have to try—that we're even having this conversation based on something I didn't do and had no control over. On the other hand, the consequence is nothing short of life-ending.

"I understand."

She stands briskly. "Excellent. Let me show you around, then." She reaches for the file folder in my lap and leaves me to take the thick notebook of rules and regulations. A painted picture of Greystone Academy covers the front. It's a shame such a horrible place is so freaking pretty.

I stuff the booklet in the lone book bag I brought with me. I was told to pack a separate bag that would be forwarded to my room. Despite myself, a nugget of intrigue blooms in my stomach. I've never been away from home. Never been away from the harsh comments and constant arguments. This seems like a way to start a brand new life.

Ms. Ebon opens the door, and I follow her out into the hall. "Pick up your discarded clothes, Miss Walker."

Trailing the clipped sound of her heels bouncing

off the hall, I pick up the scraps of fabric, placing everything in my book bag, and race to catch up to her.

She shows me the common areas first. The cafeteria and gymnasium are huge, at least five times the size of Lunar Pack School. The juxtaposition of old world with modern flares makes everything seem so foreign. "No one is allowed on the first floor after seven p.m.," Ms. Ebon instructs. "There are common areas in the different wings if you would like to socialize. I'm sure I don't need to tell you this, but there is no sexual fraternization of any kind. If you're caught doing so, both of you will automatically be cast out. It's not a problem we usually have since your instinct will forbid it, but it has happened."

"Well, there goes my plan for tonight," I joke.

Ms. Ebon stops, and I almost run into her backside. She turns yellow eyes on me. "That is the worst threat to our kind. I don't find that funny at all."

I nod once, feeling the dread in the pit of my stomach boil up. Trust me, I get the whole we-need-to-mate-with-our-bonded-one-so-we-can-prolong-our-race thing. It's another reason why I'm certain I'm the product of a mated pair. If I wasn't, I should've come out fucked up or something, right? Otherwise, what's the big deal? Despite my inner beliefs, her words ring around in my head. Could anyone really blame these

33

wolves for taking solace in another when they've just been through the biggest hurt of their life?

I guess in Greystone Academy's eyes, you can.

"Noted," I mutter, slinking back. I barely listen as she points out several more rooms in the tour.

Her reaction to my joke is just more evidence that I don't actually belong. No one thinks like me.

4

*M*s. Ebon leaves me outside a room in the Lunar Pack wing, handing me a rather modern-looking key despite the castle-like appearance of the corridor. The echo of her retreating heels bounces off the walls as she descends the winding, stone staircase, leaving me alone to peer inside my new digs.

It's bigger than my bedroom.

The bag I packed sits inside the doorway. Against the far wall, lying horizontally, is a full-size bed, and to my left sits a simple, dark wood desk. I suppose I'll be able to study whatever the academy feels necessary to learn in order for me to win Jonah's heart here. I fake gag, and my wolf practically rolls her eyes at me. At least she's paying attention instead of hiding in her own self-misery. To my right, a big TV is attached to the wall above a massive dresser. Adjacent to that is a closet and a door to my very own en suite. I don't know why I'd expected a roommate to be waiting for me. Maybe because that's how they depict dorms in movies? Thankfully, I don't have to deal with being around someone twenty-four seven on top of getting my heart broken.

Honestly, this room is ten times nicer than home. My parents are so far down the pack line that we have the worst house in Lunar. It's a small two-bedroom surrounded by woods. It's furthest from the center of town where all the other wolves live, but I've always loved how out of the way it is, like a built-in sanctuary. Plus, I love the expanse of land. There's so much space for growing my plants. I might have a bit of a green thumb, which is as weird for shifters my age as it is for humans.

Oh well. No one has ever accused me of conforming. Obviously.

Lunar Pack linens stretch across the mattress, our moon crest taking up the foot area of the charcoal comforter. The midnight-blue sheets are the perfect complement. I trail my fingers over the soft fabric, then plop my book bag down in the center. It's late, and I've had a shitty day. My eyes are itchy and begging to close now that everything is settling down. The shifts are getting to me.

Twice in one day on my first day. That's unheard of.

On top of that, instead of celebrating with my parents, I was sent away. At home, others are commemorating becoming one with their wolves, and for some, their new mates. I was so preoccupied with finding my own, and subsequently being rejected, that I didn't pay attention to who else mated.

In my world, today is one of the most important days of the year. Graduation from our primary studies is coupled with becoming one with our shifter form. It's symbolic to becoming adults. Even I was looking forward to my initial shift, and I don't look forward to anything pack related.

For a few minutes, my wolf and I were gleefully happy together romping through the woods. But when we caught Jonah's scent, everything changed. He sent us into a spiral, leaving us at odds again. Since I was a pup and she started to awaken inside me, we've fought. She wants to belong to the pack, while I've shied away because I knew what waited for me if I tried.

I unpack my things into the dresser, and in the process, find black socks and shirts donning the Greystone Academy crest already folded inside. I don't think much of it until I move to the closet. A whole slew of skirts and sweaters with the same crest are tucked inside. I pause, my fingers tightening around my one fancy shirt from home. "No fucking way."

I immediately bring out the booklet from my bag, scanning through the index until I find the dreaded word—*uniform*. I quickly turn to page seventeen, and sure enough, we're required to wear matching attire. A pleated skirt paired with a polo and a sweater in the winter.

A knock sounds on my door that I don't recognize at first because I'm in shock. It gets louder, and I march toward it, tugging the door open, prepared to tell Ms. Ebon exactly what I think about school uniforms. A petite, brown-haired girl has her hand up, preparing to knock again. When she sees me, her eyes round.

Instantly, my fury drains away and is replaced with apprehension. "Oh, sorry."

She chuckles. "Let me guess. You found the uniforms."

I track my gaze down her torso to find she's wearing the same sweats I am but with a Hello Kitty shirt. Prior experiences with shifters my own age have made me standoffish, so I narrow my eyes, waiting for her to talk first.

This new girl is undeterred. "I'm Mia," she tells

me. "Daybreak Pack." She hikes her thumb over her shoulder, indicating the far end of the hall. "I've been waiting for you to get here." Pulling out a basket from behind her, she shoves it between us. A box of tissues, an inordinate amount of chocolate, and a glittery unicorn journal are all packed prettily inside.

"What's this?"

"I made you a welcome basket. Though...." She appraises me. "Looks like you don't need the tissues. Most people are a hot mess when they first get here."

I lean against the doorframe. "Too pissed to be a hot mess."

She shoves the basket into my chest, forcing me to take it as she walks inside my new domain. She sits down on the foot of my bed like we've been friends for years. The hair on the back of my neck raises, and I wonder if this is what it's like to socialize with people. I've seen it from the outside, but I know nothing about friendly meetings.

Hanging out? Is that what this is?

"So, what's your story?" she asks, peering around my room. When I don't respond, she peeks at me. "You might as well tell me now. This place leaks like a sieve. We're all the castoffs, so we have to find consolation in each other."

"My mate rejected me," I answer stupidly.

She rolls her eyes. "Duh." Sighing, she says, "I'll go first. My mate is a piece of shit who's been dating the same girl for years. When we all shifted for the first time and he didn't get matched with her, he rejected me. Oh, and she rejected the mate she'd been fated to also. We're both here."

My mouth drops. "No shit." I had no idea people could be rejected for the dumbest fucking thing. Actually, I *should* have realized that. My rejection is fucking ridiculous, too.

"Your turn." She leans forward eagerly, brown hair falling over her shoulders.

"My mate," I snarl. Yep, still having problems saying that out loud, "rejected me because he thinks, and I quote, 'Kinsey Walker has never tried to become part of Lunar Pack.'"

She grimaces. "Harsh."

"Yeah. He's security for our alpha, so apparently he wants a mate who will just do whatever he says." I smile at the new girl. "That's never been my thing."

She smirks. "I like you, Kinsey. We should be friends."

My wolf lifts her head. Just when I think she'll most likely be avoiding others for the rest of our mutual life, she suddenly gains interest. Her ears flatten, attuned to what's going on. It's weird because I can feel the move rather than see it. Evidently, she loves the idea of being friends with another wolf, even if we're not in the same pack. "I'm not going to lie, Mia. I've never been friends with anyone before, so I'll probably be a lot more trouble than it's worth."

She laughs, the sound ricocheting around the bare room. "Don't take this the wrong way, but you're the weirdest wolf I've ever met."

If it weren't for the light in her eyes, I might have taken offense, but really, I'm fine with that assessment.

I hold up the basket. "So, chocolate?"

"Girl, I thought you'd never ask."

I break open all the bags and have a seat on the bed next to her. "Best part about being a wolf," I proclaim, shoving a piece of chocolate into my mouth, "you never get fat."

"I went on an eating spree once, just to make sure. I swear, I ate so many freaking calories I almost didn't touch food for a month. It was around the time when that human swimmer Michael Phelps was all over the news for eating an insane number of calories a day. I was sure there was a threshold where I would start to put on some fat. Nope. Nothing."

My wolf likes Mia, settling down as my possible new friend and I go back and forth about the positives of being a shifter. Before long, I lean against the wall and study my new surroundings. Reality starts to set in. There are a bunch of cool wolf things, but I'm stuck at Greystone Academy. "How long have you been here?"

She presses her lips together. "I'm not a good one to ask if you're wanting a Cinderella story."

That makes sense. The fact that she's here means things aren't working out for her. A blush creeps up her cheeks, and I hurry to assuage her worries. "Hey, I'm not going to judge. None of my pack likes me, so...." I trail off, hoping she gets what I mean. I'll probably be here forever, too.

"Over a year." She clears her throat, her face hardening. "He's pretty fucking stubborn. He only shows up for his mandatory meetings, and we don't even talk."

"Mandatory meetings?"

She wipes chocolate from the corners of her lips. "It's all in your manual. Pass me a pillow, would you?" I reach over to grab her a pillow, and she stuffs it behind her back before reclining against the wall. "Basically, there are mandatory meetings, almost like family visitation in human jail. Mated pairings are forced together to make it work. A lot of us try, and he pretended in the beginning, but that only lasted a few months."

I mull over her words and what she's previously

told me about how she ended up here. Fated mates aren't allowed to be with anyone else. "But..." I hedge, not wanting to call the only person who's attempted to befriend me a liar, but something doesn't add up.

"But why would he keep shunning me when he can't technically be with her? Good fucking question. I can't seem to get it out of him."

I shake my head. "That's fucked up."

"Truly," she snarls.

I bite my lip. At least I don't have to contend with another girl in the picture. For all Mia's bravado, that must hurt like a bitch. Whatever our brains might want, our wolves—our very nature—will only want our fated mate. "I mean, they can't be... together," I say, putting it delicately. I'm well aware of this shifter rule since it's the very reason I'm looked down on.

"They're not supposed to be fucking, but who knows? I'm not there to spy on them."

"Christ, Mia. That means—" I cut myself off. I don't need to tell a girl I've known a whole five minutes that she's going to end up Feral. I'm sure she already knows. "How long do you get here? To make it work before...?"

She shrugs. "Your mate has to officially fill out a form that states there's no hope for your pairing. He hasn't done that yet. Trying to 'spare me'."

"Fuck him," I growl.

"Cheers to that." She holds up half a Snickers bar, and I toast her with my Dove chocolate.

A warmth spreads through my belly and over my limbs. My wolf sits up—as interested in this new friendship with Mia as I am. I never let her have the chance of bonding with others back in Lunar, so she's already anticipating running free in the forest with Mia, jumping over tree branches and wrestling in fields. Hunting down prey. You know, wolf stuff.

Me? I'd love to just sit and watch a movie with someone. Talk boys, maybe. A big part of my life was taken away when no one wanted anything to do with me. A smile forms on my lips as I realize I *am* talking boys with someone. Sure, we're discussing how they dissed us, but it still counts.

"Your advisor probably told you to read that whole Greystone Academy manual, and you should. Just in case you were thinking of bailing on it like I did. It's actually pretty informative." She crumples up the Snickers wrapper after she finishes the last bite. "No one ever thinks they're going to be in here long, but...." She shrugs.

"Well, I was thinking of skimming it, but if you say so."

She smirks and shimmies toward the edge of the

bed. "Tomorrow, I'll introduce you to a few people. It's not all bad." She reaches inside the basket she made me and pulls out the tissues. "Looks like I need these more than you, though." A sad smile tugs at her lips while she moves toward the open door, clutching the tissue box in her fist. "I'll stop by before breakfast, and we'll go down together. Yes, you have to wear the uniform. Roll up the hem a couple of times."

She winks, and I nod. "Night, Mia."

"Goodnight, new friend. I'm at the end of the hall if you need me."

I wave to her, and she disappears behind the closing door. With a groan, I collapse on my pillows, kicking the basket of chocolate off the bed in the process. I glance out the unopened window to my left. Hundreds of twinkling stars dot the night sky, and a blanket of clouds roll in, partially obscuring the moon. On days when it felt like I was kicked by everybody, I'd enjoy a night of dumb comedies on TV with my parents in our small, rundown house. Everything on the outside wouldn't matter because at least we had each other.

Loneliness creeps in, seeping to my very core. I sit up to sift through my bag and find my cell phone. A couple of texts in the group chat I have with my parents wait for me. **Be strong, Kinsey**, my father writes. My mother responds with, **I love you.**

I take a deep breath, willing myself not to cry. **I love you both**, I text back. **I'm settled in my room for the night.**

After I hit send, I shut my phone off. I don't want to be disturbed by sad messages the whole night which might make me want to march down to Mia's room and take back those tissues. I've been dealing with shit my entire life, so I can take this, too.

As soon as it's quiet, however, pain sinks in. My brain replays the absolute elation filling my very being upon realizing I had a fated mate. *It's natural*, I tell myself as I bask in the warmth of the memory. But afterward, when the rejection plays out over and over again, it rips my heart in half. It's so cutting that I'm thrust out of my own body. Mate rejection is abnormal. It's wrong.

Well, if Jonah Livestrong can fight off his own instincts, so can I. The thing is, giving in to my stubbornness will ruin me. I'll be relinquishing my family, my life. Can I really do all that to get back at my supposed mate?

Christ, I'm only nineteen years old. This is some heavy shit to unpack.

Despite trying not to, I fall asleep to Jonah's handsome face. Each time I attempt to wipe it away, it reappears. Memories stick out in my mind of Lunar High: Jonah the big jock; Jonah in the inner circle with the future alpha; Jonah never looking at me twice until we shifted for the first time.

I hope his head is as filled with me as mine is with him. That should teach him a lesson.

Ignoring all rational thought, I burrow down into the shirt he gave me. His scent helps me drift into a dreamless sleep.

5

"Knock, knock, Newbie," Mia calls through my closed door.

I woke an hour ago, unable to sleep any longer with the weight of today sitting heavy on my shoulders. The first thing I did was tear Jonah's damn shirt off, hating that I used it as a lifeline last night. I threw it in the back of the closet and slammed the door shut, hoping I'd forget about it.

However, a half an hour later when I went to dress, I saw it all crumpled up and decided to pull it out, fold it, and sit it on an interior shelf. The good news is, my closet smells delicious. The bad news is that it's Jonah's scent. And right now, I can't stand him.

I rise from the bed and slip my phone into my bag. When I peer down, I don't even recognize myself. I woke so early, I had time to blow-dry my hair until it landed in auburn waves over my shoulders. I'm in a pleated, midnight-blue skirt, a tucked-in, black polo shirt, and sensible flats. I feel so bleh. I'm more of a t-shirt and jeans kind of girl. I can't even remember the last time I wore a skirt.

Pulling the door open, my new friend Mia waits on the other side. She studies me, starting at my feet and working her way to the crown of my head. "Did you roll it twice?" she asks.

"I'm kind of tall. I only rolled it once."

She shakes her head. "Roll it again. This isn't a convent."

I smirk. "Won't Ms. Ebon yell at me if I screw with the school's uniform?"

Mia widens her eyes. "Shit, I forgot you had Ebon. You should probably lower it, actually."

I scoff. "Yeah, I'm not that much of a rule follower, I just don't want my ass hanging out. Who invented this outfit? The director of Britney Spears' *Baby One More Time* video?"

"We could be so lucky." Mia holds out her elbow. She chuckles when I hesitate. "Come on, girl. Bring it in. This is normal."

I laugh at myself for being weird. Who would've thought I'd have to meet a girl outside my pack to show me what it means to actually have friends? "Like this?" I slip my arm through hers.

She pats my hand playfully. "I'm about to introduce you to the other misfits. Everyone likes to talk about how this place is all fucked up, but the people are nice. I mean, we all have something very important in common. The hard days are when your friends get to leave and you're stuck here. They don't let you keep in touch."

I kind of expected that, but a twang hits my gut anyway. Mia and I are very new friends, but I'm already hoping she doesn't get to leave, which is horrible. If she leaves with her fated, she gets to go back to society instead of becoming Feral, so I should be hoping she does.

While we walk to breakfast, Mia gives me the real lowdown on Greystone Academy. "Daybreak and Lunar are in this wing, second floor." When we get to the first floor, she points down a hallway identical to the one we came from. "Horizon and Eclipse Packs are that way. The opposite wing accommodates the other packs. Moonstruck and Twilight on the first floor. Galaxy and Sunflare on the second."

More voices echo through the cavernous halls. The closer we get to a place with activity, the more my stomach clenches. I tell myself that Mia's right: we're all here for the same reason. We're all outcasts here.

We round the corner, entering the cafeteria. My short peek into this room last night didn't do it justice. Rays of sun shine through an enormous glass room, illuminating everything in a halo of light. Stone columns run up the walls, anchoring huge plates of glass that continue up and into a vaulted ceiling. Decorative ironwork melds the plates together. It's absolutely breathtaking. And in my opinion would make a way better greenhouse than a cafeteria.

My gaze drifts to our right where I take in a buffet line filled with steaming food, and a kitchen just beyond that. How is this Greystone Academy? It seems way too fancy for rejected shifters.

A squeal pulls my attention away from the room itself and finally settles to the people scattered about the tables. I stop, making Mia grind to a halt as well. I blink at the scene before me, taking in the other students dressed like me. "How many people go to Greystone Academy?"

Mia peers out over the semi-filled tables. "About fifty at capacity. Our numbers start to dwindle as the year progresses."

Fifty fucking rejected mates. That seems impossible. How many people are willing to do this to someone else?

"Some wolves don't stay very long. Rejections can be caught up in pack politics or power plays." She leans over and lowers her voice. "You should hear the dumbass reasons some of us are here. The dumber the rationale, the sooner they get to go back. There are a lot of faces here now, but a third might return within a month."

The fact that anyone would use fate as a power play boggles my mind. I knew I hated people. I swallow at the new information. "How many wolves from Lunar are here?" I quickly scan the tables for anyone I recognize but come up empty.

"One."

Okay. One. Let's see.... I start to scan again but stop. "Wait,"—I turn toward my new friend—"I'm the only one?"

"Your advisor's kind of a freak." Mia presses her lips together. "She has a very good reputation."

A warning tingle shoots up my spine even though that could mean good things for me. My wolf doesn't like it either. Her ears perk up, paying as much attention to what's going on as I am. Let's hope Ms. Ebon's only an overzealous advisor with an uncanny ability to bond mated pairs back together and not the kind that likes to send wolves Feral.

"This way," Mia says as a guy stands from a table in the middle of the room and waves at her.

She waves back but leads me toward the buffet line, which has so much more food than I ever dreamed of eating for breakfast. I'm usually a cereal-in-the-morning kind of girl, but there are so many choices. Eggs, bacon, toast, pancakes, yogurt, fruit, and an entire cereal section. Determined to get something out of my stay here, I load up on bacon and pancakes, then grab some fruit, too. Our last stop is the drink counter where I'm bombarded with a bunch of juice choices along with milk, chocolate milk, and strawberry milk. I opt for chocolate and then follow Mia further into the glass room.

I get caught up into peering at the clouds hovering in the sky that I almost walk right into a table. "Woah there," a masculine voice calls out. I glance over at him, and he grins at me. "New here?"

"Very."

Mia nods toward the oblong, wooden piece of furniture that almost made me a klutz. It's massive and must be at least ten feet in length. Benches run up and down the sides, so I take a seat across from Mia and the guy who stopped me from making an ass out of myself.

"This is Nathan," Mia tells me. "The other shifter in my fucked-up love quartet."

I grimace. "That sounds like a nightmare. Sorry guys." They watch me as I pick up my fork, and it's as if I'm on display in a store window. I've never eaten breakfast with anyone but my parents. Hell, I've never eaten inside a cafeteria with anyone before. During lunch at Lunar High, I took my food outside and ate by myself.

"What are you in for?" Nathan asks.

He's a handsome guy with dark hair and a line of stubble down his cheeks and across his jaw. He's not as built as Jonah, but no one is. Just looking at him, I can't imagine why no one would want to snatch him up. The same goes for Mia, too.

When I tell them as much, they laugh.

Mia clutches her stomach. "That made my whole week. My whole month. I'm going to tell my little sweetie pie asshole that the next time I see him."

Nathan chuckles and rolls his eyes. "You do that." He bites into an apple and peers back at me. "So?"

Oh, right. Me. I blush. I'm really screwing up this friend thing. "I'm Kinsey. Rejected for not fitting in, I guess."

Mia helpfully supplies the true answer. "Her mate said she didn't ever try to fit in with the pack."

"And he thought that sending you to the place for the ultimate castoffs would change that?" Nathan squeezes the apple in his hand until it splits in half with a crunch. Mia pats his shoulder while he drops the remnants of it right onto the table and glances away.

Behind us, someone sniffles. We all turn to find a girl with blonde hair entering the room. Complete despair mars her face as she peers around, wide-eyed. We instantly sober. My wolf mirrors the girl's emotions, mewling inside me. I rub my chest, and Mia frowns. "It'll get better."

"Sometimes worse," Nathan adds unhelpfully.

Mia hits him. "Don't tell the newbie all the bad things."

He doesn't listen. His face sours as he watches the blonde girl. "Wait until the first counseling meeting when you see him for the first time since the rejection."

He's not kidding about that. Last night in the hall, the same horrible despair ripped through me. "I already saw him again." I place a sliver of pancake in my mouth and start to chew. It takes a moment for me to notice that they're staring at me slack-jawed. I hurry and swallow. "What?"

"You saw him already?"

I shrug. "During my meeting with Ebon, I kind of

shifted. Accidentally, of course. I ran out into the hall, and he was there."

Mia grabs Nathan's arm. "You fucking shifted in the academy?"

Heat blooms on my cheeks. I peer around to make sure no one's listening to us, then turn back. "Yeah, it was an accident. I got mad."

Nathan watches me quizzically as if he can't figure me out. Mia picks up on his face and says, "I know, right? I dropped by her room yesterday. No tears."

"You have a heart of steel." He studies me even further before staring right into my eyes. "Even I shed a few tears on my first night."

"Please, you were a wreck," Mia points out, poking him playfully.

I glance down at my plate. "Just used to people not liking me, I guess."

Nathan groans. "Sorry, Kinsey. I didn't mean anything by it. I'm shocked is all. I'm sure your mate is an asshole."

"Aren't they all?" Mia muses.

"Yep," Nathan sighs, popping the p. "Perfect, hot assholes with an ass that just, mmm," he bites down on his knuckle while his eyes seem so far away. "I could sink my teeth into it."

I guess his response answers one of the questions I

woke up with. Judging by the looks of longing on Mia's and Nathan's faces, it doesn't get any easier to think about your fated mate. "This isn't fair," I grumble.

"Aww, you already figured out Greystone's true motto."

The corner of Nathan's lip curves up and then flattens. "The fucked-up part is, if she walked through those doors right now, I'd be on my knees in front of her, begging."

His words cast a somber feeling over the whole table. Eventually, he demolishes the rest of his food and gets up. He doesn't even utter a goodbye, but both Mia and I watch him leave. My heart feels like an anchor in my chest as he walks past the crying girl at a table all by herself, grabs strawberries from the buffet, and drops them next to her. She peeks up at him gratefully, and all he does is smile and nod before leaving the room.

"He goes through mood swings," Mia informs me. "We all do. One day we'll want to rip their throats out and roll around in their blood. The next, we just want to jump them."

I spin back toward her. "Is there anything you guys can do about your situation?"

Mia heaves a sigh. "We've tried, but nothing yet. We're the ones who ended up here, so we're supposedly the less trustworthy ones. We literally have no sway here. No rights. We're at the mercy of our mate. I hear that's a thing that happens now. Newly fated wolves write up a Mate Rejection Slip so the other can't do it to them first. Then, they sort everything out during the initial meet and greet."

"You're kidding."

Mia shakes her head. "Happens a lot in families who've had a sibling end up here. Think about it, your brother or sister is banished to Greystone and then goes home to tell you how awful it is. To save your ass, you fill out the form so it can't be done to you."

Fear trickles in. Rejected mates is a much bigger problem than I ever expected. "It can't be that hard for someone to watch your two mates back at Daybreak and figure out the truth, though."

Mia's face falls. "You're forgetting the other part to the bond, Kinsey. If we do that to them, and they're cast out, made to go Feral, what will that do to us? Sure, we might be leaving here, but only to face a life without the one thing that's supposed to hold us together." She shivers.

I blink at her. I never thought of that. We really are fucked here.

Mia lets out a breath. "I know. Heavy shit. It's always heavy shit. I hope you brought Xanax."

We eat in silence until a woman in a business suit approaches our table. Mia gazes up first, and when the woman clears her throat, I peer up, too. "Miss Walker, Ms. Ebon would like to see you in her office when you're done with breakfast."

My heart sinks. "Thank you," I tell the woman.

Her friendly smile unnerves me. I watch her leave, and Mia informs me it's the academy's secretary. She works for all eight advisors, and of course, the head of Greystone.

"Who's the head of the academy?" I ask, kicking myself for falling asleep instead of reading the manual.

"Sister to your alpha." Her lips thin. "She hates all of us."

My stomach plummets, and everything I just ate threatens to come right back up. That would be Lydia Greystone—the worst accuser of my parents' relationship.

That's fantastic. The woman is already predisposed to hate me, so this should end well.

6

*D*eflated and annoyed, I trudge to Ms. Ebon's office after breakfast. Mia has to give me directions, but there are handy signs on some of the walls, so I should learn my way around sooner rather than later and not have to ask where I'm going all the time.

I knock heavily on the gigantic, wooden door. "Come in," she calls.

The door creaks as I swing it open. Ms. Ebon stays behind her desk and gestures toward the chair across from her. I take a seat, the wood protesting under my weight. When I asked Mia what she thought my advisor wanted to meet me about, she said she didn't know but guessed it had something to do with my schedule if I hadn't gotten that yet.

Instead, the first words out of Ms. Ebon's mouth shock me. "I need you to fill out this questionnaire about Jonah." I take it from her, and after quickly scanning it, I peer back at her with a frown. "Are you kidding?"

"That's the second time you've asked me that. I'll once again assure you, Kinsey, that I have a very important job to do. My methods work, so if you would please fill out the questionnaire, I will share some information with you."

I tap my feet against the floor and read through the paper again. This is different than anything I could've imagined. *Do you find your mate attractive? What could your mate do to help you find them more attractive? Do you like his/her personality?* This sounds more like I'm signing up for online dating.

I study Ms. Ebon from the corner of my eye, but she's already moved on to other work. This seems like a freaking waste of time. We're talking about fate here, right? What does it matter if we find them attractive when it was meant to be?

With a sigh, I resign myself to filling the form out. I pluck a pen from her mug of writing utensils and get to work.

Do I find Jonah attractive? A part of me wants to get revenge and say "no, he's a petty asshole." But

Jonah is a god, to put it lightly. I've always lusted after him, to be honest. Every female wolf did. It's actually shocking that Jonah would have a problem with his mate. Which means, obviously, I am the problem, aren't I?

The form leaves a huge space for me to answer the question, but I don't feel particularly loquacious about this topic, so I just write **Yes**. It kills me to do it.

What could your mate do to help you find them more attractive? I smirk. Ha. That's easy. **Don't be a dick**, I write in the box. Then, because apparently I am talkative about this topic, I keep going. **It would be nice to have a mate that was open-minded and wouldn't jump to conclusions. I find that really sexy.**

Do you like his/her personality?

Ha. Another good one. **Not particularly. I was treated like an outsider since I was a pup due to something that's not true and completely out of my control.**

I tap my pencil against the wooden desk, thinking. My statement is entirely accurate. However, thinking back, Jonah was always nice and respectful to others. I can't remember a time when he participated in talking shit about me either. He didn't stop it, but he didn't actively participate. He just ignored me. I bite my lip and add: **But I saw him be nice and respectful to other people, so that's not all that bad.**

I fill out the rest of the form, trying hard not to roll my eyes at some of the other questions, including *What would you want to do on a date? What do you like to eat? If you could go anywhere, where would you go?* There are more questions concerning him, too, as well as abstract ones like *What would you want in an ideal guy?* To that, I answer: **Just someone to come home to that will accept me for me.**

It's a little too much like a dating profile, but I go with it. Ms. Ebon has awesome statistics, so she must be doing something right. At least, I have to tell myself that because the alternative is too scary.

"Finished," I tell Ms. Ebon.

She holds her hand out. "Excellent."

I pass the form back to her, and she reads it over while leaning in her chair. I take the time to study her room more. There are a lot of textbooks about human personalities and interpersonal relationships. She has one book that stands out called *The Study of Love.* Maybe I need to check that one out. I could use some pointers.

I want to smack myself as soon as I think it. The warring part of my personality is arguing that we shouldn't have to work to be someone else for our *fated* mate. This is all bullshit.

Ms. Ebon stands. "Come with me, dear." She walks from her office, and I follow. Other shifters traverse the halls now. Everyone peers at me curiously but shies away from Ms. Ebon. It's her stark appearance, I think. She's very prim and proper. She doesn't look like someone who ever lets her hair down to have fun.

When we're at the end of the hall, she swings a door open, clutching my file to her chest. I walk in and freeze. She nudges me further, the big door thudding closed behind us. We're in a salon. A legit salon with a wall full of mirrors, a barber shop chair, and beauty magazines. The place smells like hairspray.

"Come sit," Ms. Ebon demands, gripping the back of the salon chair.

I stare at my frantic blue eyes in the mirror surrounded by a plain face. I always envied the girls who wore makeup. I was never big on it because I assumed it would make me stand out, like I was trying to conform, but also because makeup wasn't in my parents' budget. My auburn hair ends in waves past my shoulders. Since I actually styled it today, it looks pretty awesome.

My feet are lead weights as I slowly trudge toward

the chair. I step up on the little, silver footrest and sit back. Ms. Ebon looms above me. She studies my face, and I just know I'm about to get a rude awakening.

If I filled out that paper, so did Jonah.

Maybe he prefers blondes? Someone thinner? Bigger? All I know is that I really shouldn't fucking care, and if my advisor is about to spout some bullshit on making me look like Jonah's ideal girl, I will not be responsible for what happens.

"This is my own little studio that I use on my advisees. You already filled out the questionnaire, so you've probably guessed that Jonah filled out the same one. You'd be correct."

My stomach twists. I shouldn't have eaten all that food this morning.

"Would you like to see what Jonah wrote about you?"

My eyes narrow. I stare straight into my reflected eyes as if I could see inside my own soul. Everything in me is screaming *Fuck no*. Instead of swearing freely, I smile at my advisor through the mirror. "No, thank you."

She takes out the paper and shoves it into my hands anyway. "Too bad."

I don't want to look. *Please don't look.* But curiosity gets the better of me. I glance down. Sure enough, it's the exact same form I filled out minutes ago, neat hand-writing penned across the page. I read the answer to the first question.

Do you find your mate attractive?

His answer: **Yes. Kinsey is beautiful. She just never lets anyone see it.**

I choke on air. Is that air? Because I'm pretty sure it's not supposed to be this hard to breathe when I've been doing it all my life.

"We're here because I want to leave anything further up to you. For the record, if he had written that he didn't find you attractive, I never would've shown you the paperwork."

"Yeah, well, how many of them actually say they don't?"

She grimaces. "A fair few do but appearances aren't everything. Love can be borne from many things. Eventually, you start to find things to love about your partner that you never saw before. Maybe the pig nose you said they had becomes the thing you love about them most. Personality quirks. Conversation. I bring my students in here because I believe that confidence does a lot for the soul." Ms. Ebon studies her own appearance, and a slow smile creeps across her lips. "This part of the process isn't for your mate. It's for you. I have a hairstylist, a makeup artist, a designer on call. Would you like a change? Or would you like to stay the way you are?"

I press my lips together, and our gazes meet in the mirror. "Is this a trick question?"

"Absolutely not."

I give her a short nod and then study myself. "I love my hair," I tell her, pulling my auburn strands over one shoulder. Then, I look at the plain features of my face, and my gaze drifts toward the beauty magazines where girls are all wearing makeup and look completely put together. "I've never had makeup. It might be fun to try that. I don't have any money, though," I tell her.

Ms. Ebon settles her hands on my shoulders. Surprisingly, her touch soothes me. "It's absolutely free. Our pack cares a lot about our wolves. I'm getting the feeling you may not have experienced that before, but I hope that you will here. We're strict, but it's for a reason. Give me one second, and I'll get my makeup artist in here."

She turns her back and sends off a text. Within minutes, a supermodel walks into the room. She has dark, wavy hair that falls to her shoulders. She smiles, her lips painted in a pink that looks absolutely fantastic against her darker complexion. "Look at you," she says. Immediately, she gathers my hair back, running her fingers through it. "What a beautiful mane. Let me guess, you're a red wolf?"

I nod. "Red like fire."

"I bet you're gorgeous. I'm black, obviously. We would be like flame and smoke standing next to each other."

Ms. Ebon butts in. "Grace, this is Kinsey Walker. She's interested in your makeup expertise. Why don't you go ahead and explain to her what you want, Kinsey?"

I blush, but all Grace does is wait for me to speak. The back of my neck heats, and my fingers curl around the arms of the chair. It feels weird to have people looking at me and not telling me what a disgrace I am. It's kind of nice.

"Well, I've never worn makeup before. I was kind of hoping you could teach me how to put it on. Maybe a natural look so I don't, like, stand out?"

"So the exact opposite of me?" Grace asks, striking a model pose in the mirror and pursing her lips.

I laugh. "I'm not sure I could pull off pink." I cringe because I honestly don't know what I could pull off. "I just don't want people staring at me, you know?"

"I hear you, girl. I got this." She turns to the corner of the room where a whole beauty bar awaits. Her gaze tracks back and forth from my face to different colors and then she returns with a whole mess of things I only know by name from TV.

She goes through step-by-step, keeping the look minimal like I asked. She doesn't just put it on for me, she teaches me how to do it myself. She applies the makeup to the left side of my face while I do the right using her technique. When we're finished, I stare in the mirror at someone who looks like an upgraded version of me. A slightly refreshed, invigorated version that's somehow still me.

Grace runs her finger under the side of my lip where I messed up a smidge of the natural red color. "There," she finishes. "You're so pretty, Kinsey. You were already pretty before, now you just have a little snaz added." She drops my new makeup items into a bag and hands it to me. "Good luck getting your man back."

She spins and leaves, and I'm left frowning at her through the mirror. I'd somehow forgotten I was in here for Jonah. It felt like I was at some luxury spa, and here I am, being thrust back into reality. "I didn't do this for Jonah," I say to no one in particular.

"I know you didn't," Ms. Ebon states. "Like I said, this was for you. Come on, we have other things to do today."

I swing the bag by my side as we walk from the

room. There are a few stragglers in the hallway once again. They all stare at me, and this time my cheeks bloom, most likely darkening the very little blush we applied.

I spend the rest of the meeting with Ms. Ebon reading what else Jonah said in the paperwork. She tells me it's a way of getting to know him without all the pack pressure surrounding us.

At odds with her words, I don't actually feel any pack pressure. All I feel is distrust and hurt.

His words on the sheet in precise, careful hand-writing only eases my worries a little. He's quite open and authentic, which makes me glad I filled it out the same way. His only real complaint is that I don't act as if I'm in a pack. Our initial meeting is going to be an eye-opener because I'm not going to be quiet when we have that conversation. I didn't do anything wrong, and I won't have a problem telling him so.

If they want me to lie to get into Jonah's good graces, that's not happening.

When I get back to the Lunar and Daybreak wing, I peer down its length. I don't know how many Daybreak wolves are here, but I know I'm the lone Lunar. Dozens of doors line this hallway, and I'll be happy if most of them are empty. In a way, though, it feels like I'm secluded again, singled out for being different.

My nose twitches when I open my door. Jonah's scent is everywhere, emanating from the closet. There have only been a few times in my life when I haven't appreciated my superior sense of smell. This is one of them.

Placing my new makeup on the desk, I drop to my bed and disregard the enticing aroma. I need to get some Greystone Academy manual reading done since I lied to Ms. Ebon and told her I'd already started.

But before I begin, I turn my phone on, expecting there to be texts from Mom and Dad. I'm not disappointed. They have always been the hovering kind. They believed they could shelter me from the shitshow that was my life. In a way, it was nice to have them always asking me how I was and making sure nothing happened at school that day. But when I got into my preteens, parents sticking their noses into school situations only made the bullying worse. According to my wolfpeers, not only did I deserve to go Feral, now I was a tattletale. So, my parents haven't known what I've dealt with as I got older. The constant name-calling, the ostracism. I kept it all to myself. I think they wondered why I never had friends over, but they were probably happy about that, too. One less person around meant one less person to explain things to.

Instead of answering each of their messages, I decide to call the house phone. My mom picks up like she's just run a mile. "Kinsey?"

"Yeah, it's me." I shake my head. My mom has this uncanny ability to know when I'm calling. When I was younger, I thought it was magic that she always knew when I was calling. But when I got older, I realized it was because no one else ever calls them.

Time drags on like an anchor trudging through sludge while I wait for her answer. "How are they treating you?"

"Well," I breathe, "my advisor is okay. I think. She's going to do her best to get Jonah to accept me." My face burns as I say it, and I can't mask the mixture of horror, disbelief, and uncertainty. Especially not to my mother.

"I can't imagine what you're going through." A choked sound bubbles in the back of her throat. "Your dad and I never wanted this for you."

Well, of course not. No parent would want this for their child. It just is. Instead of going into that, I change the subject. "I made a friend. She's from Daybreak. She's been here a while."

"I don't know if making friends is a good idea, honey."

I bite my lip and roll toward the wall. As usual, I evade and avoid. "The rooms are nice, and I have my own bathroom," I whisper. "We have to wear a uniform."

"Kinsey, what are they telling you?" Mom asks, as if she didn't hear what I said.

My stomach twists into a tangled knot and squeezes. I was trying to avoid this conversation, but seeing as it involves the Pack Council, I don't think I can. If my parents are going to be investigated, too, they should know about it ahead of time. "Well, there are two different things. Jonah says he rejected the bond because I never tried to make myself part of the pack. Since his future job relies on the pack alpha, he wanted me to come here to reform."

"And the second?" Mom asks, and I'm no emotional expert like Ms. Ebon, but I can guess she's already figured it out.

I sigh. "Mom, you know. My advisor let me read the form from the Council, and their opinion on my bond is that I have questionable lineage."

My mother's breathing deepens before panting filters through the line. Like mother like daughter with angry shifting. Shifters can move into their wolf form at will, but during certain heightened emotions, the shift can take hold of us, and we can't stop it. We're supposed to be able to—especially someone my mother's age—but apparently she's beyond control.

"Calm down," my father's voice demands in the background. A weening cry sounds from the phone and then the line muffles. I sit up in bed, clutching a pillow to my chest. Two seconds later, my father pipes up, "Kinsey?"

"Yeah, it's me. Is Mom okay?"

"She needs to go for a run. She hasn't gone in hours. She's been waiting to hear from you."

I don't bother telling my father what Mom and I talked about. They're mates, and despite the fact that he was right next to her, they can also communicate telepathically. I used to hate that fact when I was a kid because they would always have silent conversations in their heads, mainly about bedtime or if I could get dessert, and I'd always be stuck in the dark.

Thinking about my childhood makes my heart ache. I always saw their love. The accusations that my mother strayed outside of her bonded mate seemed like such an out-there theory.

"I know this is hard, Kinsey. Your mother and I will convince the Council...again. You just need to worry about Jonah because we want you to come back to us."

A howl sounds in the background, and a jagged crack splits my heart. "I love you, Mom," I whisper.

"She knows. We both love you."

My mouth feels thick, like my tongue is too filled with the truth to speak, and my father won't want to hear it anyway, but I can't stand not to be honest with them. "Dad, it's not fair. I'm supposed to win Jonah back when he—" My voice breaks.

"Kinsey." Dad's voice hardens, taking me off guard.

"You love Jonah. Jonah is your mate. This is a hiccup in the beginning of everything you will be together. Think of all the shifter babies you'll have. How you'll bless the pack. It's a miracle. You'll do anything to fix this, right?"

His voice is strained so hard it could cut steel. He's never spoken to me like this before. I pull the phone away to make sure I'm still talking to the right person. Sure enough, the screen reads *Home*.

That's not true anymore either, though. Greystone is my home now.

"Right?" my father insists.

"Right," I respond, matching his own tone. "I'll talk to you later, Dad."

Right before I hang up, I hear his long howl that gets cut off when the line goes dead. I groan in frustration and throw my phone on the bed. Those weren't my dad's words. He was saying them, but they weren't *him*. It was as if he was trying to convey something to me in them. Maybe I should be as steadfast as he is. It doesn't matter that it's not fair. If I don't find a relationship with Jonah, I'm gone. That's the reality of the situation.

A knock sounds on my door. Mia and Nathan's voices filter toward me, so I call out, "Come in."

They enter the room as if we've been doing this for weeks. Months, even. Relationships made here are fast-forwarded since you never know when that person might leave. Mom said she didn't think I should make friends. Is this why? Because I'll miss them when I'm gone? Or because making friends means I've resigned myself to staying here? I wish I'd had the opportunity to ask her before she lost control.

"You look...sad," Mia hedges.

"Just having an existential crisis," I mutter.

"Oh, did someone only now realize where she is?"

Nathan laughs while he sits in the chair in front of my desk, and I smirk at Mia as she sits on my bed. Another form follows them into the room, and I cut off my reply and stare at the newcomer. It's the girl who was crying this morning in the cafeteria.

"This is Nadia," Mia informs me. "Horizon Pack."

During Shifter History at Lunar High, I learned about the eight different packs, but I've never once traveled to any of them. That's for the alphas and the higher-ups. The rest of us stay within our own, making sure the pack itself is self-sufficient and sustaining. It would be nice to see some of the others one day.

Nadia waves, and even that is sad. My heart goes out to her. Maybe if I was normal, I'd be broken, too, just like Ms. Ebon suggested.

"What's this?" Nathan asks, peering into the bag on the desk.

My face colors again, heat creeping up my neck. "New makeup."

"Forgot to pack it?" Mia asks.

"Nope. Today, Ms. Ebon took me into the salon. Apparently, I'm lucky enough that my mate thinks I'm good looking, but she asked me if I wanted anything anyway."

Mia blinks at me. "You *what*?"

"The salon? You know, with the hairstylists and the makeup artists?"

She shakes her head. "There's no salon."

I give her a dubious look. "Um, yep. Grace did my makeup."

Mia flies to her feet and stands in the middle of the room, her hands turning to fists. "You're kidding me. You got a makeover?" She leans into my face, and I pull away, hitting my head on the wall.

"Space," Nathan warns Mia.

She automatically backs up. "My advisor never offered me that. What the hell?"

I peer around the room. Nathan's gazing at me expectantly. Nadia seems interested, too. "Seriously? So, no one gets the same treatment here?"

Mia groans, throwing herself on the bed again. "No, all the advisors have their own way of doing things. Damn. I wish I'd gotten that opportunity."

I press my lips together, nibbling them in thought. Ms. Ebon certainly seems as if she has her own unique style. Now I feel bad that I brought it up.

"So, what's this about your mate thinking you're good looking?" Nathan asks.

Again, my heart swells of its own volition, no matter how much I try to temper it. "He filled out a questionnaire, and Ms. Ebon showed it to me."

"I bet that felt good," Nadia offers, speaking up for the first time. Her voice is so low and sweet. My head snaps toward her, and she nearly jumps.

I've been trying not to process how that felt because I didn't like the initial wash of warmth his compliment gave me. My mate thinks I'm beautiful. A twist of pleasure sinks into my chest. I seek out my wolf, wondering if it's coming from her, and it isn't. It's coming from me, which makes it worse.

Nadia's lower lip wobbles. "I'd kill to have any kind of information."

My eyebrows draw together as I watch her dissolve into tears. I sit there while Mia goes to her, giving her a hug. I peek at Nathan, and he's staring at the new girl with pity and something akin to understanding. My wolf sighs, watching the show with a tortured expression. Her own feelings overwhelm me, and I push them down again. Is it wrong to think that I've already given my pack enough tears? Spending any on someone who's supposed to be my bonded one screams wrong.

Eventually, Nadia sniffles, and Mia gives her a little space. She whispers something to the new girl, and Nadia gives a soft smile and nods. "Sorry," the new girl chuckles nervously after she's pulled herself together. "I can't seem to stop crying. My advisor told me to come back when I did, so hopefully that will happen soon. I can't wait for the first meet-and-greet where I get to see him again." She swallows.

I harden my heart. It's as if I physically reach into my chest cavity and squeeze the pumping muscle to keep it from wrenching further apart. I'm nothing like this girl, but that doesn't mean I'm a heartless bitch. I feel for her. "I'm sure everything will turn out okay," I offer.

I've never had to console someone before, so hopefully my attempt doesn't ring insincere. I feel for everyone in this place, but it's not pity or grief—I'm mad on their behalf.

"Let me walk you to your room," Mia suggests. She leads Nadia out with an arm around her shoulders. "See you tomorrow," she calls out behind their retreating bodies, waving over her head.

"See you tomorrow," I agree, frowning at my manual. I guess it's time to get to work.

Nathan stands. He lingers at the door until their footsteps start echoing down the stone hall. "Nadia's *mate*," he snarls, "...is her best friend."

"Wait. What?" I snap.

"I know," he growls. "Fucked up, isn't it?"

"What a dick." My hands sink into the sheets. What kind of asshole sends his best friend here?

Nathan sighs, shaking his head. "See you tomorrow, Kinsey."

I nod as he leaves the room, and I can't believe that someone would send their best friend here. It just doesn't compute.

Mentally stewing, I pick the manual up and start from the beginning. The first chapter is basically a long list of rules. Some of them I've heard before like, "access to the communal first-floor areas is forbidden after 7 p.m." There are also rules about the uniform that don't take long to internalize as they're pretty basic. Don't make any alterations. Got it.

The last rule piques mine and my wolf's interest, though. Shifting. There's a minor reference that states shifting in the academy is forbidden, and I cringe; however, that's not the one that pricks my arm. We're allowed to run in the south lawn until 10 p.m. but going outside Greystone Academy's perimeter is forbidden.

"Good to know." My wolf raises her head, panting, as if she's excited about the prospect of stretching her legs. I am, too. I've only shifted twice, and neither one of those instances led to anything fun. Even though I'm at odds with my wolf most of the time, I need to become one with her. Shifting will hurt less, and plus, it would be nice not to fight with myself over every little thing.

There are horror stories about shifters who've gone mad because they never bonded with their wolf. I shiver at the thought, and my wolf reassures me with a gentle nudge.

After that, I try to read the manual like a good little Greystone Academy student. I really do. But now that the temptation is out there, it's hard to ignore. We get restless, my wolf's back arching as if she's already limbering up. I read a whole page and realize I was never paying attention, so I start it three more times before giving up.

"You want to run? Let's run," I finally say, sighing as if this is the greatest hardship.

My wolf sees right through my bullshit.

Since I was little, I dreamed about traipsing through the woods near my house, chasing after my parents. When they used to go out, I'd watch them shift from inside the doorway, envy pulsing through me. Since I'm here, family outings have been taken away, at least for the time being, but the idea of running for fun shouldn't be stolen, too.

A quick peek outside tells me it's still early. The sun hangs low in the sky, burning a bright pink-orange in the tree line. I toss my manual to the side and leave the room, heading toward the main doors. I smile at other students who happen to be milling around the building, and almost unbelievably, they return the favor.

I'm on such a high when the warm air welcomes me as I step outside. Anticipation burrows into my stomach, popping my nerves in excitement. I make myself walk casually to the south lawn. Luckily, a row of little changing huts are lined together. I've seen similar things around Lunar back home. They're places to get naked so you spare your clothes during the shift.

Spotting an empty one, I step inside. A whole set of directions and rules is posted on the interior of the door, most likely so students can't feign ignorance. Everything the paper says is already explained in the manual I just read, so I carefully peel my clothes off and set them on the bench. My heart pounds. Butt naked, I stand in the center of the room and reach out to my wolf. "Ready?"

Like that's even a question. By the time we're old

enough for our initial shift, our wolves are panting for it. The only reason there are rules against shifting early is so a true bond can take place between human and wolf. Shift too soon and the wolf can take over and run free, never returning to human form. Try to suppress the wolf and you'll never be able to shift.

It's a constant worry I've had over the years, but luckily, my wolf is as strong-willed as I am.

She doesn't let me prepare for the shift before she rushes to the surface. The tingling in my arms from my coat coming out to the breaking of my bones happens in a split second. A scream rips through me as I fall to the ground.

Thanks for that, I grumble.

Tongue lolling, my wolf smiles now that she's in control.

She pushes free of the swinging door and trots through the grass, claws sinking into the damp earth. The wind rustling through the trees tickles her auburn coat. The blades of grass tickle her feet.

Then, a familiar smell hits her.

My wolf immediately perks, her ears standing at attention. That sweet, sweet aroma captivates her very being.

She smells *him*.

8

*H*er copper paws dig into the ground as she races. The wind whips through her fur, making it ripple all the way to her tail. His scent is faint, but she follows it anyway. Nose in the air, she sniffs the wind to gain direction.

There are a bunch of cool things about being a shifter, but one of the negatives is that when human-Kinsey is walking around, I'm in the driver's seat, completely operating our form. However, when we're shifted, my wolf is in control. I can try to talk to her like she does to me, but it's of no use. As we get to know each other, we'll become one being, one mind, but that's not the case right now. So, though I'm trying to tell her that Jonah's scent is most likely from yesterday, she doesn't listen.

A part of me is worried, too. What if it is fresh? I don't know if I can take another rejection right now.

Since she's not listening to me anyway, I quiet and become the audience to what's happening around me.

My wolf stretches her legs, strength and agility flowing through her. She dodges trees and skillfully jumps over fallen branches. She moves completely on instinct. To be honest, it's a nice reprieve from having to think all the time.

She scents the air, shifting direction. She's getting closer.

At the same time she thinks it, I feel it. I try to remind her about the school's boundaries, but she has a one-track mind. The fated bond is hardest to ignore, which is part of the reason why the academy is so unfair.

My wolf stumbles over a rock and growls. She's telling me to shut the fuck up and stop distracting her as she gets her feet under her again. A twig breaking nearby makes her pause. Ribcage expanding and deflating rapidly, she waits. If she smelled him, he had to have smelled her, too.

A branch moves to her right, and she spins. Coming out from behind a bush stands a russet-haired wolf that dwarfs us. My wolf whines as he approaches, muzzle in the air. Treading steadily, he moves closer until they're nearly nose to nose. His eyes are a green-yellow in wolf form—a striking difference from his normal brown with flecks of emerald.

That familiar pull comes again. It's like high-powered magnetization, tugging them to nudge each other, to play.

My wolf moves in, butting their muzzles together, then resting her head around his mane. He sniffs her, and my heart constricts when his wolf responds with a warm, *Kinsey*. The sound, masculine and strong, is foreign from my own thoughts but natural at the same time. It's as if it was always missing from me, and now that I've heard it, it's clicking the last few pieces of my soul in place.

My wolf preens. *Jonah*.

Mine, he growls, and his wolf rumbles the sound from deep within his chest.

His rough word heats my core, and I can't tell if it's wolf-me or human-me that's turned on. Probably both.

He licks the side of my wolf's face and then takes off, speeding through the woods. She runs after him, nipping at his legs playfully. He's fast and strong, but she holds her own, staying right with him. Her chest feels like it's going to explode as they race through the forest. They bound over streams, calling out their freedom into the night with howls of satisfaction.

When they tire out, Jonah leaps at her, nibbling playfully. They wrestle for a little while, but my wolf is as much of a hussy as I've always wanted to be. She doesn't play for long, it turns into something more. Nuzzling and soft cries emanate from deep within her throat. She's practically melting in heat, panting with need.

Jonah stands over her as she's sprawled on her back, her coat mixing into the grass. He sinks lower, resting his body on my wolf, licking her face until our hairy muzzles are gone, and Jonah and I are wrapped in each other's arms, kissing like we can't control ourselves.

His tongue delves into my welcome mouth, and I moan low in my throat as the world around us disappears. He lowers his hips into mine, and if I hadn't become completely coherent before, I am now.

His cock presses against my entrance.

We both seem to realize it at the same time, and he scrambles away from me, crawling back on all fours until he stands. My gaze drops to his dick, and I stare for an awkward amount of time. I've never seen one in the flesh. Hell, I've never even been kissed until now.

He cups his erection, hiding it from my view. "Kinsey."

His hard voice breaks me out of my spell. I sit, my

bare ass sinking into the grass now, but all I can feel is his lips on mine, begging for more, nudging for more.

And I fucking liked it. Hell, I fucking loved it.

My wolf is watching with bated breath, and a part of me wishes Jonah and I were both in that form where there isn't all this extra baggage between us.

"You should turn away," he huffs, avoiding my gaze like he's trying to protect my innocence.

"Why?" The only thing I plan on doing is standing and wiping the grass off my ass. "We're mates, right? It's not as if seeing me like this is wrong."

"What we just did was wrong," he replies.

I flinch.

I have to admit, that one fucking stung. My first kiss. My first *anything* with a guy. Of course it was wrong because it involved me. I swallow the hurt threatening to pour out.

When you're a wolf, you can do whatever you want until you're mated with someone. Then, you're stuck with that one person. In school, I'm well aware that my wolfpeers had relationships. Like with Nathan's and Mia's mates, it was fine for them to have a relationship. You're just supposed to forget about them when fate pairs you with someone else. Lots of times, you end up with the person you were with, but not always. I envied my wolfpeers for that bit of freedom, that rite of passage of being a teenager. I've never made out with a guy, and the first time I do is with my mate who doesn't want me.

The area behind my eyes heats, tears pricking. I've been so good throughout all of this, but I'm at my limit.

"What are you even doing outside the school?"

My hackles rise, and I get to my feet. "We're allowed to go for a run."

"Outside the perimeter?" he asks, still pointedly not looking at me.

I know because I can't take my eyes off him. His chiseled chest and abdomen muscles. His throat working as he tries not to peer my way. The sharp line of his jaw and cheeks. His mussed hair from just shifting is sexy as hell. "I didn't know I was outside the perimeter."

"You are," he barks. "You're damn near Brixton."

My eyes widen. I hadn't realized Brixton and Greystone were that close. "You're attending there?" I ask even though it should be a no-brainer. It's where Lunar shifters go for post-primary education. I'd be attending there if I wasn't stuck at Greystone.

His shoulders tighten. "Yes, partly. Most of my training is with my father, though."

My wolf whimpers, and a bit of it escapes my human form and fills the air between us. Finally, he turns toward me. He lets his stare drop, taking in my human form briefly before meeting my eyes and not letting them budge. All I needed was that short perusal for my body to heat again and then I say the dumbest thing anyone has ever said in the history of humans and shifters. Hell, I'll even throw in aliens, but it's not fair that I'm internally freaking out, and he's ignoring me. "That was my first kiss."

Jonah blinks. His lips part, and instant embarrassment hits my cheeks. For a split second, sorrow bleeds from the green specks in his eyes until they harden up again. "It shouldn't have happened. We can't control ourselves in our wolf form."

"Shouldn't have happened?" It comes out far more hurt than I want. "Our wolves are our truest form."

"Says the girl who only shifted for the first time a couple of days ago."

"*You* only shifted for the first time a couple of days ago, too, asshole," I snap. His eyes flash. But I'm not backing down from him. I did enough hiding and retreating at Lunar, I'm not going to do it here, too. And especially not in front of my mate. I take a step toward him. "Besides, you think I'm beautiful."

He eyes me warily. "She told you that?"

Everything in me tells me to go to him, but I

restrain myself much better in my human form. "I'm sure she'll share my answers with you."

"She already has. Does *'don't be a dick'* ring a bell?"

I chuckle. "Looks like you didn't take my advice."

His brows furrow as he takes me in. "I'm not a dick."

"Really? You just told your mate, that her first kiss shouldn't have happened. That doesn't ring dickish to you?"

He bridges the gap between us. "What should I have said? That I wanted to take it further? That I wanted to sink my cock into your wet heat so badly that I'm still fucking hard as a rock?" Breath whooshes from my lungs, but he ruins it in the next second. "To get your hopes up when it's a real possibility that nothing like that can ever happen between us?"

My wolf howls inside my chest. It's so loud that it shakes me to my core. My legs almost give out from underneath me, but I don't let it show. Instead, I incline my head. "You know what that will do to me."

He doesn't answer for the longest time. We stare at each other, unsaid words tangling between us. When he doesn't respond, I shake my head. Everything he does only solidifies that I was right to avoid my pack like the plague. Spinning, I let my wolf take over. She obliges, singing out her own slew of growling barks that echo behind her as she tears back through the forest. She runs as if she can somehow out-race the pain slicing through her drumbeat heart.

My wolf gets us to Greystone Academy safely. Behind us, a familiar scent trails, staying in the tree line as we break through the grass and continue toward the small changing hut. She nudges the swinging door open with her muzzle and then shifts, letting me take control. I collapse onto the ground, staying there with my chest heaving, feeling as if I'm bleeding out onto the worn grass.

Neither one of us wants to be in control right now. The hurt is too damn much.

I'm just going to say it. Fuck fate. It dealt me the wrong hand. Screwed me, actually. Feral is looking like it might be my future.

As I've been doing all my life, I pick myself up, dress, and beckon strength to me. A wolf howls in the distance, and a shiver makes its way up my spine. It could've been any wolf, but something in me knows it was Jonah. And that howl was for me.

The school has helpfully supplied a full-length mirror to the right of the door. I get all the tangles out of my hair and grimace at the dried dirt coating parts of my exposed skin.

A nice hot bath or shower might help wash away all this emotion. I step outside the hut, peering toward the bushes where I left Jonah, and a shadow moves. My sight is better than a regular human's, but I still can't confirm if it was the wind or a big, beautiful, brown wolf who passed in front of the tree.

Turning away, I march back toward the stone building. Instead of admiring it for its architectural qualities, I appraise it as the fortress that it is. It looks standoffish, secluded. Inside, it hides away the same type of unwanted creatures.

To think that I'll have to sit through more meetings like the one I just had with Jonah again and again until he makes his final decision.... I might tell him to put me out of my misery now. If he never plans on building our supposed fated relationship, he might as well let me go. I don't want to be like Mia and Nathan—having to deal with this shit for a year.

I'd rather take my chances as Feral.

The walk back to my room seems to take forever. When I finally get there, I gorge on Mia's chocolate while I finish reading the manual to keep my mind off what transpired. There's a map of the grounds, and judging by this, yeah, I was totally outside the perimeter of the school. There is no mention of Brixton anywhere on the sketch, and I can't help but think that omission is on purpose. For those of us who have a mate that close, it could break us.

Not me though. I know my place now.

When I finally lay my head down to sleep, Jonah is all I think about.

His bruising lips against mine.

The head of his cock nudging my entrance.

He was ready to take what he wanted, and I would've given it to him willingly.

It would've been a big mistake, of course. If we'd gone that far, Jonah still could've spoken those words to me. If that had happened, I probably would've gone Feral myself.

Hey, that's an idea. Why wait for him to make the decision? I could escape this place any time I wanted. Guarantee no one would come after me.

9

*T*he next morning, Mia's knocking rouses me from sleep. My head hurts, my limbs are tired—my first real run with my wolf has taken everything out of me.

"You in there?" she calls, knocking again.

I groan an unintelligible sound. A few moments later, though, I drag my ass out of bed and stomp toward the door, whipping it open.

Mia's already half-turned away from me when she glances over her shoulder. Her eyes widen. "Girl, that's some wolf hair if I've ever seen it."

Wonderful. I lock eyes with her. "I'm late. Obviously. You want me to meet you down there?"

She pushes past me. "No, I'm sensing a story and I want in."

I close the door behind her and lock it, then move into my bathroom, still wearing the same outfit from yesterday. I frown at my hair in the mirror.

Taking a deep breath, I tell her the whole story, not leaving anything out. In opposition of where my thoughts had headed yesterday, I can't go Feral. I can't willingly leave this place. Even though I'm not happy, I won't do that to my parents. It would devastate them. Plus, I've adjusted well to having a friend. It really does become like second nature.

By the time I get the knots out of my hair, I've finished the tale. I peer at her through the mirror. "I'm taking a quick shower."

She spins, giving me some privacy, but continues to talk to me as I disrobe. "You met up with him in wolf form? Holy shit."

"Yeah, holy shit," I mimic as I turn on the faucet, standing just out of the spray while I wait for the water to heat up. I can't believe I fell asleep with all this gross shit on me. Those bedsheets need to be cleaned and sterilized as do the clothes I wore. My literal bare ass was in the dirt last night, and I didn't mind because Jonah was on top of me. Not remotely how I pictured my first kiss, but somehow, I can't complain. About the kiss, anyway. I have a long list of complaints about the kisser. Mainly the fact that he's an asshole.

"What are the odds that he would be out for a run the same time you were out for a run?"

Now that she mentions it, what *are* the damn odds? And how come we didn't stumble across anyone else in our romp around the forest?

"I bet it was fate," Mia yells.

I laugh as I run shampoo through my hair. "Isn't it all fate? That's what got us in this predicament anyway."

"No, what got us in this predicament is dumbass wolves who think they know better than fate."

I shrug even though she can't see me. I agree with her sentiment on the dumbass part, but I don't know, I feel like people should have their own thoughts. If he doesn't want to be with me, fine. The messed-up part of that scenario is that if he doesn't, I have to leave the pack for good. But that's a stupid Pack rule, not from the divine.

Then again, the argument would be: If fate made it so, it should be so.

Tou-fucking-ché.

Now that I've had a whole argument with myself in the shower, while my very first friend waits outside, I groan.

"What was it like?" she asks.

I stare at the clear water now running between my toes as I wash the conditioner out of my hair. I almost don't want to answer. I finish the shower without uttering a word in response. When I shut the faucet off, she hands me a towel around the shower curtain. Taking a deep breath, I steel my shoulders. My wolf is already on board with my answer. I can feel her contentment. "Amazing," I whisper.

"I was afraid you were going to say that."

I wring my hair out and tie the towel around me. Mia turns her back again as I get out. I swallow. "Have you ever...." I can't bring myself to finish the sentence. If she hasn't, I don't want to hurt her.

I can't see her face, read her expression, and it makes the silence that grows between us stretch. Finally, she states, "No, we never got that far. I asked him if we should once. I thought that if he'd felt it with me, maybe he'd see how right it was. But you know, part of me is glad he said no."

My throat constricts. I know exactly what she means. I'll never forget that kiss. Ever. "Yeah," I rasp, moving to the sink to brush my teeth. "I think you're right."

The pain is so fresh and new, I don't know what to do with it. I stand in front of the sink for who knows how long until Mia plops my academy outfit on the closed toilet lid. "Here. Picked out your outfit for you."

I meet her stare in the mirror and smirk.

She smiles back. "Hurry up. I have some calories to eat."

Exiting, she closes the door and gives me some space to change. Thankfully, at some point last night, I put my new makeup in the bathroom, so after running my hands through my damp hair, I decide to let it dry naturally and spend what little time I have doing my makeup like Grace showed me. When I'm done, I can't say it looks as good as yesterday, but it's not bad for my first time solo.

As soon as I swing the door open, Mia rises from my desk chair and hikes her bag up on her shoulder. "Hurry. Nathan's texting me every few minutes."

I grab my own bag, and we both head out, traveling down the Daybreak and Lunar corridor until we hit the stairs. Once on the first floor, we make our way to the glassed-in cafeteria. The food choices have changed today. French Toast instead of pancakes, scrambled eggs, bagels, sausage, and more fruit. I scoop whatever looks good onto my plate and follow Mia to where Nathan is sitting with Nadia, who surprisingly, doesn't have red-rimmed eyes this morning.

She holds a cup of orange juice in her hands and

gestures with it. Immediately, I can tell that a smile does her justice better than a frown. It lights up her whole face.

I sit next to her while Mia takes her place next to Nathan. "Blame me," I tell him. "I wasn't up when Mia knocked on my door."

"Late night?" Nathan inquires.

Mia acts as if she's not paying attention, so I decide to keep what happened between me and Jonah private. Well, private between me, Jonah, and Mia. I don't feel like getting into another big discussion. Especially after seeing Mia's reaction to the kissing part. Whatever I say is going to make them think of their own mates, and we already do enough of that.

Instead, Mia and Nathan start discussing something about an upcoming project in one of their classes, and Nadia breaks out a notebook and begins to write in it. The date is written on the first line, and she begins to freehand, scribbling down sentences on the paper. I glance away in case it's private and not something like a list of how to get revenge against her best friend who completely abandoned her. If it's a revenge list, I'm on board with helping her.

Mia's gaze travels over my shoulder. "Incoming," she singsongs under her breath.

This time, I'm shocked to find Ms. Ebon towering

above our table. I almost come to attention in front of her. It's the aura she gives, making me want to obey her right away. "Miss Walker, I need to see you directly, please."

I stare back at my plate. I was done a while ago and just moving food around to pass the time, so I stand. "Of course, Ms. Ebon."

I grab my bag and start to follow her out of the room when I peer over my shoulder. Mia grimaces at me, and Nathan wears a furrowed brow as he watches us walk away. I shrug. At this point, I don't know what's going on, and I can think of like three things that I've done wrong and could possibly be getting in trouble for, so there's no sense in worrying about it yet.

Her heels click ahead of me as we march down the corridor to her office. She stops at her room, gesturing for me to go inside first. I don't know if this is a social meeting like our first or more of a school meeting, so I refrain from sitting until she moves around her huge desk after shutting the door behind us.

She sits, placing her forearms on the wood top in front of her. Leaning closer, she stares at me straight in the eye. "I was alerted to some unfortunate news this morning."

My heart pings painfully in my chest. My first thoughts are of my parents. I forgot to look at my cell this morning to see if anything had been said since yesterday, but her next words erase all those worries. She swivels her monitor until it faces me and presses play. The clear image of a forest appears. Not three seconds into the video, a copper wolf barrels through the frame and exits it. It happens so fast, I'm pretty damn impressed with myself, but when I glance at Ms. Ebon, I can tell she's not about to commend me for my superior speed.

"This is the video at the perimeter line. If you move out of the frame, you are no longer within Greystone Academy's grounds."

I close my eyes and breathe out.

"Are you going to deny that's you?"

"No, that was me," I tell her.

She straightens slightly as if she wasn't expecting me to tell the truth. "Did you read the handbook or the signs in the changing huts to know that going outside the perimeter is in violation of our policies?"

"I did read that. I can't say that I knew where the perimeter was when I did it, but I knew that crossing it was wrong."

Ms. Ebon spins her monitor back to face her, then leans in her chair, steepling her fingers in front of her. "When anything triggers the motion cameras, they go right to our security which reports directly to the administrator." She raises a brow as she appraises me, and it makes me wonder if she knows the tie between Lydia Greystone and my family. "Mrs. Greystone herself brought it to my attention."

When I don't respond, she moves her monitor back around. Opening a separate tab, she clicks play on a new video. This time, it's of two different wolves who triggered the cameras. One copper and one brown. I frown hard. Seeing Jonah in that form pains me. My own wolf, who's been sulking, whines because she feels the same way I do. The wolf we can tolerate. The human, we can't.

"Who is this wolf?" She plays the video again, pointing him out like I wouldn't know who she was talking about.

"That's Jonah Livestrong," I inform her.

She recoils. "Your mate?" She watches me for a long time before asking, "And how did it happen that you went for a run with your mate?"

I sigh. "I didn't set out to go for a run with him. My wolf wanted out, so I shifted. As soon as she smelled him, I had no control over her." My wolf sniffs, and I can feel her contempt but it's true. "Trust me, if I had been in control, I wouldn't have—" I break off because my first reaction is to say I wouldn't have gone after him, which is completely and utterly true. But that's not the reality I should speak in front of the woman whose job it is to get me and Jonah back together. Correction: *Reform* me so that Jonah will be content with me as a mate. I try to cover up the break as quickly as possible. "If I'd had control, I wouldn't have broken the rule," I finish.

"We might be able to work with this," Ms. Ebon states, turning her computer around and typing furiously on her keyboard. "You are a pup. You caught wind of your mate and couldn't control yourself." She stops typing and glances at me. "You do know those cameras are miles away from the south lawn. Upwards of ten miles in some areas. How on earth did you catch his scent from that far away?"

I shrug. "Is that weird?"

"It's peculiar," she answers. Returning to typing, her fingers banging against the keyboard until she right-clicks on the mouse with a final punch of power. "There," she smiles. "You'll still have to be punished, but let's hope the penalty won't be expelling you from the university and a mark on your record.

Fear slices through me. "Expelled?"

"We take our jobs very seriously here, Miss Walker. On first inspection, it was unclear what other wolf you were running with. Had it been another male, that would have been clear grounds for expulsion."

"It was definitely Jonah," I grind out. No matter how much I wish it was different, I can't think of anyone but him.

Her computer pings, and Ms. Ebon returns her stare to the screen. She cocks her head before clicking several times, then her eyes scan. I almost come out of my skin waiting to hear what's going on. I move to the edge of my seat to see if I can get a better view, but it's no use. The computer is angled too much.

"Interesting," she murmurs. Turning toward me, she says, "That was an email from Jonah. He was confirming your story. He and his father placed those cameras, so he knew they would've captured you both." A light shines in her eyes, and I get the feeling she's thinking way more into this than she should. She must believe he's come to save the day.

She's sorely mistaken if that's the case.

"I'm sure his email will also help smooth things over with Lydia."

Highly unlikely if Lydia has it out for my family, but I'm not going to burst her bubble. Especially if it lets me off the hook more easily.

Ms. Ebon does a few things on the computer before facing me again. She leans over the desk, clasping her hands. "Kinsey, I'm going to need you to tell me everything that happened on your run with Jonah."

I blink at her but she's not remotely joking.

Horror races through me. If I have to explain to an adult what happened in the forest with Jonah, I'll die of embarrassment. "You're kidding...."

*M*s. Ebon's words settle in my stomach like bricks holding down a decaying corpse.

"At this point, you really need to stop saying that to me."

We sit there mute, neither one of us giving an inch. I have a feeling she could literally do this all day, so eventually I give in. In my own way. "We played. We shifted. We fought."

She purses her lips, her elegant, red lipstick creasing. "What did you fight over?"

I panic for a moment.

"Same old stuff. He said he didn't want to get close to me because we still might not be able to make it work. I got mad. I shifted and sped through the grounds."

Ms. Ebon taps her pen on the desk for a couple of seconds and then drops it again. "Kinsey, I need you to think about something long and hard. Do you want to live Feral?"

"No," I respond immediately.

"Exactly."

She keeps staring at me which spurs me to ask, "Exactly what?"

"I understand your anger. I get your hurt, your pain. What I need you to think about right now is the hurt and pain you'll feel if you can't ever have Jonah. If he rejects you for good, and you go packless, living out in the wild, which will eventually lead to death. I say all this not to scare you but to make you wake up. Jonah isn't a choice. He's your savior."

My wolf perks up, but I slam her right back down. Figuratively, of course. But honestly, I'm interested in Ms. Ebon's thoughts. Some of it rings true. Some of it makes me want to sit up and take notice.

"Think about being out on your own in the wild. Do you think your stubbornness is going to save you from longing for Jonah? Do you think your superior ability to compartmentalize your feelings is going to allow you and your wolf to live in peace when your heart will only beat for the one person you can't have? I can give you statistics. I can give you all the numbers in the world. We've studied fated pairs who live Feral for what little time they survive. I can break out testimonies from wolves who've lost their mate. Think about your own parents. What would happen to one of them if something happened to the other?"

Damn. She is good. I blow out a breath. "He doesn't like me. I've never been able to get anyone to like me," I confess, voice wavering.

"That's not true," Ms. Ebon states, gesturing toward the door behind me. "You have new friends. Hell, I like you. You're kind of a pain in my ass, but I like you. Don't let your past ruin your future."

Her words feel as if they were shot out of a barrel of a gun aimed right at my chest. *Don't let your past ruin your future.* "I don't know how to do that," I admit.

"Firstly, trust my process. Be honest. Be open. Even if it hurts. Even if it feels as if it's tearing you open from the inside out."

I swallow, leaning back in the chair. I'm not going to like this one bit. I already know it.

She stares at me for another little while, and when she nods, it's as if she's telling me I'm ready for the next step. "Now," she says. "I have your schedule." Turning back to her computer, she hits a few buttons until the printer to her left kicks to life. "I'm warning you now, you're not going to like some of it. But you have to put your trust in me. I know what I'm doing."

I'm not sure her warning me ahead of time is going to do any good. I still am who I am regardless of what I'm told to do.

"I'm going to also let you in on a little secret. It isn't always the case that mates are so hands-on when it comes to their bonded ones being here. As I'm sure Mia and Nathan have told you, some of them try to remove themselves from the process completely. Jonah hasn't."

Hmm. Look at that. I still can't find a will to like him.

Liking and wanting to kiss are now two officially different feelings. When he's kissing, his mouth isn't screwing anything up.

I brace my shoulders. "Alright. I'm ready. Give it to me."

Ms. Ebon moves the paper in front of her and peers down at it. "As you heard on the first day, everyone's classes are different. In fact, sometimes it's not even a schedule in the traditional sense of the word. There's not a lot of moving from one class to the next as you're used to."

This all sounds like a fancy way of trying to butter me up for when the real kicker comes. Like she'll just slip in the bad news when I least expect it. My nails dig into my skirt.

She flicks her gaze to meet mine. "Jonah has requested that you go on outings together. You'll be required to attend dinners and parties at the alpha's house while you're here since that will be part of your life when he takes his position in security."

Dread squeezes my stomach. Just picturing the wolfpeers that I would have to see there...the same ones who made my school life miserable. "He's trying to kill me."

My advisor shakes her head. "Quite the opposite. Exposing you to the role you would be a part of is fantastic. To go along with that demand, we've put you in etiquette and social classes."

I close my eyes. "You what?"

Ms. Ebon frowns, dribbling her fingers over my schedule. "Kinsey, you haven't had the most luxurious upbringing. If you show up at the alpha's house not knowing which fork is which or how to properly drink without offending anyone, you can't expect to make a good impression."

"He wants to...refine me? Like I'm some sort of Feral wolf?"

My advisor's face hardens, and I realize I'm pushing my limit with her. "You will also take Pack History and political lessons so you'll be able to speak eloquently in front of a room full of people. Jonah has also expressed an interest in helping you learn different security and enforcing techniques so that you'll understand more of his role in the pack."

I have to interrupt her there. "Okay, where's the part where he gets to know me? Should I come up with something? I have a few things I'd like to teach him about the real world."

"Your concerns are common. I can't say that any of my students have ever expressed them as bluntly as you do, but we've already covered that, haven't we?" She huffs, leaning back in her chair. "While you do these things together, he'll get to know you. Spend the time training with him to talk about yourself. Spend the dinners showing him how you act in social situations. You don't have to lose your entire self, Miss Walker. No one wants a cookie-cutter mate."

She could've fooled me. My leg starts to bounce up and down. If he's going to teach me enforcer things, maybe that means I can get a few shots in at him. Then, I can be all *oops, I accidentally did that on purpose*. Maybe it won't be all bad....

Ebon continues. "In addition, I've made notes from

your previous education in Lunar and have taken the liberty of enrolling you in some general science classes with a self-study in Botany. My hope is that we can get you out of Greystone Academy within enough time so that you can start your education at Brixton as soon as possible."

I cock my head. "You got all that from my Lunar transcripts?"

She clears her throat. "I wish we had more opportunities for everyone's tastes, but that's not the case here. I'll be your mentor in your self-study, so we'll have to meet weekly on that as well. I have spoken to our landscapers, and they have agreed to give you a section of the grounds so that you can conduct experiments, or whatever it is that you want to do."

She finishes unsure, as if her statement is more of a question. I have to say, out of all of that, this is the best news I've had. The forest, trees, plants, and flowers are my friends. In a perfect world, I'd run a greenhouse. Maybe a flower shop, but no, a greenhouse would be more my style. Once you get the flowers at a flower shop, they may be beautiful, but they're already on the last leg of their life. If I had a greenhouse, I could grow different plants, sending them out to continue brightening the world.

"I think that's the first real smile I've seen from you, Kinsey Walker."

I blush. "I'm sure you're right about that."

"Just a hint," Ms. Ebon says, leaning over her huge, wooden desk. "Open up about your tastes, what you're passionate about. My aim isn't just to get you and Mr. Livestrong together, it's to get you to be happy about it too." It's her turn to blush. "Our happiness is of the upmost importance. Now...." She gets serious again as she pushes the schedule toward me. "You'll have to excuse me. I need to read up on what the hell botany is so that when you show up and start spouting off technical terms, I'll be able to keep up."

She gives me a smile, and I pick up the paper and stand. I wouldn't say my schedule is an entire waste. Only three quarters. I'm not sure what forcing Jonah and I together will do instead of giving us more opportunities to fight, but I'm willing to try.

I give Ms. Ebon a short wave before leaving the room. Something she said resonated with me. Part of this is getting him to know me more. I'm not going to hold back, that's not my personality. I held back for too long, and that's just not me anymore. It's time to be the girl I was in my parents' house everywhere. I'm not going to retreat into my shell in Jonah's presence as I was prone to do in Lunar. It's not happening. If he has to decide whether he accepts me or not, he might as well know the whole truth.

The hallway stretches ahead of me. A quick peek at my schedule shows that I could make it to one of the science classes today. Just as I'm about to find a directory, a door slams to my right.

Mia runs from the room. I catch her red face and glassy eyes. As she rounds the corner and out of sight, a guy walks out of the same room. He swaggers down the hall dressed in real clothes. His face is pure calm—the complete opposite of my new friend's. His gaze barely meets mine before he saunters toward the exit, hands in his pockets.

I'd bet fucking anything that's her mate.

I don't think, I react. He's tugging the huge doors open when I start running to catch up with him. He's halfway down the steps when I take them three at a time, knocking our shoulders together at the same time he takes a step so he's off-kilter. He stumbles forward, loses his footing, and has to pull off a true wolf move to save face so he doesn't trip down the stairs.

I keep running. "Sorry," I call out over my shoulder. "I'm in a rush."

He mumbles behind me, but I can't wipe the smile off my face. Dick doesn't deserve my friend. What he deserves is a hell of a lot worse than almost falling down the steps.

I wait until a bright red car ambles down the driveway before walking back into the school. Science can wait because my friend needs me, and apparently I have a lot of upcoming socializing to do anyway. I better start preparing for it now.

After picking my book bag up where I left it in the middle of the hallway, I follow her steps until I find the library and walk in. Sure enough, in the back of the stacks, Mia and Nathan are huddled together.

Mia glances at me over Nathan's shoulder and turns away, wiping the mascara from under her eyes. Nathan turns, and when he sees me, he relaxes. I sit next to him, dropping my bag on the chair to my right.

"Typical meeting day," he grinds out.

Looking at Mia now, I know I don't want the pure turmoil Mia is going through right now. Ms. Ebon was right in some respect. I don't want to always pine after a guy who doesn't want me. That can't be Mia's future, can it? Mate or no mate, couldn't she find happiness with someone else? Screw pack laws. Screw mate laws.

I don't utter any of this out loud— instead, changing the subject and telling them all about how I almost got kicked out of school on my third day.

It turns out, laughing at someone else's problems is

a huge mood booster. After about ten minutes, Mia's whole demeanor has changed.

I might have to bring her on a date with Jonah. At least I'll be able to prove to him I do have some social skills and, *gasp*, some people actually like me. For me. Little old doesn't-want-to-contribute-to-pack-life me.

Over breakfast, Nadia and I compare our schedules. We both share Pack History, but that's it. She doesn't have Etiquette or Sociology classes. In fact, she gets to take a lot more educational courses because her mate doesn't have a problem with her social abilities. The only bug up his ass is the fact that they're best friends.

I don't know. I'd be all about shacking up with my best friend. At least you know you like each other. Who's to say you couldn't learn to love each other in that way eventually?

Nerves twist my stomach as we make our way to our first official Greystone Academy class. Nathan and Mia informed us that everyone has to take this class so we'll see all the new shifters who just got here. Now that I've learned some of the stupid reasons people are at Greystone Academy, I'm utterly curious of everyone else's stories.

A classroom that matches the rest of the academy's decor opens in front of us when we step inside. With the stone walls and wood accents, I'm playing out my castle-living dreams. A fireplace sits empty in the front of the room, the desks lined up in rows before it. I start to head toward the back, but Nadia goes right for the front. I hesitate, unsure of what to do. I'm more the type of girl who sits in the last row and watches everybody. When I'm not in everyone's face, I become a harder target. My wolfpeers had to go out of their way to say nasty things when I was in the rear of the classroom, and they did, but it would've been a lot worse had I been front and center.

But I can't leave my new friend here to sit by herself....

I grudgingly plop into the seat next to hers, the hairs on the back of my neck rising. My wolf raises her head as if she can sense a threat but immediately settles down when there isn't anything in the room that's going to hurt us except my own insecurities. I start to squirm, peeking over my shoulder.

Nadia, however, doesn't seem to be having the same problem. She chatters beside me as she brings out a notebook. A couple shifters file into the room. Both girls. They take seats behind us, and my foot starts bouncing up and down. I'm convinced they're going to do something to me.

"You okay?"

I nod once, closing my eyes to tell myself to calm down. I'm not in Lunar anymore. If anything, I belong here with the rest of the misfits.

I give myself something else to focus on as more wolves enter the room. There seems to be more females here than males, and I make a mental note to ask Ms. Ebon, Queen of Greystone Statistics, what the male to female ratio is for rejected mates. I'm beginning to suspect the numbers are skewed in the male's favor.

Shifters aren't in this century in regard to feminism, and this is added evidence to that fact. We're all about the strong, alpha males in Lunar. We pride excellent virility and genes. My mind drifts to Jonah. He's everything a female shifter would want in a mate. His very physical being screams protection and safety and, let's face it, fucking sex. It's in our genetics to lust after the strong ones, and Jonah is arguably at the top of that list.

Now that I've kissed him, I'm finding it damn hard to concentrate on anything else. My mind pulses with the memory of him. His lips. His body. His cock. All of it calls to me.

An older shifter waltzes into the room, and I'm thankful for the interruption. He introduces himself as our Pack History professor, Mr. Lyme, then launches into his lecture for the day with vigor, and unfortunately for my current sex-crazed mind, I find it as tedious as I'd imagined. We learned Pack History in primary school, so this is repetitive. A quick scan around tells me no one else is taking notes either, so I can't imagine it was only Lunar Pack that had a good educational system. Fortunately for my brain, the professor is interesting and humorous. He doesn't seem to take himself seriously, which is in the plus column, and he keeps me interested enough so I can shove Jonah into the back of my mind for now.

When the class nears completion, Mr. Lyme lowers a large projection screen on the wall. Turning to face us, I recognize a change in his face—his features have fallen. "It's a mandatory requirement for this class that I show you this video. It's my least favorite thing to do. I add it to the beginning of the course so we can get it over with. I am sure none of you will end up in this predicament, but since we have already covered an overview of the pack system, this video discusses the often unspoken wild wolf community known as Ferals."

He retreats to the rear of the room, and after a few moments, a video starts to play. A slice of fear shivers down my spine. My wolf also perks to attention, ears straight up. Not a lot of human life grabs her interest, but she knows what this means.

In true documentary-like fashion, the filmmakers go out in the wild and record different scenes and interviews. We're shown huts in the woods, frail, primitive humans feasting on woodland creatures. Slide after slide portrays a subset of wolves that is so unlike our own pack system. Living alone. Hungry. Some of them caged. Some of them living in filth. Brutal fights over food, housing, and territory. It's like watching a documentary on parts of the United States ravaged by war or a fantasy world set in the apocalypse.

They definitely never showed us anything like this in Lunar. Our Feral imaginations were the horror stories, but this movie is far worse than any story I've ever heard.

During one particular scene where a shifter in her human form is eating some sort of dead animal, Nadia leans in. "Have you noticed there are no children?"

I blink at the screen. I hadn't noticed. I was too stuck on the fact that Feral is a real possibility for myself and my new friends, but now that she mentions it, I haven't spotted a single child in human or wolf form. There are no families either. Just lone wolves.

I feel sick.

I was always the outsider but never like this. I still had my parents. I still had a house, no matter if it was the worst in the village. There was a spot for me to always lay my head down and bathe and eat—and there were people who loved me.

While I watch, I don't notice that I've partially shifted. My fingers have turned into claws digging into the top of the desk. Nadia elbows me, and pointedly glares at my hands. I stare wide-eyed, then close my eyes. *It's okay.* I console my wolf as she freaks the fuck out. *That won't be us.*

Slowly, she starts to retract until my claws return to fingers—the same needle-like sensation coursing through me as I change. When I'm fully human, I lean against the back of the chair and place my hands on my lap in case something like that happens again. When the class ends, I hightail it out of there, leaving Nadia behind calling my name.

My wolf is begging to be set free. I need to get the hell out of Greystone Academy and give in. I practically race through the halls, exiting out the main doors and rounding the side of the building where the huts are in view. Someone calls my name from behind me, but I don't register that they're talking to me until a hand yanks back on my arm. I spin, growling—the sound more wolf than human. My heart batters my chest, singing a song of agony and fear.

Jonah stands in front of me. He takes a step back and raises his hands in surrender. A black polo shirt pulls taut over his broad chest. His biceps burst from the sleeves barely containing his muscles. Glistening, brown hair styled to the side shines in the sun beating down on both of us.

"What are you doing here?" I bark. I can't tell if I'm mad that he's here, that he's so gorgeous, or that he's interrupted me from running. Probably a mixture of all three. The last thing I want is to be attracted to someone who doesn't think I'm worthy.

"Ms. Ebon and I have a meeting to schedule your class with me, but I saw you running out of the building." He studies me, and for once, he doesn't do it with disgust. His gaze roams down my uniform, then travels up to meet my eyes. "What's wrong?"

I laugh, but it almost comes out like an exasperated sob. How could he be asking me what's wrong? Everything is obviously wrong. "I'm stuck here, away from my family. Away from anyone who loves me. I had to sit and watch a grotesque video about living Feral, as if it's some sort of warning to us all, and the guy who put me here is asking me what's wrong. That's what's fucking wrong, Jonah."

He rubs at his chest, and I wonder if he can feel the pain coursing through me. When a wolf is really hyped up, they can transfer their emotions to others in the same pack, and the bond between fated wolves is supposed to be stronger than that. The higher up you are in the pack, the easier it is to transfer emotions, so this is most likely our bond making Jonah wince. "I was told you could talk to your parents while you were here."

I blink at him to make sure he's serious and then lose my shit. "Oh, really? I'm lucky, then. Tell me, can you only just talk to your parents while you're attending Brixton? Or can you maybe go see them whenever you want?"

He roars in my face, the sound pricking my skin. "Why do you fight me at every fucking turn?"

"Because you're ruining my life!"

Jonah moves fast. I cower as his hands stretch out but instead of the attack I thought I was getting, he grabs my forearms and crushes me to his chest. His arms wrap around me, squeezing. The warmth of his huge form envelops me in all directions. He's stiff at first, like a boa constrictor who doesn't know his own strength. Eventually, his muscles retract until it's just his two giant arms holding me to him in an embrace. "Relax," he whispers. "I feel like my heart is tearing right out of my chest. I need you to calm down. Please."

With his one hand bound around my shoulder and another around my back, I can only move my head. I tilt it up, peering into his unsure eyes. My heart slows. "You feel me, don't you?"

He avoids my stare. His throat works, the cut of his jaw feathering. "Yes, I feel you."

Almost instantaneously, my mood shifts. My wolf is content being barricaded in our mate's strong arms, and she no longer threatens to burst free from my human form or be the accelerant to my temper. I lean my head against his chest because even though I hate that he gives me comfort, I need it right now. I crave him like a bad idea that will hurt later but in the present moment, you just don't care.

Little by little, his hold loosens, but he still doesn't let me go. His heartbeat, once erratic, returns to normal, mirroring mine. It's far past time one of us should be stepping away from the other, but we don't. For once, I give into nature and instinct, and let what I need carry through me.

Finally, he asks, "Do you have classes for the rest of the day?"

I shake my head, my cheek pressing against his shirt. "I was going to start my self-study work, but I'm free." My words reach out to him like an olive branch. I hold my breath, waiting for him to shove them right back in my face.

He reaches up and works his fingers through my hair, tugging on the ends slightly until I'm peering up at him. "What's your self-study in?"

My heart lodges in my throat. He's holding me like a lover. Tentatively, I reach my own hands up. I clasp his waist, which feels oh so right but I get nervous, so I move them up, then down, then I finally drop them in exasperation. Evidently, I don't have any idea how this works. How do two mates, who are supposed to be each other's forever, get over being hurt?

"Don't," he murmurs, untangling his fingers from my hair. I think he's going to back away, but instead, he grabs my hands and returns them to his hips, holding them there until he returns his grip to my hair. "Now," he breathes. "What's your self-study in?"

"B-botany."

He raises a brow, a small smirk playing over his lips. "You're a science nerd?"

I cock my head. Years of teasing have taught me to lash out, but I hold it in. "Not really. I just like the forest, trees, plants, but mainly flowers."

As we're standing here, I can't help but think that I'm doing as Ms. Ebon told me to. I'm introducing myself to him. I'm laying bare the parts I hid from everyone. The ones I held inside knowing that if they never accepted me as a pack member, they wouldn't like the weird parts of me either—the parts that would rather sit outside with my hands in the dirt than go to pack parties or meetings.

He watches me for the longest time before pulling away. My hands drop to my sides, and my heart squeezes as he puts distance between us. My wolf doesn't feel it as much. She preens under the huge advancement we've made, but I'm not as convinced. All we did was give in to nature.

"If you're calm now, I can ask Ms. Ebon for a schedule for the gymnasium so we can practice."

"Are you going to make me a badass?"

I swear his lips quirk, a prelude to a smile. "Why? Do you think I'm a badass?"

It blows me away how proud I am that I almost made him grin. "You certainly look the part, but I haven't seen you in action." It's a taunt. I'm begging to see him sexed up and strong. It makes me quiver just thinking about it.

He gestures toward the academy. "Let's go find out."

Walking next to Jonah—my mate—on the way back to Greystone fills me with warring emotions. Nature begs me to be this close to him all the time, but there's still that little part of me that's blaring a warning not to let him in.

This slight step forward is nothing in the grand scheme of things. However, plants don't grow in a day either. It takes a lot of different factors and processes, and the same happens with shifters, too. Well, shifters of the rejected variety. The only thing I can do is hope that we keep taking steps and eventually find ourselves where we always belonged.

12

I lied when I said I didn't know if Jonah was a badass.

We're supposed to be stronger and healthier in packs but that doesn't mean there isn't infighting or arguments. I witnessed a fight between Jonah and another wolf once. I don't remember what it was about, but Jonah kicked his ass in spectacular fashion. It was jaw-dropping, awe-inspiring, panty-melting goodness.

So, I'm not surprised that when we get approval from Ms. Ebon to use the gymnasium and lug all of his equipment from his truck to the gym that he blows me away with his agility and skills. He doesn't even change into more comfortable clothes to do it either. Standing there in the black polo and jeans, he goes through what he calls a short warm-up. I have to watch that I don't get caught gawking or drooling at his fine ass.

We didn't realize until too late that the only thing I had to wear was my academy outfit. That didn't mean I got out of the workout, he just promised to bring me appropriate clothes next time. Today, I'm stretching as he goes through some calisthenics.

Thankfully, when I unroll the skirt to its full length, I'm not showing off my goods while I stretch. Then again, the way I keep watching him, I'm wondering if I should roll it twice like Mia suggested.

I clear my throat. "So, I hear you emailed Ms. Ebon about my transgression the other day. Thank you."

He stumbles, something I wouldn't have noticed if I weren't watching him like a hawk. "It wasn't your fault. It was pure wolf instinct."

I'm going to regret what I say next, but I do it anyway. "Still, administration was two seconds from kicking me out. They thought I was with another wolf."

He stops mid jumping jack, and a growl rips from his chest. It's so feral that it makes the tips of my toes tingle and arousal pool in my lower belly.

"Of course that would mean—"

"I know what it means," he snaps, shoulders

132

bunching. His skin starts to ripple as he loses control, and it makes me smile. "What are you smiling for?"

I nod toward the fur sprouting over his arms. "You don't like the idea of me being with someone else."

He grinds his teeth together, closes his eyes, and gets himself under control. A few moments later, it's as if his outburst never happened. "Of course my wolf doesn't like the idea of it."

Hmm. *My wolf.* That sounds like a cop-out, but I don't push him on it. I'm trying to be...nice. Normal, even. If that's such a thing.

When silence stretches between us, my anxiety kicks in. All of Ms. Ebon's notes are swimming in my head, so I ask the first thing that comes to mind to get to know him better. "So, do you like the idea of going into security for the alpha?"

Jonah turns toward me, the areas around his eyes tightening. A glean of sweat shines across his forehead from his exertion.

When he doesn't respond for a long time, I start babbling. "You don't have to answer. I was merely curious."

He shakes his head. "It's not that. I don't think anyone's ever asked me that question. But yes, it's an important part of our pack life, and I'll be honored to do it."

Well, that sounded like a super political answer. "I bet it makes the sacrifice worth it since our future alpha is one of your good friends." My voice comes out hard and strained. I don't mean it to, but I never got along with the three big wolves at school. Our alpha, beta, and Jonah were the kings. They never participated outright in the name-calling and shaming, but they never stopped it either. Something the alpha's son could've easily done. He wouldn't have since his aunt was one of my mother's accusers, but that doesn't mean I can't be bitter about it.

Before I can stop myself, I say, "I bet they pity you." His head snaps up, but I've already committed, so I keep going. "When you found out I was your fated one, I bet Jesse and his family pitied you."

The striking emerald in his eyes fades. He doesn't need to confirm it for me because my thoughts weren't exactly suspicions. I've watched my pack enough to know that some wolves are pitied when their mate is revealed. For me to be bonded with someone like Jonah, I'm considered lucky. It's a definite rise in the pack. But I guess what no one ever thinks about is the other side. It's not as if I somehow finagled fate to choose me for Jonah. I didn't ask for it, so I certainly shouldn't be ridiculed for it either. I'm sure they're all having a field day back home. They probably had a mourning party for Jonah.

He rubs his chest again. I try to temper my emotions, but when I can't, I groan. "Let's just get started." I stand, ready to do anything other than feel sorry for myself and have Jonah read me through the bond. "Remember that I'm wearing a skirt, and I'll try my best."

He huffs. "It's not like I haven't seen you before."

His gruff voice sends a blaze of heat up my spine. "Yeah, well, none of those times worked out well for me, so I'm hoping we don't have a repeat."

I avoid his gaze. Whatever he feels about what I just said should be none of my business. I don't want to see hurt in his eyes for fear I'll feel bad, and I definitely don't want to see relief that we're on the same page either.

Seconds tick by, and I chance a glance at him. He's still stretching, so I mirror his movements. Eventually, he says, "My parents take our work for the pack very seriously. That's why I wanted you to have a sense of what we do. Obviously, I wouldn't expect—" He pauses, pressing his lips together. "You know if this works out— Fuck," he spits, shaking his head. "I wouldn't expect you to have to participate if you didn't want to. Not everyone is cut out for it. That's all."

That's one of the first times I've seen him conflicted. "And you're wondering if I am?"

"No, I'm fine with my mate doing whatever makes her happy, so you could do your flower shit. If you want."

"Flower shit...." I chew on that one for a while. At least it's something.

"I'm trying to open up to you, Kinsey. Christ. You make everything so damn difficult."

My mouth moves, but no words come out. "I'm not trying to. This is the longest conversation I've ever had with anyone from Lunar, so—"

"Alright, alright." He holds up his hands to stop me before we dissolve into an argument again. Gritting his teeth, he says, "There's a lot of shit between us, but we have to try. I'm here. I'm willing to see where this goes. I know you have a whole bunch of opinions about me, and I have my own about you, but I'm here because I want to know if I'm right. Fate wouldn't have paired us together just to ruin both of our fucking lives. So, can we tone down the fighting? We'll never get anything accomplished if we can't."

I nearly fall off my feet. We've basically come to the same conclusion. No, it doesn't erase anything that happened to me before, but he's right. Fighting isn't going to solve anything. In fact, it's going to take me further away from what I want. Maybe there's another way to deal with my hurt, and I shouldn't place it solely on him anyway.

My lip curls. *Ugh. That was so adult sounding.*

"Is that a no?" Jonah asks, placing his hands on his hips.

"No, that's a yes. I was thinking about something... stupid. Forget it."

"Okay...." He rubs the back of his neck. "Also, I just want to say one thing before we start. I shouldn't have made that comment about your—our—first kiss. I was out of line, and I apologize. I should've realized it was your first, and I don't know, I just said what was on my mind, and I shouldn't have. I understand why you ran away from me."

My lips tingle at the mention of that kiss. My wolf, who's been happily brimming at the surface this whole time Jonah and I have been close to one another, is practically coming out of her skin in excitement. I'm trying not to wrangle her under control, and as long as this nice Jonah sticks around, maybe I won't have to. "Okay."

"Okay?"

I nod, feeling a little lighter. An apology is something.

He releases a breath and then launches into his

family's history on protecting the alpha. Some of it I know from our own pack history, but it's cool to hear it from his first-person point of view and stories handed down from his ancestors. If I had waited, I wouldn't have had to ask him if he enjoys what his life's work will be. It's clear he does. He takes it very seriously, and it's good to see this passionate side of him. Plus, his family is making a difference in our pack. I'm not going to tell him right now but it's kind of exciting.

"My aim in these classes isn't to show you how to protect the alpha's family yourself, but obviously it's something I believe strongly in. I want my mate to be able to protect herself if the need arises."

The use of *my mate* is doing funny things to my heart. "I like the idea, too," I tell him, and he pauses at my words. "Didn't expect that?" I ask.

"If I say not really will I have to apologize again?"

I chuckle. "No, you're safe with that answer."

"Good." He keeps giving me looks as he moves closer. He takes one step and then stops. Then another, stopping again before moving even closer. I wonder if he's aware he's doing it. It's as if he keeps stopping then realizing he wants to be that much closer to me so he automatically steps forward again. "So, I thought we could start with basic human defenses, then work our way into wolf defenses. Because of our nature, we'll often shift first when we're in danger, but there are some helpful things we can learn in our human form as well."

We take the next hour to go through really basic self-defense moves. I don't complain. Through this time together, I get to know him better. Not as the Jonah from school but as the real Jonah. The more he opens up, the more I find I like him. Plus, all this close contact is making my body short circuit. Since I'm determined to try instinct over mind, I *really* like when he touches me; molding my fists into the proper punching form; placing his hands on my hips when he's showing me where my power should come from. Every time he does it, a *zing* passes between us like an electrical shock. If he feels it too, he doesn't let on. He's all business as we move through the different techniques, and I'm actually really happy with how much I've learned when the class winds down.

He brings out his phone to check the time. Frowning, he relays, "I should go. Um, I was thinking, maybe we could exchange numbers? That way if one of us has to cancel or, you know, talk to the other, we won't have to go through Ms. Ebon."

"You...want my number?" My mouth parts. He's my mate and this shouldn't be surprising, but it also feels as if he's kind of hitting on me. Out of everything that happened today, this might be the most shocking.

"Yes," he replies softly, looking up to meet my own gaze. There's vulnerability in his brown eyes. We haven't shied away from touching each other, even if platonically, and I wonder if he feels the same pull I am. I dig my phone out of my bag, ignore the text from my parents, and bring up a new contact. He plucks it from my fingers. "I'll put it in."

His fingers dance around the screen, and when he hands it back to me, I find he's put his name as Mate. My heart races, and I can't gather words to speak, so instead, I shove my phone in my bag and stare at him dumbly.

He steps closer. "If you need anything, call me."

The possessive rumble emanating from his chest hardens my nipples, and it's damn good this academy uniform hides it. I'm already trying to come up with reasons why I might need to call him as a pool of heat settles between my legs. My wolf wants me to throw myself at him; to stake my claim. Luckily, the human part of my brain speaks up. "What's it like at Brixton?"

He shrugs. "A lot like Lunar, I guess. I'm not there all the time. I don't live on campus or anything. I just go to visit friends and attend a few classes."

"So, you're mostly in Lunar?"

He nods, and I don't know why I'm suddenly so consumed by what he does on a daily basis. Maybe his possessiveness is sparking my own. Our bonds are forging whether we like it or not. The more time we spend together, the harder it will be to control—in theory.

His expression morphs. "What is it?"

Wow. I'm suddenly feeling super stabby about what he does in his spare time, and I know I should keep my mouth shut, but I can't stop myself. I sigh and run my hands through my hair, my hackles rising. I don't like the idea of him being away from me, and I'm wondering *what* he's doing. I fan my face. "I got, like, a whole jealousy thing going on, and I don't know. I'm about to ask you something stupid, but you're going to have to answer me straight. Are you seeing anyone in Lunar?"

He growls. "Of course not. Are you seeing anyone here?"

I recoil. "No, I'll be freaking shipped off to Feralville."

He steps forward, looming over me. "Is that the only reason?"

His husky voice makes me swallow. I shake my head, feeling small in his overwhelming presence. "No," I squeak.

"Good." His chest rumbles.

Dear fucking heaven. This boy. My wolf is ready to lay down and have him go at it. My face flames hotter, legs weakening.

"Now that we have that out of the way...."

I raise a finger. "Actually, I have another question." He lifts an amused brow, so I go on. "I said you were my first kiss, but you never said...." I peek at the floor, unable to meet his eyes. "Was I your first kiss?"

His breathing deepens. I almost tell him to forget I asked, but my stupid curiosity and natural jealousy won't let me, and I can't stop it now if I tried. Giving into my wolf instinct isn't all good apparently. Right now, I'd like to use one of the girls he's kissed as my own personal scratching post.

He places a finger under my chin and lifts until I'm staring into his sharp gaze. "I need you to listen to me, Little Mate. My head is so filled with you, I can't remember what the others were like." A growl starts in my chest, and he pinches my chin. "I understand how you're feeling. My wolf roared in triumph when you said I was your first kiss. I wish I could give that reassurance to you. I really do."

I bite down on my lip. I expected that I wasn't his first kiss. Sifting through my memories, I can't bring an image forth of him dating another girl, but I'm sure it happened. He's Jonah fucking Livestrong, and I'm nobody. That doesn't take away the fact I wish he could give me that reassurance, too. My heart beats a mile a minute. I clench my hands to fists at my side, and my fingertips bite into my skin.

There's a mentality in young pups to have fun while you can because when you do get paired, your heart is no longer yours. But it's not supposed to be like that. Fate, the Gods, whoever it is, is the ultimate. And you don't realize that until you get older and you're staring at your mate the way Jonah's staring at me—as if he would happily strip away the past and give me his first everything.

The emotion is so powerful that it threatens to knock me off my feet.

He stares at my lips, then backs away, releasing his taut hold on my chin. The breath whooshes out of me.

The sound of heels on wood echo off the gymnasium floor, and I slide away from Jonah as if we're doing something wrong. "Miss Walker?" I tilt my head up, finding my advisor just inside the door. "I need to see you in my office."

I swallow. What the hell is wrong now?

13

*T*he clock on the wall ticks behind me as I sit across the desk from Ms. Ebon. Jonah stands just off to the side. His mere presence is a crushing sort of domineering warmth that spreads over my shoulders and down my front. Even Ms. Ebon keeps flicking her gaze above my head to the imposing figure.

"What's this about?" Jonah asks.

Ms. Ebon slides her stare to him and then back to me. "I've heard from Greystone Academy administration regarding your rule infraction. I have the punishment at hand."

My heart beats a crazy, disjointed rhythm. Mindbogglingly, Jonah steps closer. He's practically on top of me. I need to fan my face again. The number of emotions flowing through me can't be healthy. One second, it feels as if my heart is going to stop ticking for good. In the next, it's as if it's soaring off on a rocket ship.

"I explained to you that it wasn't her fault," Jonah states evenly, almost dismissively. His cool tone exudes power, and despite where I'm sitting, his confidence turns me on.

"Yes, well, Lydia Greystone differs in opinion."

A rumble starts in his chest. "I wrote her as well."

I spin in my chair. "You wrote the alpha's sister for me?" I can't believe it. Not one single person has ever interfered on my behalf. Never.

With his hands behind his back, his biceps bulge, and I trace the hard line of his body as if I could jump him right here. Unfortunately, he's not looking at me. Instead, he addresses Ms. Ebon again. "What is the punishment?"

I turn around, making myself pay attention to what's actually going on. This is serious.

She leans back, gaze tracking over the two of us. She doesn't make any outward show of it, but her studious nature must sense something different between us. When she answers his question, she looks at me. "You're forbidden from shifting while staying at Greystone."

Horror rips through me. I stand with my hands clenched to fists. "No."

Jonah's at my side in an instant, snarling under his breath. "That's degrading."

Ms. Ebon's hands tighten around the arm of her chair. "It wasn't my decision. I understand your frustration; however, Mrs. Greystone believes this is the worthy punishment for your actions."

Jonah paces, his hulking form too big for even this huge office. I glance at the floor, anger and shock rippling through me. It's as if I've taken a few huge leaps forward and then someone came behind me and put me in my place again.

Jonah moves toward me, grabbing my forearm. "I'll fix this."

"There's nothing to be done," my advisor states. "I've already argued on Miss Walker's behalf, but Lydia's opinion is final. Your interference will only make it worse."

I stare down at my hands. My wolf starts to claw at my chest now as if she's just realized how serious this is. I've only shifted a grand total of three fucking times. Three. And once was a damn accident. I grit my teeth. I'm used to putting my wolf in a box, but I've been trying to let her out, to give her more freedom. The weeks after your first shift are supposed to be when you bond with your wolf fully. Now, I can't let her take control at all.

"This is bullshit," Jonah bellows, and I swear the glass in the cabinets rattles.

"Mr. Livestrong," Ms. Ebon admonishes.

It's as if everything is happening outside my body. One good day. One fucking good day, and now this. A cruel, unusual punishment for someone who was only following her nature. This has to be because of who I am.

Two pairs of eyes watch me as I stand there in silence. The true sympathy in Jonah's gaze does nothing to deter what I'm about to say. "The only thing that's bullshit is that I'm here in the first place." I turn, giving them both my back, and stride toward the door. "I'll lock her up. Don't worry, I'm used to it."

The usually heavy door throws open easier with the adrenaline pumping through me. I have no idea how I'm going to keep my wolf inside when what she really wants to do is escape and tear into people. I speak calmly to her, reassuring her that we'll get out of this. It's taking all my willpower to keep her at bay right now, so I don't hear the heavy footsteps approaching me from behind.

A hand closes around my arm, and a growl rips from my chest, ending in a ferocious snarl. Gritting my

147

jaw together to stop the change doesn't work. My teeth elongate, pushing through my lips with a sharp pain, and a keening sound starts low in my throat.

Jonah pulls me into a dark alcove. He places his huge, meaty paws behind my head and backs me into a wall. "Shhh," he soothes, barricading my body. Instead of making my wolf tense up, it does the opposite. She starts to withdraw. His very presence reads safety to her. I breathe in deeply, exhaling in heavy pants. Eventually, my wolf calms down enough to realize that Jonah and I are close again. Close enough that I could look up and....

And I'm doing it. Fuck it.

I tip my head back, my gaze tracking from his yellow eyes to his full lips. I'm not tall enough to bridge the distance between us unless I climb him like a tree—which I'm not above doing—but I don't have to. Jonah swoops down, capturing my mouth with his. He thrusts his tongue inside, an invasion of my body and mind as I'm swept away by him more and more. Deftly maneuvering around my sharpened teeth, he kisses me until they retreat. He moans, passing his tongue over the cut on my lip, and my legs turn to mush, crumbling beneath me.

He plucks me from the air with ease and holds me against the wall as he strokes my mouth into pure submission. I feed my fingers through his hair, tugging and clawing, caught between wanting to keep him there and wanting to make him suffer for what he's done.

I'm damaged. I'm broken. But most of all, I'm conflicted.

He breaks away, a groan piercing the silence between us. Reaching up, he touches a spot of blood that's blooming on his bottom lip.

I bit him. Holy shit.

Pinning me to the wall once more, he runs his hands from my lower back to my neck, then down again. "Take it out on me. I can handle it. Just don't shift," he rumbles.

"I hate you," I growl as I slam my mouth against his again. I lick the length of his lower lip, catching a drop of blood before we clash. It's as if we're at war, fighting over who can invade the other first. I rake my hands over his shoulders. His muscles bunch underneath my touch, tensing while I inflict physical pain on him.

Coincidentally, other than trying to plunder my mouth, he's soft with me. His fingers massage the back of my neck while his other hand creeps down my spine, dipping lower to squeeze my ass.

I break the kiss, gasping into the air while my hips

rock forward and find his waiting cock. "Jonah," I groan, a fire stoking in my core.

He places his large, outstretched hands around my head, using his lower body to keep me suspended. With my legs wrapped around his midsection, my skirt hikes all the way to my navel. All I can feel is him.

He rolls his hips into mine and a delirious friction sparks the nerve endings between my legs. As embarrassing as it is, I whimper. I bite my lip, stifling the sob inching up my throat. The good news is my wolf no longer wants to claw her way out of my body. However, my body, on the other hand, has other ideas. I press forward, searching for him and am rewarded, once again, with his erect cock sliding against my panties. "That feels good," I moan.

Fuck. I need this. I need the reassurance of my mate. It's not just how sexy he is, it's the comfort he'll bring. It's finding solace in the one person who's supposed to be with me forever.

"Touch me. Do something." I capture his mouth again, feeding into our kiss. I push the pace until I'm moaning, dry humping his cock.

It takes me too fucking long to realize he's stock still. I peek up to find him staring at me. Indecision clouds his gaze, and it extinguishes all the fire inside my body at once.

I drop my head against the wall, chest heaving. I close my eyes, but Jonah isn't having any of that. "Open up those eyes, Kinsey." I swallow. When I return my gaze to his, he makes sure he has my attention before saying, "I can't do this with you right now. It doesn't mean I don't want to. Obviously, you can tell I fucking want to."

Judging by the fact that he's still hard, yeah, I can see that.

"I was trying to distract you so you wouldn't get into more trouble."

I flinch at his words. "Mission accomplished," I deadpan. I try to wiggle down his body, but he presses back against me, driving his hard cock into my hip.

I gasp at the sensations that course through me, and he levels a glare. "I'll make you come right now. I'll make your pussy mine. I'll give you everything you want." He slams his lips down on mine, and for a brief moment, I wonder if he changed his mind. However, this kiss doesn't last long. He pulls away. "Your first orgasm shouldn't be in some dank hallway, hidden in secret after the roller coaster of a day you've had. It should be private. Sensual. In a place where we don't have to stop at one." My pussy clenches, and more arousal floods my panties. Jonah sniffs the air and growls. "You like the sound of that." His eyes yellow, staring at me as if I'm the prey.

"I love the sound of that," I counter, giving him as much aggression as he's giving me.

He swipes at the blood on his lip, zeroing his gaze in on the spot where my own mouth is tender. "You'd let me touch you? You just told me you hated me."

I groan in frustration.

Jonah clasps my ass, holding me upright as he backs away. With his fingers digging into my skirt, he lowers me to the floor. He knows he's won. He's made me see reason through the rush of sex, and I hate him even more for it.

He straightens my uniform, making sure that my skirt once again covers all of my important parts before retreating to pick up my bag. Instead of handing it over, he throws it over his shoulder. In true, possessive wolf fashion, he says, "I'm walking you to your room."

"Are you even allowed to?"

He gestures toward the opening in the alcove. "I'm pretty sure I'm not supposed to be forcing you into dark halls either. Now, are you going to show me your room, or should I just start opening doors?"

I take a few moments to get my bearings. I don't want to attempt walking and end up flat on my face because my legs have decided they're going to desert me. Luckily, when I take my first step, they work fine except for a little wobble. "I'm on the second floor," I mumble.

I show him up the twisting, ornate staircase. When people pass us in the hall, their eyes bulge out at his hulking form, and then they glare at me as if they want to poke my eyes out with hot irons. Not because of Jonah, but because they can tell he's my mate. They most likely suspect I'll be leaving soon—that I've done what they couldn't—and they're jealous.

Hell, I would be.

"You're making a scene," I whisper.

"I'm making sure my mate gets to her room after a rough day. I don't care what anyone else fucking does."

It's too late to balk at the word mate, but part of me wants to tell him he should've thought of that before he sent me here. "This is me," I say once we get to the top of the stairs. He inspects the huge, wooden door that's big enough to accommodate his figure. I take my key out of my bag while he holds it out for me, and I unlock my room. Pushing the door open, I walk inside. "My humble abode."

He leans against the frame and peers in. He doesn't take a step over the threshold, just drops my bag inside the door and crosses his arms, watching me as I prop my hip on the desk, waiting for him to say or do something. "It's nice," he says.

"Yeah, it's bigger than my room at home. I even have my own bathroom and the buffets for breakfast, lunch, and dinner are to die for. I'm not"—I clear my throat—"used to that."

His hands turn to fists at my words. The muscles on his forearms pop out. Something I've said has triggered him. Maybe it's the revelation of my life back home? Even with the small house and being the black mark upon the pack, I'd much rather be home.

He frowns at me. "I know I did this to you. If you could not hate me while we figure this shit out, I'd be grateful, Kinsey."

I blink at him. A response doesn't immediately come to mind, so I stare into his eyes. The rawness in his words and expression squeezes my heart.

When I don't say anything after a few good minutes, he reaches for my door and starts to pull it closed. "Have a good night."

The door shuts with a soft click. How a huge man like himself can be so delicate, I have no idea. I throw myself on my bed and curl up, stuffing a pillow under my head. Scared to think about my predicament for fear I might freak out again and be unable to control myself, I, instead, throw myself into the moment I had with Jonah. My body heats all over again. I'm about to yell out *Why?* when my wolf gives me a dubious look. It's not as if I can see her, but her movements are mine, like a separate but identical entity. I can feel her emotions, and right now, she's saying, *Duh.* It's the nature of our match. I can still hate Jonah and want him to kiss me like that again.

I'd spent so much time hoping I didn't mate with anyone from Lunar that I forgot to research how it would be if I actually did get paired with someone. I wasn't expecting the whirlwind of emotions. I need legitimate, first-hand accounts of bonding with your fated one. Rumors don't help.

Do all normal shifter pairs start out with more of a physical bond? Or is it just us?

These are questions a pack could answer. Too bad mine has never wanted me.

14

*J*udging by the looks I got from some of the other residents of Greystone Academy when Jonah walked me to my room, I can't tell Mia and my new friend group that Jonah and I made out yesterday. It's not that I couldn't tell them—it's not against the rules or anything—it's that I don't want them to feel bad that they aren't making out like horny teenagers with their own mates. It'd be like telling your friend who's struggling to lose weight that you've lost ten pounds without trying. I'm pretty sure they'll want to cut me.

I wait until we're all seated with our trays at breakfast before bringing up the physical attraction talk. "So, you know how you guys are my first friends?"

Nathan chuckles. "Still think that's a little weird, but yes."

"I missed out on a lot of gossip that maybe would come in handy as we go through this whole, you know, having a partner thing." My face is already red which makes them more curious about what I'm asking.

Mia rolls her hand over. "Do tell."

I peek around us, making sure we're relatively alone before I spout to everyone that I'm a super newb at all things sexual. "So, I'm curious if mate bonds make your um...sex drive kick up a few thousand fucking notches?"

Nathan spits out his water, and Mia crumbles over the table laughing. In between bursts, she says, "Sex-ed teachers and doctors are the only people who use sex drive."

I groan. Of course that's what she comments on. "Well, do you know what I'm getting at or not?"

"Are you saying you want to flick your bean more often?"

I purse my lips, avoiding her stare now. Nathan has completely checked out of the conversation.

Mia's eyes widen when I don't answer. She doesn't say anything, but I think she's figured out that I've never masturbated. That's it. End of story.

Instead, she shrugs, "Yes, and that's what fingers and vibrators are for."

Nathan focuses on eating. Nadia, on the other hand, has a whole different perspective. "I don't know if I was ever sexually attracted to my best friend before this, but I am one hundred percent sexually attracted to him now. So, in this case, yes. It's the universe trying to get us all to make babies and preserve our race. It's natural."

"You know what would be helpful?" I gripe. "A class on how to be rejected."

"Maybe some self-love tips," Mia offers.

"Advice on how *not* to claw their throats out," Nathan adds simply.

"A whole section on separating your own thoughts and feelings from that of nature," Nadia muses.

Mia leans forward, patting her arm. "You're my hero for that one."

Nadia grins.

This talk allows me to forget about the stipulation placed on me yesterday. I haven't told them about it yet, and I don't know if I will. Strike that. I don't know if I can. I don't want to go into another downward spiral where the only thing that can keep me from losing it is Jonah's mouth...and other important pieces of anatomy.

After breakfast, Mia hangs back as we head to our separate classes. She waits until we're alone. "Just give it a try," she says, lifting her brows. "It's not bad. It's normal. No one will love you like yourself."

She winks before taking off, and I end up going to etiquette class with warm cheeks, which burn hotter when I discover I'm the only person there. As if this couldn't be any more degrading. Luckily, the instructor is nice enough. She's an elderly shifter with curly, silver hair. Her coloring probably makes for the most striking wolf.

"Miss Walker," she calls out happily. She's wearing a floral print dress that hits past her knees. Her gaudy blue stone and gold earrings remind me of the vague memories I have of my own grandmother.

I peer around the smallest room I've seen at the academy. A wall full of windows adorns one side. Antique side tables sit against the side walls, and a chandelier dripping shiny crystal flourishes centers the room over an oval, dark wood table. My instructor fits so well with the space that it makes me feel that much more out of place. I grimace. "Am I the only one in the class?"

"Yes, dear. It only means you're special enough to warrant all of my attention. I'm so happy to meet you. I'm Mrs. Graves."

Well, how could I not respond to that warm of a welcome? No matter if it was just nice words meant to make me feel less shitty about myself.

"In this class, I'll show you how to act in certain special social occasions such as fancy dinners or parties, but I'll also take you through more customary niceties such as greeting someone or small talk. There are so many things at play that can put others at ease, and I'm happy to share my knowledge with you. First," she says, looking me over. She circles me and pouts. "Drop the hem of your skirt. I can tell from here that it's rolled up. I took pains to determine the appropriate length of the female uniform, and I will have it worn correctly."

I quickly do as she demands, thankful I didn't have it rolled that extra time that Mia said I should. As she circles me again, she places her fist in the middle of my back. "Chest out, shoulders tight. Posture is key. How you carry yourself says a lot about you. It's important not only in the human world but in the shifter world as well. Having terrible posture automatically makes you appear weaker. Just look at the human teenagers on television nowadays," she ends in disgust.

I press my lips together to keep from smiling. When she rounds to stand in front of me again, she says, "You're very pretty, dear. Your makeup is perfect.

Kudos on that one. I'm not a fan of dramatic looks that seem to be all the rage today. Yours is classic, tastefully done. The only thing I would suggest is a red lip. It asserts power and dominance. Plus, it's also chic and trendy. Your figure is perfect, just watch the hunching of the shoulders." She tsks about cell phones causing all of us to have rounded backs, and I do my best to take her advice even though I'm not sure if there's any scientific evidence to support her claims. We break our bones every time we shift, so I can't imagine that cell phones would do us any lasting damage. Humans? Yeah, they're probably fucked.

"Talk to me about your mate, dear."

I internally groan. He's all I've been thinking about. "What do you want to know?"

"His status, his physical description. Anything you can tell me about why you're in this class right now. I intend on helping you as much as I can, and I take my job very seriously."

I go through the whole spiel about who Jonah is. She interrupts only once to ask if I have any pending parties or dinners to attend, to which I decline. When I get to his physical description, she nods along. "Quite a height difference between you, then? Flats go with our uniforms, but if you do not have heels, I suggest you get some and learn to walk in them. In fact, I'll add that to my class shopping list. You'll want heels that still compliment his stature without dwarfing your own. With such a beast as a mate, you want to reach his own presence. Do you understand what I mean?"

I nod even though I'm still piecing it together in my head. All in all, this isn't a horrible class. I envisioned being stuck in a room with a bunch of other girls reading textbooks, but I can get on board with hands-on learning. Unfortunately, at the end of class, Mrs. Graves brings out a booklet. "I've been teaching with this same material since 1972, and nothing has changed."

I gloss over the cover of the book. *Etiquette and Manners for the Modern Shifter.*

Kill me now.

"Read at your leisure, but I will expect you to have read it from cover-to-cover before the end of our time together. Instruction is important, but classes on real life scenarios are far more practical, my dear. Next class, we'll discuss etiquette at tea parties, but I want you to study the section about postures. Understand?"

"Yes, ma'am."

She smiles politely, dipping her head. When I stoop to pick up my bag, she curls her lip in disgust. "No, dear. Like this." She teaches me the perfect way to bend over. It's so elegant and charming that I feel like I've already elevated myself by five stations from that one move alone.

Damn. I'm practically a princess already.

She ruins my dreams when she tells me not to slouch as I'm exiting the room. Her prim and proper voice makes me smile as I walk backward, telling her I'll do my best, but honestly, I made it worse. The look she gives me as I'm backing away tells me she's horrified of my undignified exit. Why do I think our next class is going to be entirely about how to walk delicately?

Since I don't have another physical class for the day, I slip up to my room, eager to start my self-study in botany. Ms. Ebon has charged me to come up with my own topics and research experiments, and I plan on putting all that together as soon as I get to my room.

I pause with my hand on the doorknob. *Jonah.* His aroma tickles my nostrils. I peer over my shoulder, but he's not there. I tell myself I'm only smelling him because he stood in this exact spot yesterday, but my heart still sinks at his absence.

When I open the door and find him sitting on my bed, I instantly perk up.

He stands, decreasing the space by a third. I slip inside and close the door behind me. I've read the *Greystone Academy Manual* cover-to-cover, and I know for a fact having a wolf of the opposite sex in your room is against the rules, no matter if he's your mate or not. "Hey."

He launches into a one-sided conversation. My brain is so focused on how good his shirt looks draped over his muscles that I forget to pay attention to his words until he's standing in front of me. "Have you heard from your parents?"

The strain in his voice kicks my animal instincts into high gear. I talked briefly with my mother last night, and she'd sounded off, but she has since I've been here, so I didn't think anything of it. "Not since yesterday."

He takes my bag from my hands and sets it down before pulling me by the hand to my bed. My nerves kick up. First, he's actually being nice to me, which means there's obviously something wrong. "I want to— I feel compelled to tell you something I overheard today. This goes against everything I've been taught to do, but I...." He rubs his chest, jaw ticking.

"What is it?" I finally ask. His sour look threads a needle of worry through my veins.

"Lydia Greystone wants your mother to go on trial for her alleged mate crimes."

I gasp. "Her alleged mate crimes?" I echo. "Me, you mean?"

He nods slowly, interlacing his fingers through mine. "I went to the alpha mansion today to ask Lydia to reconsider your punishment, but instead, I was met with this news."

I shake my head. "This doesn't make any sense. Mom was already cleared of this after I was born. Not that anyone else seemed to care," I growl.

He places his other hand on mine, kneading my skin roughly. What he's doing works—taking the attention off my wolf threatening to burst free again and putting it somewhere else. He's awfully damn good at this. "Your—our," he corrects right away, "current situation has brought it up again."

I turn my hard gaze on him, hoping I'm searing my contempt into him with everything I'm feeling inside. "What were you saying yesterday about me not hating you? You did this."

He snaps his jaw shut. The more alpha the wolf, the more they don't take criticism well. Jonah's temper snarls at the surface, his eyes shining yellow, but he doesn't let it go. "Even if I hadn't put in my rejection slip, the council would have. You know that, Kinsey."

Fissures web across my heart. To think I could be the reason my mother is cast out.... I can't take it. I yank my grip from his and stand in the center of the room. The weight of getting Jonah to accept me, of having my parents' life be everyone else's business falls on my shoulders. Everything's crumbling around me. "Why did fate do this? I was happy being the outsider."

My wolf's claws threaten, the tell-tale needle-like tingles buzzing my fingertips. Jonah leaps for me, pressing his body around mine to keep my wolf inside. "Don't give them another reason to try to expel you."

My nostrils flare. Every time I freak out like this, it gets harder and harder to keep my wolf at bay.

"I want to help," he says. "For any part I had in this, I need to make it right." He pulls me away at arm's length. "Tell me right now if you're aware of any truth to Lydia's accusations."

My eyes widen. "You think I'm a freak?"

His answering growl sends a shiver down my spine. "I need all the information I can. I have friends who'll help. This will not come between us. You don't need another reason to hate me," he fumes. "I want to work together, so I need to know everything you know about your lineage."

I want to tear away from him, but I also know he's the only thing keeping me sane right now. "I am the only daughter of Jacqueline and Kevin Walker. It's not like we spent every day talking about how people ripped my mother and her morals to shreds with their petty accusations. We already lived a shit life because of this."

"I'll fix it."

The way he says those words, the demanding look in his eyes, it's as if the truth of his statement resonates through my body. I instantly relax a fraction. Instead of feeling as if I'm going to lose my shit, it feels like I could possibly wait a couple of hours now. I blink at him. "You just pulled some alpha wolf bullshit on me, didn't you?"

His eyes widen. "Did it work?"

I shrug. "Impressively."

He crushes me to his chest, his strong hands diving into my hair and banding around my back. "I had to tell you. It's the bond. But please, keep this to yourself. If your parents don't know about it yet, you might make them worry needlessly. This could just be Lunar gossip. If we need to shut them up, we'll get a DNA test. Hopefully, it won't come to that."

I huddle into his embrace, sniffing that sweet smell of his. "Why are you being so nice to me?"

He hardens. "Because you're mine. And no one fucks with what's mine."

"Except for you," I remind him.

He shifts his stare over my head. "You'll never forgive me."

The weight of the world returns. With as big as Jonah is, even he can't hold it at bay.

Regardless, he's not my real worry right now. If he hadn't put in his rejection slip, the Pack Council would have, and I know that. However, now our situation is threatening my family. I can't have that. Jonah is the only link I have that might be able to do something for us, so instead of keeping him at arm's length, I have to hold him close.

My situation—and my wolf—demands it.

15

Sociology is possibly the worst class I have. I thought it was going to be Etiquette; however, after spending forty-five minutes listening to the instructor drone on about interpersonal relationships, I kind of want to have a close and personal relationship with his carotid artery.

How can Ms. Ebon be fascinated by this? Ugh, people suck.

Even with the way Jonah and I left things last night, I can't wait to get out of the class and meet him in the gym. I spoke with my parents before I went to bed, and they didn't give any indication that anything was going on. After thinking about it, I realized Jonah was right. Why worry them if we don't know for sure something is happening?

I was too young to see the toll it took on my parents the first time around, but I've been privy to their reaction when it's been brought up. I've witnessed how timid they are to go to pack festivities. During school activities, when their attendance was required, they were always on the outskirts, like me. Watching and waiting. And also like me, no one paid them any mind unless it was to make some snotty remark.

I can imagine why Jonah wouldn't be thrilled that I was his mate. My family's reputation might take his down.

I mope to the gymnasium. The huge space is empty when I get there, so I lean against the wall and slide to my butt. Pulling my knees to my chest, I wrap my arms around my legs and place my head on my thighs, shutting my eyes for a moment. My breathing deepens as I relax, batting back the emotions threatening to drown me.

Suddenly, my heart speeds. The contrast is so dramatic that I pick my head up and stare at my chest like my heart is going to pound right out of it. My wolf perks, and we survey the huge room, searching for a threat. Nothing's here, but the feeling doesn't abate. Sweat dots my forehead until it feels like I'm going to crawl right out of my skin.

My wolf tilts her head. *Jonah.*

I dismiss the thought but he should've been here by now. I unzip my bag to fish out my cell, and without warning, the gymnasium doors bang open. I pop to my feet in a crouch, my wolf hovering just beneath my skin.

Jonah barrels inside, nostrils flaring. My wolf vision keys in on the tight lines around his face as he marches forward. His whole demeanor reads danger. When he reaches me, my first inclination is to cower. He places his hands on my ribs and forces my back to the wall. His hot breath caresses my face as he drops his forehead to mine. My own breathing matches, shallow and quick. Tension snaps around us as if it's a living, breathing thing.

After several long moments, Jonah asks, "Where were you?"

My hands have somehow found his sides, and my fingers tighten their hold before I release him. "What do you mean?"

He lets out a breath. "You didn't get my text?"

I shake my head, uncertainty threading through me.

He sighs. "I sent you a text to meet me out on the grounds for training today."

I move back, causing him to pull away. I rest my head on the wall and stare at him. "I put my phone on silent for the most boring class imaginable. I forgot to turn it on before I headed straight here."

His deep brown eyes score mine. The green in his irises sings today, striking against his usual muted color. "I was worried."

I reach up to touch my chest. "I think I felt it."

He pulls back even more, cocking his head.

"Before you came in, my heart started to beat abnormally fast. I thought there was a threat in the gym. My wolf said your name, and I told her no, but maybe she knew it was you."

He walks away, running his hands through his hair. "I'm scared to death they're going to do something to you when I'm not around." He returns, holding me to him again. He's so strong, it feels as if he could squeeze too hard and snap me in half. His temper rises. I see it in the pulling taut of his muscles, but I feel it in my gut more.

I know he's pissed because his anger is my own.

"Wanting to throw you out just because you went over the perimeter. Then, deciding you're not allowed to shift," he seethes.

I run my palm up his chest, feeling his heart beat in hard thuds. "I guess it's a good thing you're here, then," I tell him.

"No matter what happens, I will protect you. My whole being demands it."

That's not exactly the confession a girl wants to hear. Nature is one thing, but we have to like each other as humans first, and I'm not sure we're quite there yet with sentiments such as that.

Once my heart beats at a steady pace again, he puts more distance between us. "I thought we could train outside today. That would give you the scenery you love and still fulfill our agreement."

A warmth spreads in my chest. I've longed to go outside, but I also worry about my wolf calling to me more out there. With Jonah around, I know I won't up and shift. He'll make sure of it. "You don't mind?"

His lips tick as if they want to curve into a smile. "I don't mind at all."

Before I can swoop down to get my bag like Mrs. Graves showed me, Jonah grabs it first. He throws it over his shoulder, and we walk out the front door to the opposite lawn that the shifters use to roam free in their wolf forms. Probably a good idea since we don't need to throw it in my wolf's face that she can't give in to her very nature.

We pick a spot in the grass next to a row of tall spruce trees. Jonah's huge equipment bag is already there waiting for us. He goes to it and brings out a stack of clothing. Turning to me, he offers me the pile. "Not that I don't enjoy seeing you in your schoolgirl uniform, but this will be more conducive to training."

My brain snags on all the wrong things. First, it's the fact that he basically just called me hot. Second, that he enjoys this getup. "You like my uniform?"

He stops what he's doing and turns toward me. "Do I need to remind you of our moment in the alcove yesterday?" He grimaces. "Ouch. And here I haven't been able to get it out of my mind."

Heat swamps me. He's absolutely right. In that moment, I actually liked the uniform, too.

His stare tracks down my body. "I'm convinced the administration does it on purpose."

My flesh heats, so I try to distract myself. "You know, it's not all girls who go here. The guys wear pants." The muscles in his shoulders ripple—a true sign of jealousy. I smirk to myself. It's fun to poke the beast. "My friend Nathan lives on my floor. He's from Daybreak."

A small rumble starts in his chest.

"Yeah, he's really nice. Funny, too," I tell him offhandedly like we're having a regular conversation, but honestly, I'm loving his reaction. "I've never had friends, so it's really great when he stops to chat. It's just, ugh, he's a night owl, so by the time he leaves, it's so late."

His answering jaw snap and growl make it all worth it. The smile on my face grows when he loses control. His chest heaves, his eyes blazing wolf yellow. His back arches, incisors poking out of his mouth. "Are you trying to make me want to rip his throat out?"

My eyes bulge. All the breath vacates my chest in an instant when long, thick claws rip through his fingertips. He pants as thick, brown fur sprouts over his arms in a wave until he's half morphed. The first breaking of bones has me backing up. He drops on all fours, ducking his head as the shift completes. He turns his wolf gaze to me, lips snarling. I stumble backward, falling on my ass. Another deeper, animalistic growl tears from his chest. My own wolf rises to the surface, begging to get out.

I scoot back as he prowls closer, but I get stuck where the spruce tree's branches reach the ground. He moves over me, his thick mane brushing my legs. His heated breaths caress my skin. I tangle my fingers in his soft coat. His eyes roll to the back of his head, and he lowers himself on top of me. His weight isn't exactly the most comfortable, but I deserve it for riling him up.

He rests his head on my chest, an act of submission as I scratch behind his ears. Closing his eyes, he shifts to his human form until there's a very naked Jonah hovering over me. "You're killing me," he murmurs.

This close, I spy the torture in his eyes—the war between his body, his thoughts, and maybe even outside forces I'm unaware of. His bare chest skims mine, making my heart flip.

I trace my thumbs over his cheekbones. "Are your parents mad about me?"

His eyes shutter closed, long lashes fanning down his cheeks. "They only know what everyone else says."

"Jonah, I didn't participate in the pack because their words hurt. Everyone's snide comments about living Feral as if they would've been just as happy to see me living in the woods with no family or dead. That's why I separated myself from everyone."

"You were selfish," he argues. "A pack means something."

"A pack that doesn't even want me?"

"You never tried." I attempt to slip out from under him, but he wraps his massive hand around my back, keeping me there. "We're talking. We need to get this out. You shunned everybody else. You went against the grain because you could, and you didn't care."

Fury rips through me. "Of course that's what you would see. You're Jonah Livestrong, third from the alpha. You have everything. A respectable family, built-in friends. No one talked shit about you."

"Because I tried."

I shake my head. He may never see my side of the story. But the thing is, I don't want to give that part of me up. She deserves to be heard. "I don't know how to convince you that I did, too. I'm not going to argue about how our situations were totally different. If you can't see it, you're blind."

I drop my hands to the grass and look away. Eventually, he rolls off me, and I avert my eyes as he searches through his bag and finds a pair of joggers to pull on. "Get dressed behind the trees," he demands.

I lift myself to my feet, grab the discarded clothing I'd dropped when he'd shifted, and retreat behind the spruce trees to change into the joggers and shirt. I emerge with my school uniform in hand and lay it on top of Jonah's bag. The fresh air caresses my skin and sweeps my hair in front of my face. He's right about being outdoors. Even if I can't shift, at least I have this.

Still, it doesn't erase the tension building between Jonah and me.

Now that I have the correct pants that don't threaten to show off everything I have, he takes me through a more rigorous warm up, then has me punch pads, once again perfecting my fist form. We also do a few hold escapes where he bear hugs me from behind, and I use my center of gravity, among other things, to get away.

It's a shame I can't shift. I'd love to see what he had in mind for training in wolf form. At some point, once we progress beyond human stuff, I'll have to watch him and take notes instead of doing it myself.

All in all, I enjoy our classes together, and not only because Jonah shows off his true prowess, making my wolf sing. This kind of training is empowerment at its best. The more he teaches me, the stronger and fiercer I feel. Plus, it appeases my wolf to train. I take her aggressiveness out on the pads, which also turns out to be good therapy when I picture Jonah's face while I'm punching.

As we wrap up, Jonah asks, "Does your wolf feel more settled?"

"I was just thinking that, actually. This helps keep her at bay." I frown when she whimpers. I know it's not fair, but it's the best we've got right now.

"It's not a permanent solution," Jonah agrees. "But it should help. I had anger issues when I was a pup, and my dad would train me from a very young age. It always held my wolf in."

I cock my head. "You had the urge to shift ahead of graduation?"

He nods slowly. "As you know, strictly not allowed. It could screw up the wolf-human balance."

I frown. I had no idea he went through that. My wolf was always inside, but she held back, never threatening to make her physical presence known until it was time. I can't imagine what Jonah went through to try to suppress his true nature.

"It wasn't all roses for me either," he chides.

O-kay. Here we go. I'll give him that, but there's a huge difference. Other people were okay with sending me off to die. That, in and of itself, trumps his tale. "I—"

"There's a party next weekend. The future alpha is throwing it, and I want you to attend as my guest."

My stomach turns. Warnings scatter through my mind.

No one likes me in Lunar.

They'll say hurtful things.

They'll change Jonah's mind.

"Kinsey, did you hear me?"

I nod slowly.

He sighs. "It's part of the deal."

"I know," I growl. "I'll go."

His bare chest expands as he takes me in. "It's informal. Just a bunch of people our own age."

Just a bunch of *terrifying assholes* our own age. "Informal. Got it."

He slings his bag over his shoulder, then grabs my own, signaling our time together is over. I follow him all the way through the building and to my room. His nostrils twitch as we get closer. He's smelling for another male wolf, I know it. He'll find a trace of Nathan's scent but not what I made it out to be. Like he told me before, my head is so filled with him, how could I even think about another wolf? It was just fun to tease him.

"I'll text you more details about the party when it gets closer," he says. "I'll also arrange everything with Ms. Ebon."

"Thanks," I mutter. I'm looking forward to this about as much as I would look forward to my own funeral march.

He doesn't tell me goodbye, just turns and leaves. I close the door behind him with a little more force than necessary, but I don't care if he knows I'm pissed. Does he expect me to walk into a river of piranhas and be happy about it?

Fuck.

A week and half passes with Jonah and I keeping one another at arm's length. The party gets postponed once, so naturally my mind goes to everyone hating me, and they're trying to get Jonah not to invite me. The fucked up part is, that's a real possibility.

My etiquette instructor is my saving grace in this department. She helps pick my outfit right down to the boots she buys me, telling me she'll take it off the classroom supplies budget. I hope that's a real thing since I don't have the money to pay Greystone Academy back, and I'm low-key obsessed with the outfit she chose.

When she said she would choose my outfit, I was expecting to find some sort of floral print mishmash like the dresses she wears, but the skinny jeans, boots, and long shirt are very trendy. The lengthy, bronze necklace that dangles in my cleavage rounds out the ensemble. The woman even does my nails, and as I look at myself in the mirror fifteen minutes before Jonah is due to arrive, I can't believe I've pulled it off.

I look normal.

Mia whistles from the bed. "Damn, girl. I like it."

I shift my gaze to stare at her through the mirror. "Is the lipstick too much?" I challenged myself to go a little darker, and Grace was happy to accommodate another session with me.

"No, it's absolutely perfect. I wouldn't change a thing. He's going to be kicking himself for not accepting you."

A laugh bursts past my lips. "Ha! Highly doubtful but thank you for the comedy break this evening."

She sits up, throwing her legs over the side of the bed. "I'm so jealous. We only get to go home every few months to visit, and I desperately miss parties."

Yesterday, her and her mate had another mandatory visit, and it didn't go so well. They never do. Mine and Jonah's visits aren't going spectacularly well either since we keep locking horns when he accuses me of not trying. At this point, I've stopped talking during the "mediation" or whatever fancy word they want to call it.

Hell, I'm not even in a real relationship yet, and I'm already in couple's therapy. It's fucking exhausting.

Mia gets up, placing her hand on my shoulder and squeezing. "I know this is going to be hard for you. I've been contemplating all day about what to tell you to make it better, and I don't know. The only thing I could come up with is to try to start fresh. Maybe they'll accept you more now that you're fated to Jonah? Try not to go in with old hurts and feelings. If that fails, I have more chocolate stockpiled."

I turn, wrapping my arms around her. Honestly, I don't know what I would've done if she hadn't showed up in my room that first night. I'd probably still be keeping to myself, and I wouldn't have this experience to know that having friends is actually fun. "I love you," I tell Mia, squeezing her.

My door bursts open, the wood creaking under the force. Both Mia and I jump apart, startled. Mia starts to shake, a growl ripping from her throat.

I blink at Jonah's hulking form, his chest heaving with his labored breaths. He pulls up short, taking in the two of us. "I heard you say something."

His possessive streak knows no bounds. Holy shit. "This is my friend Mia," I explain. "I was just telling her how much I appreciate the help she's given me."

Mia turns toward me, widening her eyes as Jonah

tries to calm himself. He brings his hand up, frowning at a bouquet of yellow daisies that are now in disarray, half the petals falling off.

She clasps my wrist and pulls me in for another hug. "Good luck, girl. You got this."

"Thanks," I whisper, trying to hold on to her encouragement. It's not looking good so far.

She backs away and gives Jonah a wide berth. "Nice to meet you, Kinsey's mate. Hope the door's okay. I might call maintenance while you're gone to make sure."

I chuckle as she leaves the room with a look on her face like Jonah is fucking nuts. At this point, I'd agree.

"It's nice to meet you," he mumbles.

Her footsteps eventually disappear down the hall, and Jonah offers me the disheveled bouquet in his grip. "I got you these."

I smile as I take them. Sure, they're practically barren now, but the thought was there. A trail of yellow petals litters the hallway behind him. "They're pretty." I move toward the bathroom and grab a cup I stole from the cafeteria, fill it with water, and arrange them on my desk, smiling. Flowers are customary on a date, but I'm hoping it's a step further than that. I've already told him how much I love plants and the outdoors.

"You look really nice," he says.

I peek over my shoulder to find him staring at me. His gaze drifts down my legs, up my ass, and across my torso to my face. I took the time to blow-dry my hair so it lands in dark waves over my shoulders.

While he watches me, I take my time ogling him. He's wearing dressy, dark jeans and a midnight-blue polo that stretches across his taut shoulders. His short hair is styled to the side. Dammit, he's hot. He looks good enough to eat.

My wolf agrees, her fur bristling, making the hair on my arms stand to attention.

Down girl.

"Shall we?" he asks, gesturing toward the door.

I grab the small, crossbody purse Mrs. Graves ordered for me, and we walk into the corridor. Jonah shuts the door behind him, inspecting its hinges as he does so. "I think it's going to be okay."

I start to chuckle, and it turns to a full-on laugh. "Who exactly did you think I was saying I love you to?"

He glares at me, eyes morphing to yellow before returning to brown. It sends a shiver up my spine. Silence engulfs us as we make our way to Jonah's truck. Ms. Ebon approved our outing, but I do have a curfew like a lame ass wolf pup. I have to be back by midnight. I've never been to a party before, but I've seen enough on TV to know that that's probably when the fun parts start.

Jonah opens the truck door for me, then gets in on the other side. The engine starts smoothly, and as he steers past the stone and iron gate, I peer over my shoulder. This is the first time I've consciously left the academy grounds, and a thrill shoots through me. I'm going to do as Mia said. Start fresh. Start new. I can do it.

I'm repeating those thoughts in my head when Jonah starts talking. It's as if he's bound and determined to start fresh, too. "The party is in Lunar. Jesse's throwing it at his parents' lake home."

I used to hear stories about parties at the future alpha's house on the lake, but of course, I was never invited. "Sounds fun," I tell him, trying to infuse as much enthusiasm as possible.

"They know you're coming."

"Great. Can't wait."

Jonah sighs. "You don't have to lie to me, Kinsey."

I take a deep breath and let it out. "I'm not trying to lie. I'm trying to think happy thoughts. Obviously, I can make friends, so I'm thinking positively."

He glances over, appraising me. "Mia seems nice."

"She is," I tell him. "Her mate sounds like a dick, though."

"You probably think all the mates are dicks."

I press my lips together. "Actually, I do."

The rest of the ride passes with small talk about my classes and his security studies. When the roads we turn down start to feel familiar, I lower the window. The aroma that hits me sends a knife into my gut. Lunar should smell like home, but it doesn't. I quickly roll it up and lie back.

"You're nervous," Jonah states.

I rub my stomach unconsciously, wondering if this is all my nerves or if Jonah is feeling it, too. "Of course I am."

Reaching over, he places his hand on my thigh. "I'll be right there."

The worst part is knowing that I'm going to be judged on this excursion, too. It's bad enough that I have to be thrust into the same vicinity as these people but the fact that Jonah will also be watching me to see how it goes makes my stomach turn over.

I'll be pulling triple duty tonight. Trying to forget past hurts, attempting to get people who've hated me all my life to like me, and making sure I don't commit any huge faux pas. All those etiquette classes might actually come in handy. Mrs. Graves' handbook talked about how to react when someone's being a douche, and I must have read that section a hundred times.

Mind you, that wasn't the actual title but it should've been.

I turn my head toward Jonah. Straight lips and a feathering jaw greet me. He looks about as nervous as I am. I want to ask him what will happen if I don't pass his test, but I already know. If I don't get out of Greystone, it's Feral living for me.

A lot is riding on this night.

Every step forward I take with Jonah is followed by multiple steps backward. The tension between us is too much, but in a lot of ways, I'm relying on him tonight. "You'll stay with me, right?" He's already said so, but I need to make sure.

"Until you feel comfortable." He casts a glance over at me, then returns to watching the road.

His answer doesn't sit right with me, but I can't very well tell him not to leave my side. That isn't the purpose of this party. This party is to show him that I can be a part of the pack, so I have to try.

My heart thumps while we drive into town. We skirt the outermost side streets and then head toward the lake. I press my nose against the glass as we pass the public parking where Mom and Dad have taken me before, and we keep going until we've almost circled the body of water. Jonah pulls over on the side of the road behind a line of cars.

Would throwing up count against me? I'm pretty sure it would.

My wolf straightens her shoulders, and through her, I gather some strength. It honestly doesn't matter what these people think of me. Fate paired Jonah and I together, so everyone else will have to get over it.

Jonah opens my door and helps me out of the truck. We turn toward the massive, modern house, and I loop my arm through his. He freezes at first, but then he brings me closer, tucking me into his side while we make the trek over the loose-pebble driveway.

Music drifts outside as a guy steps out of the doorway ahead of us. "'Sup, Jonah?" he calls, but when he sees me, his face falls.

Instead of letting that be it, I smile even though it's the last thing I want to do. "Hi, Spencer. Good to see you again."

He mumbles something unintelligible in response, and I'm totally putting that in the plus column. Maybe if I act as if I've been friends with these guys all along, they'll be so shocked, they won't talk to me. That's a win-win scenario.

Jonah pulls the door open, and we step inside. It's the typical scene I've devoured from movies. One area —the living space, in this case—is for dancing. The bar in the kitchen is lined with drinks. A slider on the opposite wall opens to a deck where more people are hanging out. In the grand scheme of things, there aren't a lot of people here. There isn't much inter-pack mingling until you get older, and even then, it depends on the position you hold.

"Do you want a drink?" Jonah asks.

I shake my head. "Ms. Ebon went over the rules with me. I'm not allowed to consume alcohol."

"A soda, then?"

"Sure."

We walk toward the kitchen. I ignore the way my feet want to lag behind, and instead, stay with Jonah by plastering myself to his side. I almost don't let him go so he can grab two cans of soda from the fridge but when I realize what I'm doing, I let go of him with flaming cheeks.

Jonah glances at me and smirks. My wolf and I are getting better smiles from him, but they're still not full-blown, ecstatic ones. He pops the tab on my drink and hands it to me. I take a few huge gulps and then stop myself. If I down this, I'll have to use the bathroom, and that's one place Jonah won't follow me.

"I want to say hi to Jesse. He's probably outside."

My stomach squeezes, but I don't linger on it. I smile at Jonah, and we pass through the slider that opens to a large deck. The lake lies beyond, the moonlight playing over the surface and reflecting the night sky above. It's so beautiful that I stop and stare.

Jonah pulls his hand from me and greets someone. I'm not paying attention because I'm too busy staring out at the water. It isn't until he nudges me in the ribs that I shake my head and bring myself back to reality.

The future alpha stands in front of me. He and Jonah are about the same size, but I'm pretty sure Jonah beats him by a little. I plaster a smile on my face and remember what Mrs. Graves taught me. Greet and compliment. "Jesse, hi. Good to see you. I was just admiring your view. The lake is so beautiful."

His gaze travels down the length of me and back up. Waiting for his response starts butterflies flapping in my stomach. He frowns but says, "Hello, Kinsey."

Jonah relaxes next to me, threading my arm through his again, and they start a conversation about alpha family things. I follow along fine until Jesse's girl-friend pops up. I try to keep the smile on my face but I'm sure it wavered. She was one of the biggest bitches with the loudest mouth. She graduated with us and she didn't bond with anyone in our class. No doubt she's waiting for Jesse to shift next year to see if they're true mates.

She puckers her lips, kissing Jesse on the cheek. "Hey, babe. Jonah," she says giving him a huge smile.

I tense. I'm in a shifting ban, but all bets are off if she tries to hug him or something. I will literally rip her head off. Luckily, she has enough sense in her airhead brain. "Kinsey, look at you."

"Hi, Laura," I force out. "Good to see you. How are you enjoying Brixton?"

She blinks at me, her eyes narrowing before turning to Jesse. "Do we have to do this?"

It's evident she said it loud enough for me to hear. She'd be getting an F if Mrs. Graves were here. Total bitch.

"Yes," Jesse whispers back. To me, he says, "I'm sure Laura meant to tell you how much she's enjoying Brixton."

The shifter in question rolls her eyes, so Jesse tugs on her arm and they walk away.

When they leave, I shake my hands out, close my eyes, and take several deep breaths. The wind off the lake helps calm my nerves. When I open my eyes again, Jonah is watching me. "That went well."

I refrain from rolling my eyes like the Queen Bitch just did. "Swell," I tell him. "Lovely."

"They're just not used to you talking to them. It's going to take a bit for them to warm up to you."

I practically bite the end of my fucking tongue off.

I know, they were so busy picking on me that they

didn't have time to get to know me. But that's not what Jonah wants to hear, so what-fucking-ever.

We walk to another group where more hard eyes land on me. People start whispering behind their hands, and it drives a wedge between me and Jonah. Once again, I feel like I'm on my own.

Well, this should be fun.

I've been in plenty of situations before when I realize I'm the butt of the joke, and this is exactly like that. So *help me, Fate.* I plaster a damn smile on my face the whole time even though my heart beats like crazy. When the group Jonah is in decides they're going to go for a swim, he turns to me with narrowed eyes. "You need to chill out."

He pointedly peers at my hands which are basically squeezing into his huge biceps, and I relax them. "Sorry," I mumble.

"It's going fine," he reassures me.

I swallow, gazing around. No one seems to be paying attention to me at the moment, so maybe it really is me. Since we're off to ourselves, I tug on my lower lip and stare up at him through my lashes. The boots Mrs. Graves bought me are really working with the height difference, but in actuality, I kind of like that he's so much bigger and stronger than me. Especially tonight. He makes me feel protected.

"Am I doing okay?" I hate how uncertain my voice sounds, but I put on a brave front anyway. He filters his fingers through my hair, his thumb passing over the shell of my ear.

"Yes, you're really trying, and I appreciate it."

The doe-eyed look on his face makes my core heat. Is this party like television? Do couples find rooms and go to town on each other? Can we move on to that experience? Because that sounds like a hell of a lot more fun.

"I'm going to grab us some more sodas. Meet me at the dock?"

I nod. I can get behind a trip to the lake. It's so beautiful. He leans down and feathers a kiss across my forehead. It's not the domineering, mind-melting kiss I've felt from him before, but my eyelids flutter closed in response like I'm trying to soak it in. In a way, it's more intimate. Rough kisses are spurred by our natures, but that? That may as well have come from human-Jonah.

His hand trails down my arm, and I open my eyes to find him disappearing through the slider. I take off down the deck and onto the lawn, my lips tugging into a smile. Forty yards of grass extends in front of me until a dock juts out into the lake. A few bodies are already standing there, and as I watch, one dives into the water at the excitement of the cheering crowd.

I won't be going in the water, but I don't mind watching the fun. It beats being at Greystone, and honestly, it's just nice to be with Jonah. Part of me is happy to be staking my claim here. I didn't want to come, but if he'd gone without me, I would've been a jealous bitch.

Don't ask me about shifter feelings. I don't understand them myself.

The stars twinkle above my head. A thread of excitement buzzes down my spine as I make my way toward the dock. Footsteps come up behind me, and I relax thinking they're Jonah's but tense when the scent is all wrong. I move out of the way, but the shifter falls into step beside me. I peer over and find Rachel, Laura's best friend. I tamp down my first reaction, and instead, say, "Hey. How's it going?"

She smiles, but it's cruel. "Hey, Kinsey. I heard you were coming."

I don't know how to respond to that, so I keep my mouth shut and continue on my same path. Jonah will be coming soon, and at least he'll be a buffer between me and anyone else. He may be blind but he's also not going to let anyone do anything to me either.

"Us girls are actually heading over here," she says, steering me down a separate path. She winds her arm with mine like Mia does, but it feels all wrong. Her hold is too tight.

"Oh, but Jonah—"

"Jonah said he'd be coming, too. It's a better spot to sit and relax. You know?"

My gut instinct tells me this is a bad idea, but I can't go running to Jonah. He'll just think I'm not trying. "Sure. Cool." We keep on the path that threads through a forest of trees. The canopy above us blocks the stars and the moon, but our wolf vision makes us see more than the average person, so we easily traverse the landscape. Remembering Mrs. Graves' lessons, I ask, "So, are you at Brixton, then?"

"Yes," she answers, a sliver of ice threading through that one word.

My hackles start to rise, suspicion building between my shoulder blades. "You know," I start, about to tell her I'm going to wait for Jonah on the main lawn, but she pushes me into a clearing in the woods.

Yellow, beady, wolf eyes stare back at me. I spin, and several human forms surround the clearing in all directions. They move in closer, surrounding me. It's the same few bitchy girls from Lunar that used to gang up on me, and they're doing it again now. Here.

Laura chuckles, the sound sinister in the back of her throat. "I can't believe you went through with it. Coming here was a risk."

"I'm here with Jonah," I remind them. "You know, my mate."

Her gaze narrows. "Aren't you the lucky one? Elevated by about a couple hundred spots."

"*If* he lets her out of the academy," Rachel offers smoothly.

Laura tsks. She's always been the head bitch, acting as if her shit doesn't stink, and using Jesse to do it. Her claws are sunk so cleanly into him that if he ever matches with someone else during graduation day, whoever that girl is will end up at Greystone Academy. "Do you really believe you have a chance of him choosing you? If you'd been made to go Feral with your family when you should have then at least he wouldn't know this shame."

Her words sink into me, and I hate her for them.

"You're pathetic," one of the other girls snarls. "You should just go Feral so you don't put him through any more of this. His parents won't talk to him. They're trying to do everything to not have him tied to you and your disgraceful family."

My heart beats painfully in my chest. I breathe in steadily to try to calm myself. Back at Lunar High, I'd walk away or lash out. This time, I decide to stay and face it. "I don't want to be anyone's enemy," I say, trying to keep my cool even though it feels as if my wolf is beating a door down inside my chest. "Fate chose this. Not me. Who are we to decide she's wrong?"

"*You're* wrong," Laura snaps.

"If I'm not a product of my parents," I growl, assuming that's what she's getting at, "do you really believe Fate would've matched me with someone at all? Not to mention someone like Jonah."

"Fate gets it wrong all the time," Rachel concludes. "Why would we need a place like Greystone Academy if it didn't?"

Because there are people out there like you.

Behind me, someone snarks, "Yeah, what's it like there, anyway? Eating out of troughs?"

I snicker at that. If they only knew how nice it was. Not to mention that the people there are one hundred times better than the ones at Brixton. "Something like that."

Laura's eyes glow in the dark, snapping from her normal color to her wolf teeming at the surface. "You find us funny? Someone really thinks highly of herself now."

A growl tears from my chest. My fingertips throb, and I close my eyes to talk myself down. *Don't do it. Don't do it.*

Keeping my wolf in check goes against our nature, though.

A ripping bark sounds from behind me, and I spin to find a wolf launch through the air at my head. I fall to the ground, and it flies over, landing on all fours behind me. A whine bursts from my lips as the overwhelming urge to shift and defend myself laps at me. Shifting hurts like a mother, but nothing hurts worse than holding it in.

"Just shift, Kinsey," Rachel calls, laughing. "How come you're still human?"

By the echo of giggles rising up, realization dawns on me. They want me to shift. They want me to go against Lydia Greystone's orders because they know what will happen if I do.

"Pathetic," Laura cackles. "She's deformed. Did anyone even see her on graduation day? She probably walked around half shifted like the freak she is."

I snarl. "Yes, Jonah saw me on graduation day." Peering around, I search for a way to get the hell out of here. Nothing good is coming from this. I march toward the girl who's in front of the path, but she gets in my way. I try to walk around her, but she shifts closer, staying in my face. My wolf roars in my chest, and the sound comes out right in her face. My incisors elongate, and I physically remove her from my way and start down the narrow trail.

A hand grabs my hair and yanks backward. Searing pain emanates from my skull, and I fall to the ground. "We didn't say you could leave, bitch," Rachel thunders.

A figure emerges out of the tree line. A flood of relief flows through me at the sight of the larger-than-life form, but I quickly realize it's Jesse Greystone wearing nothing but a pair of joggers. He was the wolf who flew at me. He leans down and locks lips with Laura in a searing kiss. She pats him on the chest. "Let's get this over with. Send her to where she's belonged all along."

Jesse swaggers toward me. He gets down on all fours and scoots next to my side. I try to move away from him, but two hands on my shoulders pin me in place. "Smile," Jesse teases.

"The fuck?"

Someone tugs my hair again and yanks me against Jesse's shoulder. A flash lights up the forest, and I blink, waiting for my eyes to return to normal.

Jesse jumps to his feet, clapping his hands together. "Good enough? I want to go for a swim."

Laura lowers her cell. "One more thing," she says. The group of girls descend, walking toward me. The one girl still has me by the hair, keeping me in place. My heart ricochets around my chest. They loom closer and closer. Rachel swoops to grab a rock protruding from the ground, and Laura's fingers turn into black claws. My wolf batters at me. My deep breaths turn into pants through clenched teeth. "Get your cameras ready," Laura calls out, smiling at how much I'm losing control.

I gnash my teeth together, a rumble emanating from my chest. But it's of no use, I'm going to play right into their little act.

Behind the head bitch, a wolf launches into the clearing, landing in front of me. Jonah's huge, brown wolf howls, a snarl ripping through his chest. Laura takes several retreating steps, knocking into one of the other bitches. Backing up, Jonah turns to the girl behind me who drops her hold on my hair. I don't see her run away, but branches crack in the forest.

Jonah settles alongside me and shifts, ending in a kneeling position right next to me. Rachel drops her rock, and her eyes round. He moves to his full height, and they all look like they're going to shit their pants until Jesse moves into view. "Dude. You growled at my girlfriend?" He puffs his chest in true alpha fashion.

"They were ganging up on my mate."

Jesse laughs. "Please. They were only having some fun."

"Respectfully," Jonah snaps. "They were being bitches."

"Well, you should see this," Laura says, trembling. She brings out her phone, and my heart sinks. A fake sob erupts from her throat. "We were on our way to the lake when we saw Kinsey lure Jesse this way." She finds the picture and tilts the screen toward him.

Jonah drops his head. "Don't bullshit me."

"It's true!" she shrieks. "She came onto him. I'm telling you, there's something wrong with her, Jonah. She doesn't feel the bond. She doesn't care."

One of the braver girls says, "Yeah, it's because she's not from a mated pair."

Jonah reaches his hand down, and I place my own in his. He helps me to my feet and then wraps his arm around my shoulders. "If you'd paid any attention in school, you'd know that mated pairs can feel each other's emotions. I felt what was going through her, and it wasn't that she wanted to seduce the alpha. Nice try, though."

Laura drops her hand. She sighs as if lying is no big deal to her. She's been lying all her life. "We were just trying to get her to shift. Damn, Jonah. Forget it."

A rumble emanates from my mate's chest. His angry stare flicks to Jesse, and his friend's presence grows bigger under his scrutiny, his own growl ripping from his throat. "You four, leave," he commands. When the four girls don't go anywhere, he bellows, "Now!" They cower under the weight of his words. Even Laura's shoulders hunch as she cringes. Apparently, she isn't big enough to withstand the future alpha's commands either. They walk away, the Queen Bitch herself peering over her shoulder to administer her final dirty look, but I don't take the bait. She's a petty cunt.

Jonah squeezes my hand as Jesse approaches. "You told them about Kinsey not being able to shift?"

Jesse has the decency to look a tad grieved. "I may have let it slip."

"You wouldn't let them hurt my mate, would you?" Jonah asks. His body vibrates in anger. I can feel the tension gathering in him from here, but I also catch the steady clip of his words. He's trying to keep himself in check in front of the future alpha. No one is allowed to go against him. Not even a friend.

"No," Jesse snaps. "Of course not. Laura said she had a way to get Kinsey to show her true colors so that you would know whether to let her out of the Rejected Mate Academy. I would never hurt your mate."

I scoff, and the future alpha turns daring green eyes at me, but I don't cower. I don't refute him either, though. I'm actively trying to fight against going Feral.

"Again, with all due respect, that sounds like a bunch of bullshit. I'm surprised you would fall for it. I know my mate better than anyone, and I don't need someone else's help in deciding what's best for the two of us."

"Fair enough," Jesse offers, raising his arms in true diplomatic fashion. "Let me go get you some trunks, and we'll forget this happened."

Jonah rubs his fingers up and down my shoulder. "No, we'll be leaving." He turns to me, so much apology in his eyes. "Ready, Kinsey?"

"Jonah, come on. They were only having a bit of fun."

"I don't find anything about what happened here fun, funny, or helpful. I saw a bunch of wolves who know better pick on someone who's done nothing but try today."

Jesse sneers. "Sometimes it's too little, too late."

"And if this is how she was treated, can you see why she didn't try before?" Jonah snaps.

"Watch yourself," Jesse warns.

"I plan on it. Which is why we're leaving." He turns, and instead of taking the path to the house, we hike through the woods. Footsteps leave in the other direction, and when they're out of earshot, Jonah says, "I'm shifting. You'll ride me to where we're parked."

It's as if he's human one second, then fur sprouts and bones break simultaneously before he drops to all fours and regards me with the specks of green illuminating his eyes. He nuzzles me, nipping playfully at my hand, and then I do what anyone would do in this moment: fulfill my fantasy of riding my mate through the forest.

What? Doesn't everyone have that fantasy?

*O*nce we're at the car, I climb off, and Jonah shifts to his human form. I'm sure my hair and face are dirty, not only from the ride but from the altercation in the clearing, but Jonah backs me against his truck anyway. "Are you okay?"

Inside, my wolf is still at the ready, waiting for something to happen. I soothe her until she settles down. "Peachy. Why wouldn't I be?"

His lips thin. "I didn't want to say anything in front of Jesse, but I felt your fear. It's why I came running."

I shrug. "It's what I'm used to." As I'm sitting there talking to him, my walls start to close. I watch it happen, numb. When Jonah peers quizzically at me, I really have no idea what to say to him.

He reaches over me and into the trunk. Joggers

drip from his hand when he brings his arm back. He steps into them, and my heart beats harder in my chest. Only, I know this reaction isn't coming from me, it's coming from Jonah. "I, for one, am fucking pissed."

My teeth clench. I hate that I'm so connected to him right now. These are the moments when I don't want to feel anything, and yet, I'm standing here feeling his emotions. "They're catty bitches."

"They wanted me to believe you hit on the future alpha, Kinsey. They wanted you to shift. All those things end with you in a place I can't think of right now."

I level my breaths as his increase. "It's pretty much par for the course for me. They've been telling me I was better off going Feral since I was little."

"Kinsey," Jonah grinds out as he stands in front of me. "You're breaking my heart right now." His naked chest reflects the moon. If he were a movie poster, he'd definitely be some sort of werewolf god.

He reaches for my hands, but I set them on my hips and glance away. I don't know what he wants from me. I already explained this to him. I could've predicted most of what just happened. Well, maybe not the Jesse part. That was interesting, but they tried to cover it up so well, didn't they?

He tips my chin up so I can meet his eyes. "What do you need from me?"

"Just a ride to Greystone, I guess. I mean, they didn't get me with anything, so I'm probably still welcome there. You'll make sure the photo doesn't go anywhere, right?" I cringe thinking of what that would do to me. Lydia already tried to take me down with the film of me and another wolf in the woods, I can't imagine what a posed picture with the future alpha shirtless would do.

"Fuck!" Jonah shifts again. The rip of bones settles in my head before he bounds off through the forest. Luckily, his truck is unlocked, so I climb into the passenger seat and wait. If this is how normal Lunar Pack parties are, I'm glad I was never invited. I was much better off being alone in my room watching movies or tending to my little flower garden.

A few minutes later, a huge beast of a wolf lands in the rear bed of Jonah's truck. I spin to find my mate grabbing another pair of joggers and changing before jumping to the road. He throws his car door open, the hinges protesting, then he slides in, clenching steering wheel as if he could rip it out. "Her phone is now in the bottom of the lake."

I smirk, but that's about as much feeling as I can muster. Serves the bitch right. The only thing that would've made it better is if he shoved it down her throat.

Jonah starts the car and turns it toward the way we came. Instead of settling in for a long ride back to Greystone Academy, he turns left into the public parking for the lake. He pulls over to the side and shuts the engine off. We sit there for a moment until my heart pinches. I reach up to rub my chest, wondering if it's my own pain threatening to come out. His next words clue me in to its origin. "I owe you an apology."

I grind my teeth together. "You can't control them."

"But you tried to tell me."

"Like you said, maybe if I'd attempted to befriend them earlier—"

"Forget what I fucking said," he seethes. "I heard some of what they said to you. I don't know if it was through you or my wolf hearing, but I wanted to rip their heads off for it."

"I'm glad you know I wouldn't have come on to Jesse. Respectfully, he's a jackass."

Instead of glaring at me, Jonah smiles. He actually fucking smiles. It lightens his face. It's so breathtaking that I almost forget to breathe.

"He can be, and in this situation, he definitely was. Laura's a ringleader who has him so pussy-whipped.

She can basically do anything she wants. She can make anyone the enemy and he'll believe it."

"I'm so happy I'm in her sights, then."

"Would you please say something? Anything?" he pleads. "I'm getting this closed-off feeling from you, and that's the last thing I want."

I peer out the windshield at the moon that hovers over the lake, thoughts flying everywhere. If I could just pin one down, I might have something to say, but I've found that sometimes, it's better not to feel.

He reaches out, plucks a leaf from my hair, lowers the window, and drops it outside. I chuckle. "I'm a mess. I hope Mrs. Graves doesn't get mad at me if this outfit is ruined."

"Your Etiquette teacher?"

I nod. "She bought me all this, put it on the classroom supplies tab."

He blinks at me, then rubs his hand over his jaw. "I never stopped to think that maybe you didn't have anything to wear to the party."

"Well, unless holey jeans with my *Live, Love, Plant* shirt would do, then no. I didn't have anything appropriate. I was worried she'd make me wear the school uniform for a hot second there."

Jonah threads his fingers through mine. "I put a lot of blame on you, and I shouldn't have. I'm sorry."

His apology is a shroud that hovers over my shoulders, but I don't let it in. "Words are so empty sometimes," I tell him. "Not saying yours are. I'm not even saying you owe me an apology either. I mean, maybe you do for not believing me, but can I really blame you for believing that your friends would treat me like your mate? No. That actually sounds logical. It's just that I know them. I figured they would do something like this."

Jonah turns my chin so I'm looking at him. "Will you get mad at me? Do something? *Say* something?"

"We've been arguing for damn near a week. Now you want me to get mad at you?"

His answering growl fills the truck. Reaching over, he unbuckles my seatbelt, then grabs my thighs, drags me over the seat, and spins me so I'm straddling him. "I have to elicit some emotion from you." With that, he wraps his fingers around the nape of my neck and tugs me toward him. He meets me in the middle, our teeth damn near clashing as he probes my mouth open, then swoops his tongue past my lips, delving inside with passion.

I fall forward, my hands resting on his chiseled chest. I've been to this same spot at the lake quite a few times with my parents, and in no way had I ever dreamed of making out in a car with Jonah Livestrong.

I moan into his mouth, and he praises me with a small nip on my bottom lip. The pleasurable pain shoots straight to my core. I try to shift closer, but he holds me at bay, keeping his attention on my mouth. We kiss until my lips are swollen, until I can't think of anything but him. It's as if he's branded me with his tongue, teeth, and mouth; never taking it any further than fingers tangled in my hair and down my back.

When he finally breaks away, his smile has returned. "Now that's feeling." He lowers his palm to my chest, placing it just above the swell of my breasts. My heart practically sings. "Do you accept my apology, mate?"

My throat closes at his choice of words. "I accept that you didn't understand, but you need to trust me from now on. Okay? Accept that I might know something you don't."

"I can do that for you," he breathes, clutching my shirt in his fist, my necklace twisting between his fingers. "You'll have to deal with them, you know?"

I know what he's saying—if we're to be mates, I'll be surrounded by that same group of people my whole life. "You're right." I grimace. "Maybe you're not worth it." His eyes round, and I shift forward, kissing his despair away. "Kidding." I bite his lip, pulling it between my teeth before it pops free.

"That was evil." He settles his grip on my hips. "I mean it though. I'll always protect you, but I won't be with you all the time."

I wrap my arms around his neck. "I'm glad you get it now," I tell him honestly. That's the one good thing that came from tonight. I'm not saying I'm blameless in turning my back on the pack, but at least he sees that I had a reason, and that I'm not some anti-social, freak wolf. "I know it doesn't change anything, and I'll still have to see them and be cordial even though I want to rip their throats out, but at least you see it now."

Jonah tugs at my hand until it frees from behind him and places kisses over my knuckles. "You could still change their minds. We should get a preemptive DNA test. We can prove to them that you're exactly the wolf you should be."

My chest tightens. "Would that stop them, though?"

He shrugs. "It couldn't hurt. We wouldn't even have to tell anyone but at least we'll have the proof if anyone decides to bring it up. You could just drop it and leave."

"Like a mic drop? I like the sound of that."

"It would be a bit more epic than a mic drop, but sure, we'll go with that."

I squirm on his lap. There's something I don't like

about that idea. Getting the test could solve a bunch of problems, but it also means we felt the need to do it. No one else in Lunar has ever had to prove their parentage like they're some sort of freak. "I'll think about it."

"I'm not pushing," he says. "You can do whatever you want." He pulls me forward again, sealing our mouths together. My lips are tired at this point, but he makes it all worth it. Unfortunately, he stops us a few minutes later. "I need to get you to the academy before I do something we shouldn't."

"Does it involve touching me? Because I really want you to touch me."

He groans, shifting so our foreheads touch. "It involves that and so much more."

We breathe in each other's air before he carefully maneuvers me to the other side of the truck. Reaching around me, he grabs my seatbelt and clicks it into place.

When we have these moments together—when he says things like that—I want to ask him if he's going to save me from Greystone. I mean, he calls me his mate. He tells me I'll have to deal with the bitch squad. I know that technically the decision is out of his hands since the Council is involved, but I want to know what he's thinking. That means more to me than a bunch of middle-aged shifters with bugs up their asses.

I'm too chicken to ask, though.

The drive to Greystone is solemn despite my puffy lips. Other mated pairs are settling in at university or they're back at their packs together. They're discussing their futures, but with us, things are still up in the air.

"How did you keep from shifting?" Jonah asks.

I shrug. "I locked her away like I always do."

"You should be careful," he tells me, frowning. "You don't want to do that too much."

"Well, once I get myself out of this ridiculous punishment, I'll be happy to let my wolf out and devour all those bitches."

He snickers. "That won't be good PR for the Livestrong name."

"Probably not," I agree. "You mean, I can't ever put them in their place? Maybe once? You can give me one time, right?"

He shakes his head. "I'll have you take your aggression out on me. That sounds like a much better use of our time."

"What did you have in mind?" I ask, my belly tightening at his words.

He squirms on the seat. "Things I can't think about right now or you'll be late for curfew. And we don't need to give anyone else a reason to take you away from me."

My lips part at his words. I stare at him, but he makes no comment or acknowledgment about what he's just said. My heart pounds in my chest all the way back to Greystone.

He drives through the gates at 11:58 p.m.

Pulling to a stop, he peers at the formidable building. "I suppose walking you to your room is against the rules?"

I nod slowly. "No shifters of the opposite sex in rooms after 11 p.m."

He turns and grabs my chin. "You better get in there, then, Little Mate." One solid kiss later, he releases me, and I almost fall out of the truck, except he's come around the other side to help me to the academy's entrance. He leads me all the way up the steps and then stands there as I slip past the huge, wooden door. He watches me with a saddened expression. "I'll text you."

I nod, walking away in a dream-like state. He said he didn't want anyone else to take me away from him. That sounds promising.

I climb the stairs with his words in my head, and even my wolf agrees that's a positive sign. For some reason, all the kissing we're doing doesn't register as important. Not that it isn't, but the physical bond is inherent in our natures. If we can have more moments where we actually talk without wanting to kill each other, that will be better.

I slip into my room and pull my phone out. I promised Mia I'd text her, so I send her a quick message to tell her I'm home safe and that I'll tell her all about my date in the morning.

I can't wait to get undressed. I'm uncomfortably hot from all of the pent-up hormones. I strip down to nothing and lie in the middle of my bed. Squeezing my legs together doesn't help ease any of the throbbing; all it does is intensify the heat. It's so potent, I wonder if I'm somehow channeling Jonah, but he's too far away by now—probably nursing his own blue balls. What's the lady version of blue balls? Because that's exactly what I have.

Trying to get comfortable doesn't work. I throw myself back on the pillows, imagining Jonah running his hands all over me. I'm making it worse but I can't stop. My fingers trail over my hip, but then I snatch them away. I've never masturbated before. In a lot of ways, I am a young pup. Mia acted like it was no big deal; she told me it was normal. And if Jonah won't go any further, I might have to get acquainted with my own body. Plus, I can think of it as a science experiment. If I know what feels good, that will only make our first time better, right?

I press my lips together. Something makes me think I won't have to worry about Jonah pleasuring me.

I moan in frustration. The more I think about him, the worse it gets. My body is calling to me, begging for relief.

Fuck it. I'm doing it.

I move my hands over my thigh and spread my legs. Before I think about it too much, I slide my finger down my pussy and then back up, settling it over the spot where the most heat emanates. I push down and circle. A gasp parts my lips as pleasure explodes. "Oh shit," I mutter. I do it again, working my fingers until I've explored the whole area and know what gives me the greatest satisfaction.

Flicking the bean. Truth.

I moan again as I circle the apex of my core. Arousal trickles from between my legs, and my breath comes out in gasps.

Mmm. Kinsey.

I keep circling as an elaborate picture of Jonah hovering over me creeps into my head. He takes my breast into his hot mouth while his hands explore, just as mine are doing now. Jonah moans my name, egging me on.

Kinsey?

My mouth pops open as my body starts to shake. Oh God, it feels too good.

Jonah's roar sounds in my head. *Kinsey Walker, are you touching yourself?*

I pause, my eyes rounding. He calls out for me again, and my stomach sinks.

Oh shit. I just connected with my mate while I was trying to make myself come.

*H*is growl sounds like it comes straight from my own chest and bubbles up my throat.

I pause my perusal and don't dare answer. He sounds pissed.

At the same time, my heart sings in my chest. You're not supposed to be able to communicate with your mate in this way so soon. It's a bonding thing that takes time, and here I've gone and freaking pushed it over the edge while wanting to relieve the tension coiled inside me. A tension he put there, by the way. So, in reality, this is all his fault.

If Mia were here, I'd curse her out. Actually, if Mia were here, it would be really weird, but you know what I mean. She said this was normal but communicating with my mate while flicking the bean isn't normal. I mean, maybe it is. I don't know. These weren't discussions I had with my parents growing up.

My heart thunders in my chest, hands tangle in the sheets. I shoot upright when a thump sounds outside my window. Peering to my left, I gasp when a huge form stands on the ledge, completely blocking the moonlight shining into my room. Jonah lowers, pushing the window and providing just a fraction of space between the two side-by-side panes in which he uses his shifter claws to reach through the gap and open the latch.

He throws the panes open, completely naked, and jumps down, landing in a crouch, then turns to shut the window. "Holy fuck," I mutter.

His perfect form, complete with one huge erection, is washed in moonlight. He stalks toward me. "I've gone through a lot of pants today because of you."

My chest heaves, trying not to stare at his cock but failing. "What are you doing here?"

He stands at the edge of my bed, reaches out to grab my calves, and then tugs me toward him. He bends to his knees, and I make an embarrassing sound from the back of my throat while peering down my body at him. Rubbing circles on the inside of my thighs, he pries them open. "Taking an orgasm that belongs to me." Keeping his gaze on mine, he leans forward. Hot breath caresses my core, increasing the inferno raging inside my body. More arousal trickles to the sheets, and Jonah sniffs the air. "So fucking turned on."

My hands grip the side of the bed.

"Since you've never been kissed, I'm going to guess...."

I shake my head. "No. Nothing. No one's ever touched me."

"This desire belongs to me." He parts his lips and licks my slit, curling his tongue around my nub.

A foreign pleasure rips through me, and I moan. He shudders in response, diving forward with an attention that drives my excitement to the extreme. He suckles and does this thing where he flicks his tongue, and I'm lost to the budding bliss. "Jonah, oh my God."

He moans into my pussy. "You taste so good. Say my name again."

"Jonah," I rush out. I'm pretty sure I'm about to orgasm. It's way too soon, but my body is rushing to a place I've not felt before. "Oh, Jonah, I—"

"Mine," he grinds out. "Let me feel you." He sucks my clit, and I explode. A scream tears through me, and he immediately places his hand over my mouth while his lips just barely graze my sensitive skin. "Quiet, Little Mate. We'll get in trouble."

I force my lips together, breathing heavily through my nose. Shivers rock my body while my toes stay curled from the initial burst. He flattens his tongue against me one last time, and aftershocks course through me. I close my knees on his head, and he chuckles. "I'm leaving." He groans, the sound like pure sex. "I could keep going, though. You call to me. Everything about you calls to me." His fingers flex into my skin, but he retreats, closes my legs, and shifts me back up the bed, sprawling next to me.

I'm sure my expression is as wondrous as the words sprinkling through my sex-addled brain. He's a god. He has to be. I place my hand on his chest, still trying to regain control over my body.

"Did you enjoy that?" he asks, voice husky.

"Mmm," I groan. "I didn't realize how fun that was."

He quirks a smile. "Imagine when you can last longer than ten seconds."

Warmth rushes to my cheeks. "It was longer than that."

He gives me a doubtful look.

I try to hide my face in the pillows, but he grabs my chin. "It was sexy, Kinsey. You were a goddess. I've never seen anything so—"His chest begins to rumble. "You're never to take that experience away from me again."

"That sounds like a command, mate," I challenge, raising a brow at him.

He rolls on top of me. "It is."

I loop my arms around his neck, loving the way we fit together. He crushes my breasts to his hard chest, and I feel every breath he takes. "We should probably talk about how you knew what I was doing. I thought that type of communication came much later?"

He tickles his fingers over my cheeks. "I guess fate has other plans for us."

I swallow. Everything he's saying sounds so right, but I can't keep my hopes up if this is just his sexual nature talking. "Jonah, I have to know...." I lick my lips. "Taking the Pack Council out of this, do you plan on accepting me?" The squeeze of my heart tells me I'll be broken if he says no. Not because of my wolf instincts either. Because it's him.

And no, that's not the post-coital haze talking either.

"That's not the question that needs to be asked." Dread sours my stomach. I glance away, but he pulls my attention back to him. "The question is, will you forgive me enough to accept me when I rescind my Mate Rejection slip?"

My mouth snaps shut. I stare at him, unsure if I should hold back the hope threatening to take over my body. A flood of warmth fills me as if I'm standing outside under the brightest sun.

Acceptance.

It's a feeling I've not yet had the pleasure of basking in until now. "Are you sure? What about your job and your standing?"

He leans back on his legs and pulls me around him, carefully tucking his dick to the side so we're not a few inches from coming together. "I've felt so many things with you over the last few weeks. Jealousy. Possessiveness. Desire. Anger. But one thing I can't stop feeling is that you're mine. Plain and simple. It's not entirely my wolf talking. I'm obsessed with you, Kinsey Walker. Me. *This* side of me. Tonight opened my eyes, and instead of siding with the people I've known all my life, I sided with the person who *is* my life."

My lip wobbles. His response is overwhelming.

"I'd take you to Lunar tonight if I could. Just, please tell me I have a chance."

His eyes latch onto mine and won't let go. There's real worry there. I place my hand on his chest. "Your odds are very good, Jonah Livestrong."

He cocks a smile, and I follow. How could I say no to that? He kisses me, taking his time as if savoring the moment. "I'm going to get you out of here, Kinsey. I'll do everything I can."

I frown, remembering something that the bitch said. I run my fingers through his hair when we part. "One of the girls mentioned your parents were so unhappy that they were doing everything they could to separate us. Like going to the Council about my parents? Is that true?"

His brows slam down over his eyes. "They haven't been happy, but I didn't know that. If it is them, they'll listen to me." He reaches his hands up my body and then down the length of my spine. "They're going to love you. I can promise you that. They're good people. They're just looking out for me."

"I can see that," I tell him honestly.

He rubs small circles into the base of my spine. "We'll figure this out. I promise."

"You're making a lot of promises," I tell him.

"I'm about to make another one." He leads me down to the mattress. "One day, I'm going to sink my cock inside your tight pussy. I'm going to come so hard that my seed takes hold, and in this perfect stomach, we'll grow a life together." He cups my tummy, and I nearly come from his words. His fierce wolf flashes at the surface, promising a forever.

"We better start practicing."

"Trust me, my wolf is begging for it, but my rational, human side says that conceiving a child in the Rejected Mate Academy is a bad omen and something tells me you don't have condoms."

"Fresh out of those," I deadpan.

He growls, and all it does is make the embers in my core come to life. "I guess I'll have to—" He pins my hands above my head and lowers his lips to my breasts, sucking my nipple into his mouth, and my hips come off the bed. With the height difference, all I meet is his abs but, holy fuck, it's the perfect sort of ecstasy.

"Not fair," I groan.

He answers with a grunt and moves his lips to my other pebble, sucking and teasing. Holding both my hands in one of his, he reaches with his other and circles my pussy. I lower my knees to the bed, giving him as much space as he wants. His fingertips enter me. "This is the perfect torture," he breathes, teasing my entrance.

I gasp, a moan filling the room. "Jonah."

He pushes further, slowly awakening my core as my sides suction to him. "Let's see how long you can last this time, Little Mate." He moves down my body, trailing kisses over my ribs and stomach. He parts my legs again, pushing his finger in and out of me rhythmically while he licks my clit. I run my hands through his hair, keeping him in place as I lose my mind.

I last a little longer than last time but not much. His half-lidded eyes meet mine, and as I come down from my own high, I recognize the pent-up tension in his. "Move to your back," I tell him, making my own demands.

He does as I ask, then slowly lowers his fist down his impressive length. I start like he did, placing soft, teasing kisses across his body, feeling him shake underneath me. I trail down his torso, exploring his hard planes and dips. He lifts his hips into the air, a silent command, and I hover over him. I don't know what I'm doing, but I'll damn well go down with a fight until he comes in my mouth.

"Tell me what you like," I plead, whispering just over his cock.

He jerks up into my mouth. "Fuck, Kinsey." I press my tongue against his head and suck. He breathes out, groaning. "Give me your hand."

I place it in his, and he wraps it around his base where his were. Then, he wraps his free hand in my hair, applying slight pressure as I move. I squeeze his base and stroke him into my mouth.

His answering moan is evidence I'm on the right track. I continue to suck, taking cues from his body, loving when he gets a little rough and pushes me farther than I can take him. I groan at his demand and try to take him deeper the next time. His abs flex. "Kinsey, yes. Like that."

His hip movements beg me to increase my pace, so I follow suit, stroking him quicker. I peek to find him twisting his fingers in the sheets, completely caught up in his own desire. I want to make him come. I want to overwhelm him until he thinks of nothing else but the pleasure I'm giving him. He keeps calling me *Little* Mate, but I'm the one with all the power right now. I have the biggest wolf in our pack eating out of my hands.

"Little Mate... Perfect lips. Suck me harder."

I do as he asks, and we get caught up in a frenzy until the guttural noises he makes alerts me that I've done it. He's going to come.

"Kinsey." He pushes me off him and catches his cum in his fist, holding his cock tight to his torso. He reaches out for me as he jerks, bringing me to him.

I watch with fascination at the passion that rolls through him but then I pout. "I would've swallowed."

"My cum belongs in your pussy, not your mouth." He yanks me closer, crushing our mouths together in a possessive kiss. He hovers his lips over mine. "If I didn't know any better, I'd swear you were lying about not having experience."

"Maybe you're a good teacher."

"Maybe fate was right all along." He pulls back, placing a kiss on my forehead. "I need to wash up. Can I use your shower?"

"Mm-hmm."

I watch him stand, his muscled ass curving and giving way to tree-trunk thighs. The man is gorgeous as he walks away, his back muscles still pulling taut. I lie on the bed as the water turns on in the other room.

This is not how I thought this night would end. Honestly, I thought it was going to be a disaster, and I was half right. The first portion of the night sucked ass, but I wouldn't take this part away for anything.

Jonah truly likes me, and not just with his wolf nature kicking in. He actually likes me. And I feel the same way.

Also, future thought. Screw everyone who slut shames. I'm pretty sure I'll be worshipping Jonah's cock from now on. How am I ever going to want to do anything else when I could be doing this?

he smell of the earth wafts up, tingling my senses. I take a deep breath, relishing in this moment—outside, working in my new garden. A few days ago, Ms. Ebon approved my self-study: cross pollination. I want to see what I can make by crossing two plants. I have several different species of flower seeds at the ready, but first, I need to till the soil and actually plant them.

The ten foot by ten foot square I've been given will soon be filled with seeds, and then I have to research the shit out of cross pollination to make sure I don't screw this up. Etiquette and history classes are a good base, but they're not what makes my heart pound.

Now, if one of my classes was Jonah Livestrong, I'd be getting an A+ for sure. I smile to myself as I work. It took a couple of hours to stake out the plot and dip up the soil, separating the well cared for academy grass from where I'll grow my experiments. Using the spade, I draw a line a few inches deep, ready for me to drop the seeds in and cover them back up again. Nourishment will do the rest.

A shadow falls over me, and I peek over my shoulder. The sun creates a halo around Jonah's coif of brown hair. "Hey, Big Guy." My heart wrestles to come out of my ribcage. Since the night of the party, my wolf and I have been content and in complete agreement. She's not threatening to burst free all the time now that Jonah is on our side. It's done wonders for my mental health, and I'm not feeling like I'll crawl out of my own damn skin if I can't set her free.

"Little Mate," he all but purrs. Sitting next to me, he pulls one leg up and drapes his arm over it. "What are you doing?"

"Planting flowers for my self-study."

"Need help?"

"Oh, now you ask. You got out of all the hard stuff," I tease, gesturing toward the huge plot of dirt. "But to answer your question, no. I'm good. I love doing this. I don't mind the company, though." I never mind his company anymore. From the moment he jumped out of my window that night—naked, landing on all fours like a shifter god, bare ass toward the moon—I can't get enough of him. It's borderline obsession.

"Ms. Ebon might yell at me."

We both smirk at that. There are a ton of reasons my advisor might yell at him, and this seems like the least likely culprit. Showing up in my room past curfew and pinning me to the bed while he tongue fucks me are bigger issues. However, I have a feeling Ms. Ebon wouldn't mind because she can count me in her positive statistic column. Now, we just have to worry about the Pack Council.

He rubs his chest. "You're thinking about it again."

I'm so not used to having someone else in my mind —or at least all up in my emotions. It's weird. "I just don't want them to take me away from you now."

"It won't happen," he growls.

I like to think that Jonah could help, but in all honesty, we're all at the whim of the alpha and the Council.

"Have you talked to your parents?"

I shrug. "Not about anything important. They've asked how things are going here, and I'm being vague. They're really quiet. Have you heard any rumors coming out of Lunar? I'm worried they're going through something and they're not telling me."

He picks at the grass, spinning a blade between his

massive fingers and watching it dance. "I haven't heard anything since that day." He gazes up. "I'm going to start telling people I want you out, though."

My stomach twists, but I hold my excitement in. Jonah and I still have a long way to go and one huge obstacle in our way. "Are you sure that's a good idea? What if something comes out and you're implicated?"

"What could come out, Kinsey? That's why we need proof."

He's been pushing the DNA test, and I agree with him. Asking my Mom and Dad to do that for me, though, is another thing entirely. It'll hurt them, I'm sure of it. Shifters are proud beings, and my parents have already had to deal with this shit enough. What will having their own daughter asking for proof do to them?

He reaches out, tugs on my arm, and tugs me into his lap. I dust my hands off behind his back before wrapping my hands around him. He sniffs my neck. "You smell amazing."

"It's the dirt," I tell him, biting my lip as he kisses a trail over the curve of my throat.

He chuckles into my ear. "It's you, Kinsey." He runs his palm up and down my back. It's been hard to keep our hands off of each other after we broke that first time. "If I could do it again, I wouldn't put you in here."

We both know it wasn't just him. It was the Pack Council, too. If they object to a match, they put through the same paperwork, and it doesn't matter what the fated pairs want. Sure, he did it, and he's apologized, but he was never the biggest problem. I've been holding my thoughts in about all this, but I'm bursting at the seams.

I pull back. "Can I talk to you about something?" He retreats and nods, so I blow out a breath. "Don't you think it's wrong that the Pack Council has so much say in pairings? If it's fated to be this way, what can they even object to?"

He swallows. Jonah is very pack oriented, and it's hard for him to see another way. I've been watching him wrestle with this, and I don't envy him. I'm predisposed not to trust other people, but he's basically a pack cheerleader, an enforcer. He'll be the one keeping all of Lunar safe, so to think that something might be rotten internally is a big deal to him. "That's how it's always been."

"But it hasn't, though," I tell him. "You know the history as well as I do. They only started instituting this when the packs started to die off."

"And it worked," Jonah cuts in.

"Did it? Maybe it was all coincidence. It's wrong for us to believe that we know better than fate."

Jonah's lips thin. "I'm going to say something, but I want to make it clear first that I don't think this is about you. Just as there are bad humans, there are bad shifters."

I tune him out. I know where he's going with this. It's what we were told when we were young. They're weeding out the bad apples. I stare down at my garden and the little pile of seeds I have. Some of these seeds won't make it. Some of them might grow only to get an illness and die. But does that mean that they shouldn't get a chance to live? Not planting them just because they might die seems like messing with fate too much for me.

He cups my chin and forces my gaze to his again. "I'm sorry, Kinsey. I don't know what to believe in every case, but I know what to believe in this one. You were made for me. I have zero doubt fate got it right with us."

His words make the hair on my neck stand at attention. I'll be much more appreciative of his endearments as soon as we're out from under the shade of Greystone Academy because right now, words do little else than make me feel good. I need more. I need the hell out of this academy.

"I'll get you out," he promises.

I smile at him, holding back. "Just be careful what you say to who, Big Guy."

He wraps his fist around my hair and tugs me to him, lifting his hips at the same time so I can feel his erection. "No one is taking you from me."

I bite my lip. Turned on is a constant state for us now. Fate keeps moving forward no matter where we are. We've been connecting in dreams where we fuck like rabbits. At least, I'm pretty sure it's not purely in my imagination because if it is, I'm kinky as fuck, and I didn't know it.

Voices drift toward us, and I glance up to find Mia and Nathan walking our way. I scramble off Jonah's lap, and he pouts. "It's hurtful to them," I say quickly before my two friends approach. "Hey, guys, come to help me with my garden?"

Mia laughs. "No, we wanted to make sure you weren't going to work through dinner again."

Jonah's eyeing Nathan with a hard stare, and I almost crack a smile. "Jonah, this is my friend Nathan. He's from Daybreak like Mia."

Jonah stands to his full height. He's taller than Nathan by a few inches. Of course he is, he's taller than most people. "Hello," he greets, though it sounds more like a death knell than a welcome.

Nathan glares at me, and I can't keep a grin off my face. When he turns to Jonah, he hints at a smile. "Good to meet you, man. You've got a good wolf there."

"I know."

I press on Mia's shoe to get her attention. When she peers down at me, I gesture toward the school and plead with her using my eyes. Understanding dawns right away. She grabs Nathan's arm. "Come on, we'll meet Kinsey there. We didn't know she already had company."

"Bye," I call after them. "See you soon."

Jonah turns back at me with menacing, yellow eyes. "I could take him."

I have no doubt about that. Jonah's a beast, and Nathan doesn't seem like the fighting type. I cock my head. "Hmm." I pretend to think anyway because I love it when he gets all possessive.

Jonah leans over and scoops me into his arms. "Choose your words wisely, Little Mate."

I love poking the wolf. Secretly, I think he loves it, too. He enjoys treading that fine line. "Maybe you should prove it to me with your stellar skills."

His eyes darken. "Maybe I should punish you and not join you in your dream tonight."

My stomach drops out, settling into a wildly raging

fire between my legs. "Sounds like a punishment for yourself, too."

"You have no idea." He kneads my ass underneath my academy skirt, and I moan. Peering behind him, he grins before walking that way. My legs start to shake in anticipation. Branches catch on our clothing as he squeezes between the trees and finds the stone perimeter wall. He hoists me up until my legs are on his shoulders and I'm leaning against the hard surface. Flipping my skirt out of the way, his mouth meets my panties, and I suck in a breath.

"Jonah, fuck."

A pinch on my pussy sends a wash of heat through me, and one sharp incisor shreds my panties in half, allowing him to take me fully. "Try to be quiet, Little Mate."

Mission impossible. I stifle as much as I can as he works me into a frenzy. No matter how hard I try to prolong our tryst, my pussy spasms way too quickly, and he soaks up my juices on his tongue, groaning into me.

I drop my head against the wall, chest heaving. He carefully unwraps my legs from his neck, and I slide down his body. "I take back everything," I pant, barely able to stand on two legs.

He pins me to the wall with his hips, then threads

his fingers through my hair. "I can't wait to feel that intense release around my cock."

I shudder. "The anticipation is slowly killing me."

"Well, we can't have that."

"I agree."

"Soon, Little Mate." His words make me ache even more.

He drags me back out to the garden to gather my things and helps me to Greystone Academy so I don't miss dinner. I stop him at the entrance to the cafeteria, though. "I know. I understand."

"It's just not fair to anyone here."

He opens his mouth to answer, but then the air changes. Both Jonah and I feel it—a tensing in our shoulders. We turn to find Jesse Greystone striding down the hall toward us. He smiles at his friend, and my back bristles even though Jonah relaxes. "I was beginning to wonder if you were going to make it."

Jesse looks sheepish. A few students pass us with round eyes, whispering to each other. A buzz starts over us all. There's a future alpha in the building, and everyone can taste it. "Sorry. I had to deal with some shit." He switches his stare to me. "Kinsey." He gives me a small bow, and I almost lose my shit. Why in the hell would a future alpha be bowing to me? "I'm here to formally introduce myself and apologize." He holds out his hand. "I'm Jesse Greystone."

"I know who you are."

He smirks. "Of course but we're starting fresh. So, now it's your turn. You are...."

I take his hand in mine after an encouraging nod from Jonah. "Kinsey Walker. Nice to officially meet you, future alpha."

His handshake is strong, but I don't back down. My skin warms at his touch, and my wolf howls in my head. She's ready to support him wherever he goes. "I apologize for the other night. I was wrong. I may be an arrogant asshole," he smirks to his friend, "but I do admit when I'm in the wrong. It was never about hurting you in my eyes. I wanted to make sure you were right for my friend."

I straighten my shoulders and let go of him. "Fate knew what she was doing."

He nods. "When you return to Lunar, you are welcome in my home anytime. You will not receive the same treatment, I can promise you that."

My wolf preens. Like, straight up tail in the air, fancy twirl like she's wearing a tutu. "I would happily accept an invitation to your house."

"Excellent because I have just the occasion."

I glare at Jonah as he smiles. He knew about this. Fucker.

The future alpha chuckles at my reaction, and I make myself appear controlled. "As you know, the full moon is approaching. My family would like to cordially invite you and Jonah to a dinner party." He brings out an invitation and offers it to me.

It's super elegant. A gold embellished stamp seals the back, and my name is written in calligraphy on the front. The dinner is one week from today. Holy shit.

I steel my shoulders. This will be another test, and I won't back down from it. A good word from the alpha's family might just save me.

"I accept."

21

Ms. Ebon and I sit in one of the many meeting rooms that hosts the mandatory mate mediations to go over progress. It's from rooms like this that Mia usually emerges like she'd enjoy shiving somebody...or crying. Perhaps both at the same time. The first few meetings with Jonah and I were rocky, but we're finally getting somewhere now.

I'm hesitant to tell Ms. Ebon anything without Jonah here, so while we wait for him, I take the time to update her on my self-study. The amount of research she's done on the subject so she can help guide me is awesome. Ms. Ebon is okay in my book, and at this point, it sounds as if Mia wants to switch advisors. Not that moving to a different pack advisor is allowed, but she's at her wit's end with her supposed mate.

A knock sounds on the door, and Ms. Ebon calls out, "Come in."

Jonah enters dressed in a polo shirt and nice jeans. He always dresses up while I'm stuck wearing the academy uniform. Not that he minds in any way, shape, or form. I'm pretty sure he's already planning on bringing the uniforms to Lunar with us.

"Mr. Livestrong, thank you for coming."

"Ms. Ebon." He smiles as he approaches the sofa I'm perched on and leans over to place a kiss on my cheek. A rush of warmth settles there along with a tinge of embarrassment. He sits next to me, and sure enough, Ms. Ebon straightens, eyes darting between us. She is absolutely dying over this new development.

Scribbling something in her file, she starts to ask her first question, but Jonah cuts her off. "Ms. Ebon, I would like to begin the process of removing Kinsey from this facility. Please advise on the paperwork that needs to be filled out."

She peers up, locks eyes with him, then shifts her stare to me briefly before moving to him again. "We are talking about *accepting* Miss Walker, are we not?"

Jonah squeezes my knee. "We are. I've grossly misread Kinsey, and due to her circumstances, the pack never truly tried to get to know her either."

She sets her file aside and crosses her legs. "Am I

also correct in hearing that Jesse Greystone came to visit Miss Walker?"

"He did, ma'am," Jonah informs her. "He wanted to personally deliver an invitation to the alpha's house."

Ms. Ebon smiles fondly at me. "That all sounds very promising...." However, as her words trail off, her lips thin. "The three of us know this isn't only a mate placement though. In Miss Walker's case, this is also a Pack Council placement. When you fill out the exit paperwork, you will certainly be allowed to tell your side, which will give Kinsey a great recommendation considering your standing in Lunar, but this is not as easy as signing some papers and having everything forgotten. There are serious claims against Miss Walker's lineage."

Her words get under my skin. She watches me as if I'm going to shift on her like I did the first night, but I'm in no trouble of that anymore. In fact, it's kind of scaring me how quiet my wolf has been. "I don't want Jonah involved in any of my lineage problems."

"As your mate, it's my duty to be involved in everything that pertains to you," Jonah argues.

I peek over at him. "You're cute, but no."

Ms. Ebon hides a smile at the rumble that escapes Jonah's chest. "I believe we need to tread carefully moving forward. I can help you fill out the Mate

Acceptance Form to give Miss Walker the greatest recommendation, but it will still have to go to the Pack Council to be approved."

"How long until they make a decision? Is there anything we can do to help it along?"

"All good questions," I remark, speaking up. I'm getting restless just sitting here, listening to them talk. "But let's slow down for one second." I lock eyes with Ms. Ebon. "Do you have any insight on the best course to take?"

"Unfortunately, Mr. Livestrong's words won't be enough unless he has some serious sway that I'm not privy to. I wish it were. You two are obviously fated pairs. I saw it from the moment you interacted on Kinsey's first night. Unfortunately, Lunar is very strict about pairings, putting the pack above all else. Jonah's form will help but not like real, tangible evidence as to who you really are will." She lets out a breath. "I'm afraid that's the only thing that can assist you right now, Kinsey. Although, personally, I'm very happy to see that you've come together like this."

Ice forms in the pit of my stomach. Jonah's hand on my leg aids in keeping it at bay but it never completely melts. This has been the thing standing in the way of my life since I was little. It's always been there, like a thorn in my side. "Jonah, tell Ms. Ebon what you heard at the alpha's house."

His throat works. He glances over at me questioningly, but he's come to trust me, so he does as I ask. "I overheard Lydia talking about bringing Kinsey's parents to trial."

My advisor's lips thin. She picks up the file from the table between us and shuffles through the paperwork. "I took the liberty of gathering all the information I could on what happened when Miss Walker was a pup. It never went to a formal hearing. Her parents' word was enough to put the matter to bed, and of course, the fact that they produced a healthy pup was in their favor as well Kinsey was evaluated all through her school years. Each doctor appointment was forwarded to the Council, and everything was supportive of her shifter abilities."

I blink at her. "My medical records were forwarded to the Pack Council?"

She nods, a frown tugging her lips. "It's standard practice. If you had shown no signs of having a wolf or any other defects, then that would've raised alarms."

"Surely the fact that fate paired her up also has to be encouraging evidence of her lineage," Jonah says, squeezing my knee so hard it starts to throb.

"Also in her favor includes that she was paired with

you, Jonah. In any of the other packs, this would be evidence enough, but Lunar Pack differs. They need proof."

"This is asinine," I snap, sitting back and crossing my arms. I turn toward Jonah. "Can't you talk to Jesse?"

"The alpha's family could help," Ms. Ebon states, though the tone of her voice doesn't sound all that hopeful. "But the Council is above them in this instance. In my opinion, you're going to need every-thing you can think of. The alpha's favor, Jonah's favor, and real evidence, Kinsey."

I shake my head. "This is the dumbest thing I've ever heard." Lunar is letting me down *again*. It's not enough that I was totally ostracized due to something out of my control, but now it's happening again when I need everything to fall into place. "Jonah wants to take me back to Lunar. That should be enough."

Ms. Ebon leans forward. "I'm so sorry, Kinsey. It's not."

"We could do the DNA test," Jonah offers.

"Yeah, sure. Fine. Let's ridicule my parents further by making them prove I'm theirs. I mean, what other choice does a couple of outsiders have?"

"Kinsey...." Jonah turns toward me on the couch.

My eyes fill with unshed tears. I just want to rage

at the unfairness of the world.

Ms. Ebon stands. "Miss Walker, why don't you go to your room and Mr. Livestrong and myself will conclude the meeting?" I get to my feet and turn toward the door. She stops me with a hand to my arm. "I'm very proud of you."

Her words settle around my heart, but they don't break through the unjustness currently pressing down on me.

Instead of answering, I make my way out of the meeting area, my footsteps echoing through the empty corridor as I make my way toward the second floor. I walk straight past my own room and knock on Mia's. She answers a minute later with flushed cheeks. "Um, hey."

"Hey," I grumble, walking in. Nathan is sitting on the floor, the tips of his ears red. I feel bad for even having a problem like this when they're stuck here. "Got any chocolate?"

Mia switches to lifesaving mode, pulling a bunch of bags from her closet. She dumps everything into a bowl and beckons me to the bed. "Spill."

I tell them everything, even the stuff I'd held back before. They listen and eat, and by the time I'm finished, there's a mound of empty wrappers in front of each of us.

"Fuck," Nathan says, shaking his head.

Mia echoes his sentiment. We're all quiet for the longest time before she says, "I know it's not what you want to do, and you shouldn't have to either, but you need to get that test, Kinsey. Everything rests on it. No parent wants to see their child in the Rejected Mate Academy—or worse. If they can help at all, I'm sure they will."

My heart cracks. I know they would, but that's not the point. They shouldn't have to.

I hold my hand out, and she fills it with another peanut butter and chocolate concoction that melts on my tongue. "I know," I tell them.

Nathan stands and sits next to me on the bed. The three of us line up, our backs to the wall. "I know with everything else going on that Jonah accepting you doesn't seem like a big deal, but it should be. In the grand scheme of things, isn't that the most important part?"

I sigh, shame filling me. "I'm sorry."

Mia bumps her shoulder with mine. "Don't be. We're happy for you, aren't we, Nathan?"

"Yeah," he whispers, though there's something off with his voice. "You know, I just remembered I have to catch up on some homework. I'll see you guys later."

He stands, leaving with his head down. I frown at

his retreating form, and Mia rests her head on my shoulder. "He had a bad meeting with his mate today. It's not your fault."

"Maybe you should stop calling them your mates? Maybe Bitch and Asshole would work better?"

"You're not wrong," she laments. "I'm going to be stuck here forever. And that's the good path. The alternative is worse."

I hug my friend. It's the only thing I know to do. "I hate everyone today."

She chuckles, her shoulders moving up and down against my own. "Me too. This is our *hate everyone* pity party."

We toast with another piece of chocolate before deciding to watch a comedy and forget about everything for a while. As curfew approaches, I stand from her bed and thank her for helping me.

She gives me a hug. "Any time, Kinsey. I always knew you didn't deserve to be here. You're going to make it out, I know it."

I squeeze her. "*No one* deserves to be in here."

We let those words sink in, and then I mope back to my room. When I get there, I pull out my cell and find a couple of texts from Jonah asking if I'm okay. I tell him I'm fine, then bring up the group conversation with my parents. I text them that I love them, then sit there with the phone in my hands, my heart cata-pulting around in my chest. Maybe I don't want the DNA test because I'm scared of what it will show. Mom and Dad have been acting strangely ever since I got here. My mother freaking out and telling me not to befriend anyone; my father being cryptic. I'm missing something, and that scares the shit out of me.

Maybe my parents haven't ended the rumors with a test before because they knew it would make my situation worse.

The thought curdles my stomach and makes me hate myself at the same time. My mom and dad love each other. That much is abundantly clear. They're true fated mates.

I groan. This is ridiculous. All these confusing thoughts are coming up because my pack put them in my head. If I go with what I always believed—in the special connection I feel between my parents—then *I know* I'm theirs.

Whether I make it back to Lunar or not, one thing is for sure: I won't easily become just another member. There are too many non-conforming ideas in my head that go against traditional pack beliefs.

However, my independence won't break the bond between Jonah and me. That's never going anywhere.

rs. Graves decides we need an emergency meeting before the dinner at the alpha's. Not only does she drill me on every little etiquette bullshit known to man during class, but she comes to my room to help me get ready.

It feels like it's my wedding day or some shit. Mia can't come over because Mrs. Graves thinks she'll distract me from tonight's true purpose. My etiquette instructor even sets the tone by putting on classical music and sitting ramrod straight at my desk chair. She's too prim and proper for this room. Her elegant perfume swirls around the space like we're in a French parfum parlor instead of Rejected Mate Academy. Even her dresses are too tasteful. I swear she owns dozens of floral prints of all cuts, and she hasn't worn the same one twice that I've noticed.

"When you're ready, dear," she calls out. I stare at my reflection in the bathroom mirror and gulp down breaths. I don't even recognize myself. My hair is clipped into a sweeping updo, the hairstyle showing off the curve of my neck and the exquisite dress I'm wearing. It's a tight, yet sophisticated dark slate color that hugs my body until it ends just above the knee.

I feel like a model.

Opening the door, I wait until Mrs. Graves gazes up. "Are you sure this is okay?"

Her answering grin tells me all I need to know. "Oh yes." She gets to her feet and circles me. There's not a ton of space to do that in this room, but she makes it work without falling on her face. "You look amazing. Dinner parties at houses of the alpha are all about showing off how fashionable you are in a classic way. This makes you appear older, more experienced, knowledgeable. According to your file, this is exactly the impression you need to make. We have to get them to see that you'll be an asset to the pack when you return."

My stomach churns. She's right about that. I have Jonah on my side. Now all I have to do is woo them. Should be easy, right?

I kind of want to throw up.

She returns to the bed and starts going through the bag she brought with her. Bringing out a box, she says, "I bought you these cute boots with a tiny heel since we didn't get the chance to practice walking in heels yet. With the parties you're getting invited to, I'm going to move that up in the curriculum."

After she hands the boots to me, I sit on my bed and put them on. They have cute, decorative zippers up the side that end at the ankle. I stand, and Mrs. Graves tells me to walk around the room. I take a quick turn, and honestly, they're not bad. I peer at her for approval, and she nods. "Phew," I tell her. "I was worried."

"Never show your nerves, pup. Fake it 'til you make it." She moves closer and brushes an imaginary hair up over my head. This hairstyle is clipped so tightly, there's no way anything is coming out of it. I guarantee I'll have a headache by the end of the night. I guess it'll be worth it if I can get the alpha to approve. How the hell I'm supposed to do that, I have no idea. Mrs. Graves' calm voice halts my spiral. "Kinsey." I glance up at her, and her unwavering stare helps keeps me grounded. "You can do this. Your strength pours out of you. Lean on your wolf. Look to her for how to act if you get unsettled. Her nature will be the best guide. Remember, pack life is already inside of you. I promise."

"Thank you," I tell her, getting choked up for some ridiculous reason.

She pats me on the shoulder and squeals when a knock on the door reverberates through the room. She quickly throws the two bags she came here with under the bed before maneuvering in front of me to answer the door. She mouths *Ready?* and I nod.

I'd already warned Jonah that my etiquette instructor would most likely be in the room with me when he came to pick me up, so he greets her warmly. "Mrs. Graves."

The woman blushes. "Do come in, Mr. Livestrong. I believe I have someone here who's yours."

Her words make his gaze lock to mine. A tension starts deep in my belly, tensing up my muscles, and for a moment, I forget my teacher is in the room. His possessive eyes yellow before returning to normal when Mrs. Graves tactfully clears her throat.

She stares at me expectantly, and I realize I've already messed up. I give Jonah a slight bow. "Hello," I greet him in the sweetest voice I can. "You look handsome."

My lip quirks as I try not to laugh. He does the

same, inclining his head. "Miss Walker, you're beautiful."

Mrs. Graves approves. She beams from ear-to-ear, and is so excited, it looks like she could pee through her Depends.

Jonah offers me his hand, and I take it while my instructor holds out my purse. "I'll lock the room up for you, dear."

"Thank you, Mrs. Graves. I'll see you next class."

She winks when Jonah isn't looking, and when I turn to face the hall, I have the biggest smile on my face. Out of all my teachers, she's my favorite.

Jonah wraps my arm around his, leading me down the hallway. When we get to the stairs, he lets his lips finally slip into a smile. Now that we don't have an audience, I take him in fully. Jonah is wearing a polished black suit, and suddenly, I freak out about the correct silverware to use even though Mrs. Graves practically drilled it into my head.

Jonah squeezes my hand. "I'll be beside you the whole time, Little Mate."

"I'm pretty sure you said that last time," I chide.

Instead of taking it as the joke I meant it as, his face falls. "Nothing like what happened at the lake will happen here. I can promise you that."

More promises.

We take it easy on the stairs so I don't kill myself, then walk out the grand front entrance to Jonah's truck that's parked in the curved driveway. At least that makes this more normal. I half expected to see a limo waiting for us.

He helps me into the truck and then starts the engine. Everyone is convinced that this night at the alpha's house is über-important. I've been over every different scenario in my head, telling myself I can't fail. Jonah reaches over and places his palm on my knee. "Try to relax. We don't want them smelling blood in the water."

"I'm trying," I tell him. "It's not as if I've ever been to a dinner party before, especially not one at the alpha's house."

"Remember, you are an invited guest like everyone else." He sneaks his touch up my thigh. "And if you need me to take your mind off—"

I slap his hand, pressing down on it so his fingers can't make it any further up my leg. He chuckles, and I moan. "You're so not right."

I'm lost in my own thoughts after that, and I don't realize we're pulling up to a house that isn't the alpha's until I gaze at a brick façade that's still beautiful but about half the size of the current leader of Lunar's house. "Mom and Dad wanted to meet you before you

259

officially met at the party."

I gulp, glaring at him. "Does something about me say I like surprises?"

He picks up my hand and kisses it. "You were going to officially meet them later, and the three of us thought this would make it easier so you didn't have to do it in front of everyone. Plus, I've told them my true feelings, and they're behind us completely, Kinsey. I wanted you to see it from them. I thought it might help with tonight."

"Really?" A tiny ray of hope breaks through my walls.

He nods. "Really. They're good people."

I take a deep breath as he crosses in front of the truck and opens the door for me. My legs feel like they're suddenly boneless as he leads me up the brick steps. He knocks twice on the door before opening it. A large, brightly lit entryway looms before us with the most gorgeous chandelier hanging from the ceiling. I only pull my attention away from it when Jonah's mother comes around the corner, her own heels clicking over the marble tile at our feet.

She's wearing an even more posh dress than I am, a silk scarf around her neck and ears dripping with diamonds. Her warm smile reminds me of her son's, and it helps soothe my nerves. "Kinsey, how nice to finally meet you."

I take her offered hand. "Mrs. Livestrong, I'm so glad we could connect. What a lovely home you have."

Greet and compliment. Greet and compliment.

Her smile widens. "It's Cindy. Johnathan is putting his tie on. Would you like to come to the sitting room for a moment?"

Jonah leans down and kisses his mom on the cheek. Side by side, she looks so fragile compared to her son. I'm even an inch or two taller than her, and I know Mr. Livestrong is a huge, hulking man like Jonah.

I walk through a short hallway in awe and am suddenly very wary of when Jonah meets my parents. Mom and Dad made our house up as much as they could, but it's nothing like this. It's aged, and though decorated, there's not the sense of finery that this house has.

"What a wonderful dress you have on, Kinsey. Where did you get it?"

My cheeks flame. "Well, to be honest, my etiquette teacher purchased it for me through the school. I'd be happy to ask her and pass it on."

Mrs. Livestrong doesn't miss a beat. "She has a wonderful eye. It's gorgeous on you."

"Thank you. I'll definitely tell her. I'm sure she'd be delighted to hear that."

"I think it's the girl wearing it," Jonah says softly.

His mom stands back, studying the two of us. She stares for a full minute before nodding once as if she's just made up her mind about something. "I believe you're correct, Jonah. You two complement one another well. It reminds me of when your dad and I were your age."

Jonah chuckles. "You found him infuriating."

"Then it really is like us." As soon as I say it, I want to kick myself, but the laugh that bursts from Jonah's mom's painted lips make it all worth it.

Jonah brushes his shoulder with mine, smiling down at me. A moment later, Johnathan Livestrong enters the room. He bypasses his wife and son and comes straight to me. "Kinsey Walker, welcome to our home."

His imposing figure doesn't scare me half as bad since I've been around Jonah. If I hadn't, I'd be quaking. "Thank you for having me, sir."

He shakes my hand, his grip dwarfing mine, just as his son's does. "Did I hear we were comparing notes on mates?" He grins at Jonah. "I bet you find Kinsey as infuriating as I found your mother."

Mrs. Livestrong smacks his chest good-naturedly,

and I smirk. "He does. He's told me many times," I assure him.

His deep baritone laugh calms me. This isn't half bad. If this is indicative of how dinner at the alpha's house will go, I might just make it out of there alive tonight.

We make small talk for a few more minutes until Mr. Livestrong announces that he wants to show Jonah a new gadget they got in for their business. Jonah's mom looks at the both of them as if she wants to scold them, but instead, she leads me to the couch, shaking her head as they walk away. "Never dreamed I'd have a son who would turn out exactly like his father."

"Jonah certainly takes after his stature," I muse, staring down the hallway they disappeared through. He's already left me alone again. Lucky for him, I don't believe Mrs. Livestrong is going to go all *Mean Girls* on me.

"Kinsey," Jonah's mom starts, and when I gaze at her, I detect sympathy in her eyes. Jonah may have inherited his father's physique, but he got his mom's mannerisms. "I can tell you, Jonah feels awful about sending you to Greystone Academy. He didn't imagine he was going to get a mate that night at graduation, and then when it was you...."

I wait for my instinct to lash out but it never comes.

Instead, my wolf nudges me forward. "I understand," I tell her. "I had to live with the rumors my whole life, so of course I can see things from his perspective. I was hoping I didn't get paired up." I smile but it falls flat. "What a horrible thing to wish for, huh?"

She breathes out through her nose, her face pinching. "Jonah has shared some things with me, and I wanted to tell you I was quite disgusted with the way you've been treated, and I'm ashamed to say that I never saw it."

"It was at school," I tell her. "Mostly other girls, so it's really not something you would have seen."

Her lips thin. We're already crossing into a territory that Mrs. Graves wouldn't like. She'd tell me to compliment Jonah's mom and change the subject, but it feels like this discussion needs to happen.

"If I come back to Lunar Pack, I promise I won't let people's opinions of me keep me from being involved. I have a lot of ideas for what I'd like to do in the future. I want to attend Brixton. I want—"

She grabs my hand and leans over. "You have to be very careful of Lydia Greystone. Do you understand me?"

Her fierce eyes take me off guard. She looks at me pointedly, and I nod, the breath whooshing out of me, and a different panic sets in.

Mrs. Livestrong closes her eyes and gulps in air. When she opens them again, she appears normal. "Yes, Jonah's told me about your love of flowers."

I blink at her. She keeps trying to pull me back into conversation after that, but I'm stiff and uncomfortable now. What the hell is Lydia Greystone's problem with me? And what exactly does Mrs. Livestrong know?

When Jonah's mom hears the men's footsteps coming down the hallway, she says, "Stick close to Jonah. He won't let anything happen to you. You're doing lovely."

She stands, and I rise with her until we face the two Livestrong men. I smile for Jonah because that's what I'm supposed to do, but inwardly, I'm freaking out. Again.

The brave face I put on in the wake of Jonah's mom's warning impresses even me. These etiquette classes are working. Who would have thought?

The formal introductions when we get to the alpha's house go by in a breeze of niceties, even when Laura is thrust in my face. She looks like she's been freshly put in her place and is acting the proper lady as much as I am. An outsider wouldn't even know what transpired between us.

I told Mia that no one deserves to be in Greystone Academy, but I would love to see Laura's ass in those walls, taking Ms. Ebon's notes. She'd be the worst student with too big of a chip on her shoulder to learn anything.

The night's festivities start with appetizers. Mr. and Mrs. Livestrong socialize with the other couples attending while Jonah and Jesse stay close to each other along with the future beta. If I take my past experience with the pack out of the equation, this isn't so bad. I can even converse with them without wanting to scream that they were arrogant assholes for most of my life.

It's Laura that gets under my skin the most. Even when she's being nice, I see through her carefully constructed façade. Her holier-than-thou attitude—as if I don't deserve to be at the top with them—makes me want to cunch her.

Mia came up with that word the other day when we were talking about Nathan's mate. It means cunt punch. And Laura, more than anyone, deserves a freaking cunt punch.

Now that Jonah has come out with his feelings to the school and his parents, he doesn't shy away from being affectionate, which helps me with my confidence. If I'm good enough for Jonah Livestrong then I don't really care about Laura, head of the bitches.

However, it doesn't keep me from watching my back, waiting for Lydia Greystone to arrive. Jonah's mom made a point to ask where she was when I was within earshot, and the alpha's wife explained that she would be late. We locked eyes briefly, and I silently thanked her.

Not embarrassing myself and staying away from Lydia are my two goals for tonight. When this is over, I'll tell Jonah what his mom told me and ask him if he knows what the hell it means. We both know Lydia has something against me because of my no shifting rule but his mom's warning seems bigger than that. And that's saying something.

Ms. Ebon is lobbying for me to regain my shifting rights, but I sense my wolf and I are already behind in our relationship. Around me, my past wolfpeers are discussing a reduction in shift pain as the transition becomes more seamless. Jonah steers the conversation away to save me from having to answer how my own relationship with my wolf is going, and I squeeze his hand in thanks.

After an hour, the alpha's wife announces that dinner is ready. We're a party of twelve as we take our places at the table, and thankfully, no one tries to mix up the pairs. Each of us are sitting with our own fated mates, or in Jesse's case, with the leech dressed in lipstick.

Jonah leans over as he grabs his cloth napkin from his lap. "Thank you for enduring this for me."

A smile crawls over my lips. In moments like this, I

know it will be easy to do these alpha dinners for years to come. Who knows? Maybe it won't always feel like I'm separate from them. For the first time, I want to belong if only because it will make Jonah happy.

Mrs. Graves drilling dinner etiquette into me was almost a waste of time. I could easily turn my head and see what Jonah does so I don't fall into any faux pas. By the time the dinner is finished, I can barely believe I made it out intact. I got a few funny looks at the table, but nothing that a warm smile couldn't handle. It at least forced them to smile in return, and pressing them to be nice to me, even if only for social graces, felt like it was my biggest weapon.

The alpha claps his hands together as the liquor glasses empty. "It's time for our ritual run."

I stiffen, but Jonah clasps his hand on my knee. Discreetly, he leans over. "It's okay. I've already arranged ahead of time to leave after dinner."

I give him a grateful smile. It would be unheard of to turn down a run with the alpha; not to mention that everyone would figure out that I've had my shifting abilities taken away. I don't need another rumor hanging over my head, that's for sure.

While the party congregates in the sitting room, Jonah, his parents, and I approach the alpha and his wife. I thank them for inviting me, and they're both so cordial that when we turn to leave, I can't believe I've actually accomplished the very thing I was so distressed about. We say our goodbyes to his parents by the main door, and Mrs. Livestrong even hugs me. "You did amazing," she whispers. "I'll be glad to have you as part of the family."

A lump lodges in my throat, and it stays there until we get outside. Jonah nudges me. "My mom likes you."

I smile and gaze up at him with tears threatening my eyes.

"Happy tears, I hope?"

I loathe to tell him that it feels like I'm being included for the first time, but I don't have to say a word. He gets it. I can't hide my feelings from him. It's as if we're an open energy line, and we keep sending signals upon signals to each other without trying.

He helps me into the truck, a wide grin on his face. "I'm going to talk to them tomorrow about you. I want to move forward with this, Kinsey." He turns toward me. "You can't stay at Greystone anymore. I'm going to go out of my mind."

I went from praying not to be mated to resenting Jonah and now to not being able to imagine my life without him. Call it fate. Call it a wolf's natural instinct, but honestly, I call it so much more than that. "Me too."

He gets in the other side of the truck and tucks his hand around my thigh again, drawing circles over the cloth of my dress—slow caresses that drive me wild. When he takes the backroads, I don't understand where he's going until he parks the car in front of his parents' house again. He peers over at me with a soft smile. "I want to show you something."

My heart jumps into my throat. "Okay...."

He hops out of the truck, and I meet him around front. He frowns at my shoes. "You'll want to leave them here." Without giving me a chance to take them off, he picks me up and sits me on the hood. Prying the shoes off, he drops them onto the front seat of the truck through the open window and then helps me down again. Instead of going into the house, he takes me around the rear. A fountain trickles in the distance, a blue light making the water glow.

We follow a stone path, and Jonah picks up the pace. I have to hurry to keep up with him, and when we enter the woods, my heart hammers. The moon filters through the canopy of leaves above us, lighting the path as it curves. A single light shines in the distance, and when we get close enough to make it out, my heart starts careening. It's not all of my own emotions either. It's Jonah's, too.

He brings us to a stop in front of a small, stone

cottage. "My parents and I built this house for me to live in after graduation. We knew I would want my own space, and honestly, I wasn't expecting to mate with someone so soon. Somehow, I think you might be the only person who would love this place as much as me."

I gawk at it. The single story house looks straight out of a fairy tale. Hundred-year-old trees surround it in an ethereal barricade. Even though the stone construction is new, everything is situated so perfectly that the structure becomes one with the forest. Huge, flat stones lead to a sunshine yellow door. Ornate sconces frame the entryway and match the window trim for a quaint yet dreamy style. "This is your house?"

He squeezes my hand. "I was kind of hoping it would be ours when you get out of Greystone."

Before I can react, Jonah scoops me up in his arms. "Not the dress," I protest. "Mrs. Graves will kill me."

He chuckles low in his throat. "Mrs. Graves will consider it a job well done for what I have planned for you, Kinsey Walker."

Molten heat flows toward my core. He nudges the door open, and I spot the same earthy tones and embellishments as outside. Rustic, wood trim lines the doorways and the mantle over the fireplace in the small living room. A quick glimpse inside the kitchen boasts a farmhouse sink with white cabinets and bronze finishes. Jonah's house definitely has a cozy cottage feel. Nothing like the two houses I was in today, and I'm absolutely fine with that.

"Tour later," he tells me. "I really want to show you the bedroom."

He moves straight down the hall and turns right into a large room. Kicking the door shut behind us, he sets me on my feet. I have to steady myself in the wake of the turn of events tonight took. I went from scared to death to reeling. He's thought about moving me in here. I could be back in Lunar, next to my parents, with my pack.

He yanks me toward him, and my hands land on his chest. I peer up at his heated eyes. "You haven't let me answer," I say coyly. He waits for my response as he glances from my lips to my eyes. Reaching up, he unclasps the clip in my hair, and my long waves pool over my shoulders. A smile pulls my lips apart before I even say anything.

He growls. "This is not the time to joke with me about Nathan."

Fuck. He knows me too well. "Fine. I guess I'll just have to accept your offer." I jump into his arms, and a ripping sound meets my ears when I suddenly get way more room in the skirt.

"That was you," he mumbles before claiming my lips.

His hands are everywhere, kneading my ass, slipping up over my spine, and finally in my hair. When he's finished exploring, he lowers the zipper on the dress. He moves inside, caressing the bare skin of my back, moaning when he realizes I'm not wearing a bra. I pull away, but he keeps moving forward. I have to press against his chest to create space between us. Our breaths mix. "Jonah, this is perfect. The house. You. Everything."

"So, you'll move in with me?"

He searches my gaze, and his ability to still remain uncertain makes me want to prove it to him. I shimmy down his torso and stand. Slowly, I undress him, taking off his suit coat, then his belt, and move to the buttons on his shirt. His abs flex underneath my touch when I run my hands over his bare torso.

All he has to do is pull my dress past my shoulders, and it drops down, pooling at my ankles until I'm standing there in my panties. My wolf is so ready for this, eager to solidify the bond with the wolf that lives inside Jonah.

I slip his shirt over his corded muscles and work on

his fly next. Tugging his pants open, I marvel at his erection and then shove the material down his hips. I move to stroke him, but he interrupts, pushing me backward until I fall onto the bed. He stalks closer, his eyes switching between the same brown with green accents and yellow.

"Is this where you bring me into your dreams?" I ask.

"I haven't slept here yet," he informs me. "When fate paired me with you, I held off on moving in until I knew for sure what was going to happen. Most of all, I wanted to bring my mate here so we could start this life together."

I grin. "I'm already in your bed, you don't need to keep sweet talking me."

He gives me a teasing smile before pulling his boxers down and revealing the cock that is definitely proportionate to his body. He reaches into the drawer next to the bed and throws a few condoms on the sheets. "I'm just telling you the truth, Little Mate." He grabs my chin again and forces my gaze to his. "Tonight, I intend to make good on every fantasy I have with you."

"My curfew?"

"I got Ms. Ebon to allow us extra time. She really likes me."

"Well, I guess that makes two of us."

He crawls over me, irises glowing yellow. "My wolf senses yours." He closes his eyes and takes a deep breath, shuddering. My own wolf rattles the cages of her confines. She wants out. Jonah nuzzles my neck, thick cock rubbing my thigh. "Soon," he promises her.

A breath releases from my chest, and my back arches. Fur cascades down my arms and then retreats, leaving my human hair sticking out on end. Jonah matches my movements, his russet hair tickling my bare skin briefly before it retreats.

He reaches down, moving my panties to my ankles, and I kick them off. He hovers over me, lips just out of reach. "I'm going to be as gentle as possible. I don't want to hurt you, so talk to me, okay?"

Nerves ricochet around my chest but as soon as Jonah trails his fingers across my thigh and to my heat, I've already forgotten what I should be scared about. I arch into him as he strokes and plays, dipping his fingers inside agonizingly slowly until I'm writhing against him.

I yank him down, sealing our lips together, and he has to pull his hand out to catch himself from falling on me. He moans into my mouth and reaches for the first condom. Sitting on his haunches, I watch as he tears it open, discarding the wrapper over the side of the bed and rolling the rubber down his length.

Lowering himself over me again, he nudges my thighs apart and reaches out to place a few strands of hair around my ear and stares straight into my eyes. "Little Mate, I accept you."

*A*ll my life, I've bucked against the system. I've shied away from the pack bonds, believing I was better without them. When Jonah uttered those three words, I realized that acceptance was all I've ever wanted.

A half-human, half-wolf howl works up my throat and echoes through the room. Who knew *I accept you* would mean so much more to me than the human affirmation of love?

The tip of his cock pushes past my folds. I clutch his shoulders, sucking in a breath at the feeling of him stretching me. "Jonah, yes. I accept you."

Jonah filters his fingers through my hair once he's fully seated inside. "Are you okay, Little Mate?"

I wiggle around him, getting used to the feeling of

him inside me. More than anything, I feel full...and happy. Nothing has ever felt as right as this. "I'm more than okay."

He groans. "Thank fuck because I need to move."

Jonah retreats, pulling out before sliding in again. Pressing his lips together, he watches my face, reads my body. When I start to move with him, welcoming his thrusts, he takes it up a notch until pleasure highlights every little movement. I exhale on a moan. "Is it supposed to feel this good?"

The corners of his lips quirk, and he nudges my head to the side to kiss a trail from my jaw to my ear. "It is for us." He nips my ear, grabbing my lobe between his teeth and yanking on it playfully. "Fuck. You're so tight."

His words spur my confidence. I explore his taut body with abandon, skating my fingertips over his hips and then around to his muscular back. His skin flexes under my touch in ripples of satisfaction.

My heels dig into the mattress as he crushes his hips to mine. Shifting weight from one arm to another, he traces up my side, skirting up my rib cage until he palms my breast. "So perfect."

I arch against him, and his movements stutter.

"Mmm, Little Mate. I'm trying to be good."

I reach around and clasp his ass, sinking my fingers

deep into his muscles. "Are you holding back on me?"

"I don't want to hurt you."

"Hurt me," I beg, not imagining that it could feel much better than it already does.

I was wrong.

Jonah tweaks my nipple, smirking before he starts a steady rhythm that shakes me and the bed beneath us. I gasp at his speed, reveling in the way he pins me to the mattress. Excitement threads through my very being as he consumes me completely.

He grasps my hands and holds them over my head. "This is fucking. This is what my body is demanding I do."

He slows his pace, biting his own lip before kissing the tip of my nose. He trails his expert mouth over my chin, down my neck, and to my collarbone. As he lowers further, his cock slowly retracts. Before I can protest, he sucks my nipple into his mouth.

I buck into him. "Jonah."

"This is me worshipping you," he murmurs, trailing a line of kisses all over my exposed skin. I arch into him, searching for his dick. I want more. I *need* more. "Proving to you how beautiful you are. How fucking sexy every little piece of you is." He shifts upward, entering me in one swift motion again. "And this pussy is my home."

I cry out. "Yes, Jonah. Please." He takes his time, his thrusts a steady tease. I start to shake. "I want to come around you."

"Mmm." He sits back on his haunches, dragging my lower half with him until my ass is on his thighs while my shoulders stay on the mattress. He pinches my nipples and skirts his right hand down to find my clit. With one thumb circling my nipple, the other on my clit, and his cock pumping inside me, my body doesn't know what to do with itself. It starts to shudder, pleasure lapping at me from all angles. I wrap my legs around his torso, bringing us closer as my excitement builds.

I grab the sheets, fisting them in my hands. Short cries and moans push past my lips.

Half-lidded eyes meet mine. "Talk to me, Kinsey. How does that feel?"

My toes curl. "I'm going to come. God, you feel so good. More Jonah, please."

He quickens his movements. The only thing I feel is the heightening arousal between my legs that propels me forward until I fall over the ledge in bliss. Grabbing my hips, he yanks me toward him in one intense maneuver that has me gasping. I climax around him, my heart threatening to beat right out of my chest. He shivers as he watches me, eyes closing briefly.

Jonah's expansive chest heaves. I study him as he wrangles himself under control while I come down from my high, my heart too full for words.

He shifts us until he's hovering over me once more, claiming my mouth and sucking up all the air in the room. He elicits more moans from me, breaking free only to thrust inside me again. "I felt every single squeeze." Torment crosses his face. "Kinsey, give it to me again. Give it to me before I lose myself inside you."

A sheen of sweat starts across his forehead. I work my fingers into his hair as he ravages my body. This is the Jonah show, and I'm here for it. His moans mix with mine on the bed he built and invited me into. His home. Our home.

Pelts of fur raise over his arms before he shakes them away. My own wolf rises to the surface as he drives me into the mattress. My teeth elongate, biting into my lip. "Fuck me, Jonah," I growl in a voice half my own, crazy with need, and half given way to the wolf inside me. "Make me come."

He roars, his body taking over, propelling me higher and higher. My wolf clamors to the surface, staying just below the surface. I feel her there, rippling beneath me as Jonah and I come together in a flurry of primal need.

"Squeeze me with your tight pussy, Kinsey. I want

to feel you. Fuck, I'm so close."

His excitement seeps under my skin, fanning the flames already burning there like a raging wildfire.

He cups my ass, holding me to him as he thrusts.

He hits a new spot, and I race closer to my climax. "Jonah," I warn.

He struggles to stay under control, his movements shaky. "Come with me, Little Mate," he demands as he jerks inside me, pushing me over the edge.

I start to squeeze him and cry out at the barreling intensity. He meets me, grunting out his own release. His arms give out, and he shudders over me while I kiss his chest. His orgasm keeps coming and coming, his body shaking. His cock spasms inside me for the longest time before settling.

"Fuck," he groans, dropping his head next to mine. "You're not leaving. You belong here."

I wrap my arms around him, cradling him to me. "One day," I promise, making him a pledge of my own since he's the only one who's been doing that. Being in this house, I see what life could be like here in the woods with him. Maybe we could build a greenhouse? I could start my own business. I could make a home here. In Lunar.

Something I never thought I'd have.

He lifts up to kiss me. "I'll be right back. I just have

to throw this out."

He withdraws slowly, and the both of us moan as he exits. My core is empty without him. He strides toward the bathroom, pinching the condom. The door to the en suite closes halfway, hiding his perfect body from view as the water runs for a moment.

When he returns, his cock is still erect, and my brows raise at it. "Maybe it wasn't such a good idea to have sex with you on the full moon. My wolf is raging. Are you sure you're okay?"

It kind of makes sense now that I think about it. Our wolves get carnal during the full moon, thinking only of mating, running, and hunting. "Am I hearing you correctly, Jonah Livestrong? You wish we didn't have sex?"

His eyes narrow. "I'm going to punish you for that."

"I have a feeling I'll like your punishments."

"I have a feeling you'll love them." He lies next to me on the bed, pulling me close. Placing a hand on my belly, a growl works up his throat. "You have no idea how much I wanted to tear that condom off and spill inside you."

"Full moon talking? Or does Jonah want kids, too?"

"I want everything with you."

I press my lips together. "What if the lineage concerns never go away? What if—"

He lunges forward, kissing me silent. "I don't give a fuck what anyone else believes," he fumes, barely restraining himself.

"I just don't want our kids to go through what I did."

He blinks, a frown tugging at his mouth. "I'll fight for them like I should've fought for you. I'll make it up to you, Kinsey. That, I can promise you."

I cup his face. "You don't need to promise anything more. I have everything. Except for my freedom—"

He interrupts me with a warning growl.

"—But that's coming," I say, continuing like I don't hear how possessive he is. "Your mom told me to stay away from Lydia Greystone today."

Jonah pulls back. "She did?" His brows crowd together, lines marring his forehead. "She's probably come to the same conclusion we did and realizes Lydia's out to get you for some reason. Which, by the way, there's another excuse for why I wanted to bring you here." He grins at me. "Why don't you shift?"

My heart hammers to a stop. "What?"

"Shift. I'll stay human. No one will know. I'm sure your wolf is dying to be free."

"My wolf is pretty tuckered out, actually," I smile.

His eyes glaze over with heat, but he doesn't stop insisting. "I'm worried about her. You can't keep her contained like Lydia wants you to, and I don't like what she's trying to do. You can't go for a run or anything but let her out. Free her." Tears gather in the corner of my eyes, and he kisses them away. "I'm here."

My wolf scrambles to the surface, barely giving me time to think about it before fur cascades down my arms and my fingertips grow long claws. I open my mouth in a silent scream as my bones break, back arching unnaturally. Before long, my wolf is lying on the bed, copper paws outstretched toward Jonah. He smiles, his fingers working through her fur. He nuzzles her ears, and my wolf pants, licking him.

She moves forward, crawling over the bed to lay her head on his hard chest. He reclines, petting her until her eyes close in bliss. Before long, my wolf becomes restless, though. She gets to her feet, nipping at his face, and he laughs as she swats at him, pouncing and howling on the bed. He rolls her, pinning her to the mattress while she kicks playfully, pretending to nip at his neck.

"You're feisty, Little Mate," he quips, voice throaty. She yips, animal grunts passing through her teeth. She wrestles him onto his back and lies there, sitting contentedly as his chest moves up and down. His fingers still work through her fur for an hour until she gives me back control.

It happens quickly, her need propelling me into a quick shift that still hurts like a mother. I curl into a ball, gritting my jaw until my body relaxes once again into my human form.

He frowns. "She could've stayed longer."

I straddle him in one swift movement, and his breath quickens. "We needed *this*," I tell him. Reaching down, I stroke his already hard cock. He's been hard since our first encounter, never fully returning to normal size even when I was in my wolf form.

I stroke him toward my center, and he stills. "I won't be able to stop, Kinsey."

I place him at my entrance and slide down, his bare cock filling me in the most delicious way. I'm lost to the powerful feeling of pleasure and need, pushed by my internal animal instincts.

Jonah grabs my hips, his fingertips biting into my skin as I ride him. He meets my every movement—his hard ridges massaging my core; his bulbous head driving inside me. "Fuck, Jonah. You feel fucking amazing."

He growls, reaching up to palm my breasts. "You like my bare cock, Little Mate? Stretching you. Filling you."

I keen, the sound coming from low in my throat as I

search for the ultimate climax hovering ever so close. I quicken the pace until I'm spasming around him, gasping for breath as he continues to thrust inside me to prolong my pleasure.

"Kinsey. For all the fates...." He waits until my spasms subside, then rolls my back to the bed and spins me to my stomach. Propping my ass in the air, he fills me again. My wolf howls as he takes me this way, his movements driving us forward. He places a strong arm around my middle, holding me in place as he fucks me from behind. My wolf cries out as we come together, and I'm launched into the most blissful orgasm of my life, feeling the intensity through my wolf and me. Jonah grunts. His claws come out, and I hiss as his hold tightens before filling my pussy with his hot cum.

We fall forward simultaneously as soon as he stops moving. His chest rises and falls against my back while I drag in my own deep breaths. Cum leaks from my pussy, and Jonah reaches around to cup me. "I don't know whether to say I'm sorry or take you again."

"Don't ever say you're sorry for that. I started it," I pant. "I knew your wolf wouldn't be able to stop."

He moves my hair from my cheek. "It wasn't all him."

onah grips the steering wheel hard as we sit in the driveway of Greystone Academy. In the middle of the night, the beautiful architecture looms forebodingly under the moon but some of that is my current mood.

My mate breathes through his nose. "I can't do it. I can't let you go now."

I reach over and place my hand on his thigh. He's been tense all the way here. Our coming together has stitched us closer, and I'd be lying if I said I wasn't feeling the same way. How inhumane and unshifter-like to have this reform school keeping mates away from each other. Keeping nature from doing its thing.

"I'm getting that DNA tomorrow. With any luck, this will be over in twenty-four hours. I can wait that long," he states though it sounds as if he's trying to talk himself into it. His claws come out, digging into the steering wheel.

Maybe we were reckless. I don't care. Like he said, it wasn't all the moon and the fated pull. It's Jonah and me, too.

"I'm safe at Greystone Academy," I tell him. "Ms. Ebon is here. She's on our side. My teachers are good."

"Fucking Lydia," he growls.

I unclasp my seatbelt and prop myself in my mate's lap. His arms automatically come around me, closing me in. My next words try to convince me as much as they're meant to convince him. "I'll be fine."

He pulls me to him, desperately holding me in place. It's our nature to not want to be apart from each other. "I'll take the swab first thing in the morning."

I smile. After he came inside me, he went into total alpha-wolf mode. He swabbed my cheek with a Q-Tip and placed it in a zipped, plastic bag. Tomorrow, he'll get my parents' DNA—without their knowledge—and then he'll take it to a lab to get tested.

It was my idea to get my parents' DNA without their permission. I couldn't stand to see their disappointed faces, as if I don't trust them. That's not it at all. In the grand scheme of things, this has nothing to do with them. The test is just the way to get proof that

I'll be safe, something Jonah and his wolf urgently need before they come apart.

Male wolves do this when they first mate. When they can't be with their female counterparts, they rage. We were safe from that before tonight. Now, everything in Jonah is telling him to protect me. To be with me. Under normal circumstances, it wouldn't be so bad, but since he detects a threat, he's going to go crazy until we figure this out.

"I'll kill them," he promises. "If they try to keep you from me, I'll kill them."

I swallow the sudden dryness in my throat. "You filled out the paperwork. They should be getting that soon. We'll have answers."

"Not fast enough."

He's not listening to reason. He's human-Jonah right now but his wolf is dictating his answers. "Can I see your phone?" He narrows his gaze at my request, and I sigh. "You need help, Jonah."

I don't want to regret what we just did. I refuse to.

"You can't come into the Academy like this. You're not even supposed to come up at all."

He clenches his teeth together. "I can do it. I'll be fine."

My chest tugs, and I get the feeling he's not entirely convinced either. "I'm just going to my room and sleeping. That's it. Nothing else. I'll stay there all night. We can dream together," I tell him, wiggling my brows suggestively.

His shoulders relax a fraction.

I breathe out in relief. "You can show me more positions you'd like to try?"

"I'm not sure we're veering into a territory that's helping."

I break out into a smile. He's right. We had a hard enough time getting dressed and making it all the way to the academy. "You have my number. We have the freaky mate-connection thing. I'm right here. Always," I say, pressing my hand to his chest.

I lean forward, sealing my lips to his in a passionate yet brief kiss before pushing his door open and jumping down. Jonah hands me the bag with the ripped dress in it. I'm currently wearing an oversized t-shirt of his that's like a dress on me, just not as fashionable.

"Go home, Jonah," I tell him, shutting the truck door with him inside. I reach out and squeeze his arm and then turn to walk into the school. I use every source of strength from me and my wolf not to look back, hoping he'll do the same. Logically, we know this has to happen. I have to be here until they release me. If I stayed at Jonah's, it would make things worse.

I step inside the huge, wooden door, but instead of going straight to my room, I head toward Ms. Ebon's office. I knock lightly, but as I thought, she doesn't answer. Miraculously, the knob turns in my hand, and I immediately move toward her desk, searching for my file. I find it on top. Unsurprising, since I'm currently her only student. I flip through the varying papers to find the form Jonah filled out. My stomach bottoms out when I don't see any of his personal information on it, but luckily, in a form at the back, I find one titled Mate Pairing that has all of our personal information on it, including our parents.

I use the office phone on Ms. Ebon's desk and dial the number for his parents. "Hello?" his mother answers.

"Mrs. Livestrong, it's Kinsey."

"Kinsey, are you okay? Is Jonah okay?"

I bite my lip. "Jonah's fine, but his wolf is going all alpha, and he's having a really hard time leaving me at the academy. He needs help. He's...freaking out."

"Of course he is," she says. "Where is he right now, honey?"

"I left him down in his truck. I'm afraid he might shift and do something stupid."

"I'll go get him," I hear Johnathan say in the background.

"I'm sorry," I tell her, tears threatening my eyes. I should be down there with him. He's my mate.

She sighs. "You did the right thing, Kinsey. Jonah can't help himself, and you can't help your situation. Just relax. Deep breaths. I'm going to call my son. Are you okay to go up to your room?"

"Yeah," I choke out. "I told him I was going straight there."

"Good. Go straight there. It'll help to know that you're safe."

"Okay."

She mutters a goodbye but doesn't wait for my own. I hang up the phone and put everything back in the file before hurrying to my room, the bag with my dress and shoes bouncing against my thigh as I sprint.

I use the key to open my door and walk inside, dropping everything in my path to my bed and just flop down on it. I stay there staring at the ceiling, counting down the minutes to when I think Jonah might meet up with his father. If Jonah stayed in the truck, maybe a half hour. If he started heading home, it would be quicker. If he shifted, who knows?

Forty-five minutes later, after my eyes feel as if they're sliced open, my phone rings. I answer it right away. "Jonah?"

"It's Cindy. We have him."

I breathe out in relief when I hear his mother's voice. "Is he okay?"

"His dad's talking to him, but he's home. Can I tell him that you're okay?"

"Yes, I'm fine. I've just been worried about him."

On the other end, I hear Mrs. Livestrong report to Jonah, "Kinsey is fine. She's absolutely perfect. I'm talking to her now."

The phone muffles for a brief moment. "Mrs. Livestrong?"

"It's me," Jonah's gruff voice answers.

My heart lodges in my throat. "Are you okay? Are you mad at me?"

He chuckles softly. "No, I'm not mad. I do have you to thank for a nice bite mark on my shoulder, though."

My mouth drops. "Your dad bit you?"

"I deserved it. I wasn't thinking straight."

"Like father, like son," his mom calls out.

I smile into the phone, all the tension over the past few hours slowly draining away. My body rests—finally —against the bed.

"Call me as soon as you get up," he orders. "Other-wise, I won't promise not to show up, and we'll go Feral together."

"Jonah Livestrong," his parents scold at the same time.

I chuckle. "They weren't fans of that comment."

"They never are." He's silent for a little while until he says, "Kinsey, if it wasn't clear earlier, I love you. So if you're thrust out, I'm coming with you. I don't care about all the horror stories. We're together."

My chest expands. I squeeze my eyes shut as if I can hide away in this moment forever. Acceptance and love. What a beautiful combination. "I love you, too, but we're not going Feral." I shiver as scenes from the movie they showed us in class crawls through my mind. I steel my shoulders. I won't go down without a fight. "Get some sleep," I tell him. "I'll be here in the morning."

We hang up the phone, and I force myself off the bed to grab his shirt that I keep in my closet. I pull it over my pillow and lie my cheek against the soft material, pretending I'm sleeping with him.

If I was the same Kinsey who came here, I'd want to rip my own throat out for this, but so much has changed since then.

By not being a part of the pack, I never fully accepted my wolf, and now I embrace every part of me. Every fucked-up, needy, obsessive part. If I want to pretend I'm sleeping with my fated mate, I will.

Luckily, swimming in his shirt and using the other as a pillow helps me doze much more easily. Soon, sleep takes me, forcing me into a dreamless slumber.

Falling asleep went a lot more peacefully than being jolted awake by my door slamming open. I sit up in bed, gasping as Ms. Ebon runs into the room. Her long, black hair falls over her shoulders in disarray. "Kinsey, you have to leave. Run. Now."

"What?"

Ms. Ebon grabs my arms, shaking me. "Run!" she urges, yanking me to my feet. "Lydia ran a paternity test, and it didn't come out favorable. She's coming for you now, you need to run."

Panic grips me. My heart is in my throat. Ms. Ebon leaves me standing in the middle of the room as she marches to the window and throws it open.

"Keep running, don't look back. Don't go to Lunar."

"My paternity test?"

Ms. Ebon isn't giving in to any of my questions. "Please, Kinsey," she seethes. "Run!"

She pushes me toward the open window. My limbs shake as I crawl onto the sill. Jonah did this before—

shifted and then leapt from it, landing on all fours. I peer down at the grass below, wondering how in the hell I'm going to follow in his footsteps.

The fear in my heart forces my wolf to the forefront. She's less scared than me, twisting my torso, fracturing my bones until she's soaring through the air, landing on all four paws. She stumbles but gains her footing underneath her as she surges forward.

Breaking into a sprint, she paws at the ground, kicking up dirt and grass behind her as she races across the lawn, entering the forest. She leaps over fallen trees and dodges large trunks with a focus only known to my animal side.

When she's several miles away, her wolf hearing picks up on an alarm ringing from the school, and I can imagine it was raised by Lydia Greystone when she discovered I wasn't there.

She ran my paternity test. That bitch.

My wolf stumbles. *Run now. Think later,* she grunts, and I quiet my mind as she leads me to freedom. All I have is my animal sense of direction and instinct to go on. I don't know if they'll chase after me, but she keeps running until she needs to rest. She finds a stream that she laps hungrily from, the cool water refreshing the dryness in her throat.

She stays alert, ears perking at every sound in the

distance. Eventually, she sits back and allows me to think again. We work together as we sort through the mess in my head.

He's not my dad?

If she's telling the truth, I counter, not sure if it's wolf-me or human-me talking. There's not supposed to be a distinction, so I go with it anyway.

The adrenaline coursing through me never wavers. I left with nothing, not even my mate's shirt to crawl into. A whimper works its way up my wolf's throat. Jonah. When he finds out—

No, he said it was forever.

My wolf shakes her head, fur billowing around her. It's as if she's trying to focus my attention but I can't. My mind is everywhere.

My parents. Pressing fear threatens to take me under. My wolf gets to her feet, sniffing in both directions. I have my doubts that she can take us there, but she starts off anyway. She doesn't race through the forest this time—she jogs, staying in the dense trees even though she can hear a road in the distance. It would make life easier, but it's much more of a risk.

She runs for hours, and eventually, she picks up on that familiar pack scent. It feels a little like going into the hornet's nest, but if they've found out that my father isn't really my father, then they'll go to my parents next.

She sniffs until she singles out the scent of my childhood home and then takes off in that direction. A wolf howls in the distance, and she stumbles to the ground, the sound calling to her.

Little Mate.

Jonah's voice presses in on her, but she resists. *I can't stop now. Parents need me.*

Stay, he orders.

She whines, curling up into a ball in the middle of the forest floor.

So close, yet so far away.

*a*fter my mind quiets, I feel Jonah in my chest. I was so preoccupied with running before that I didn't notice his presence. Now, my heart beats like crazy—a frenzy of mixed emotions swirling inside. My wolf stays where she is, ears flat to her head. When he closes in on us, I hear what he's thinking.

He doesn't want me to go to my parents.

Well, fuck that. My wolf gets to her feet, shakes off the forest floor, and starts running again. They need to be warned. They have as much at stake as I do.

Kinsey!

My wolf pushes past his fierce growl that nearly buckles her legs and keeps going. I need to tell them to hide, go somewhere, just like Ms. Ebon did for me.

And I also need to hear their explanation.

I'm not theirs.

I'm. Not. Theirs.

Everything the bitchy girls at school said about me when I was younger is true. I'm not a part of the pack. I should've been cast out. Gone Feral. Made to fend for myself.

Jonah won't want me now. Our bond means nothing if I'm not allowed to be in the pack.

Pack above all else.

A howl splits the air, and my wolf loses her footing again. She shakes her head, her mane billowing out around her while she gets her paws underneath her. Alert, she scents the brisk air, then changes direction, curving inward toward my parents' house.

A thrashing behind her increases. She peeks over her shoulder to find Jonah's beautiful wolf sprinting toward her, hate in his eyes. He nips at her tail, and she scurries away.

Wait!

He lunges, and she's able to change direction to make him miss by an inch. However, she's not as lucky the second time. Jonah barrels into her side, causing them both to roll, switching dominant positions until he lands on top, baring his teeth at her.

My wolf whimpers, scratching at his chest, but he

immediately lies down, dropping his head to her body. *Please. Shift.*

He does so first, leaving himself vulnerable. Standing above her, human Jonah pleads with his eyes. He knows my wolf could quickly outrun him. She could take off this second and be in my parents' house before he had the chance to shift again.

"Please," he begs.

The vulnerability in his eyes calls to me. My wolf gives way to my human side, and I land on all fours, barely standing before Jonah wraps me in a hug. I don't return it. I'm not going to draw out this goodbye. If he can't accept me for who I am, I'm not going to continue to fool my heart another second.

He pulls back, tugging at my hair to make me look at him. "Don't you dare withdraw from me, Little Mate. You taught me fate doesn't get things wrong. I don't care who you are, you're mine. Lineage or not. Don't you see? If the legends were true, fate wouldn't have paired you with anyone, so don't you dare fucking retreat from me. You're my life. My soul."

I bite down on my lip as it starts to wobble. Tears prick my eyes, and I finally reach up and hug him. "If I'm not who I am, then who am I?"

"You're my mate, and I'm going to take care of you. That's all you need to know."

"My parents, Jonah," I rasp. "Lydia came for me. Ms. Ebon told me to run, so Lydia will go after them next. I have to warn them."

"Kinsey." He sighs. "She's searching for you. You can't even be near there. They're not going to just cast you out. She's lobbying for killing you since you're an abomination," he growls.

My heart splinters at that word from his lips. Abomination. I shake my head. Unbelievable. "Lunar Pack has it all wrong," I tell him, my tongue thick in my mouth. If wolves born from non-fated pairings are supposed to come out screwed up or worse, I shouldn't even be here. "We have to talk to my parents. We need them to tell us the story of what happened. That's the only way we'll know for sure. They love each other. My mom wouldn't have strayed. I can promise you that." Jonah wavers, his hulking shoulders and bare chest on prominent display. He keeps looking around as if a swarm of Council members are going to come from out of nowhere. "I have to," I growl.

I walk away, marching in the direction of my parents' house. The clothesline flutters with crisp linens in the beautiful backyard. My flower garden is bursting with a myriad of colors, and I can't even take the time to soak in the familiarity. I pull on one of my dad's shirts from the line and then tug free a bedsheet for Jonah. Turning, I find him striding after me like I knew he would. I offer him the sheet, and he raises his brows at it. "Nothing my family has is going to fit you. I'm sorry."

He wraps it around himself, tucking it into the front like he's walking around in a towel. "We should go in as wolves. What if it's a trap?"

The back door flies open, and Jonah shifts immediately, baring his teeth. My mom stumbles backward into my father while Jonah growls at her. She presses her hand to her chest, staring warily at me. "Kinsey?"

Jonah shuffles past them into the house in his wolf form. I move forward, wrapping my mother in a hug. My father pats my back, checking over his shoulder at the huge russet wolf prowling through our small house. I pull away immediately. I'd love the time to reconnect with them, but there's something much bigger at stake. "Lydia Greystone has done a paternity test, and she says I'm not yours." My voice breaks, and as if on cue, Jonah comes traipsing out of the house and nudges me with his head. I sink my fingers into his fur for comfort.

"Oh, Kinsey," my mom sniffles, face morphing into pained anguish. My father holds her upright, lips in a thin line. I gaze between the two of them. They both look defeated but not as if this is news to them. My father, especially, would be freaking out if he hadn't already known what I told him.

"Come inside," he beckons.

Jonah nudges me again and shakes his head. I look back at my parents. "You don't understand. Lydia Greystone is coming for me. She's petitioning to have me killed."

A growl rips from my father's throat. His body heaves, and he hunches over, but my mother grabs his face. "Hold on. We knew this might happen someday. Calm yourself. We have plans in place. Look at me."

His yellow eyes return to normal, and he breathes out deeply. He shivers until his shoulders settle, effectively shaking off the shift. "I'm good. I'm okay."

Jonah licks my palm, and I peer at him. He leads me to the clothesline, and I hold the last sheet up so he can hide his shift. When he's a fully naked human, I hand it to him so he can approach my parents with a little bit of dignity.

"Mom, Dad, you know Jonah Livestrong." They both eye him suspiciously. I grab his hand, and he squeezes. "We've mated, and—"

"I'm going to do everything in my power to make sure nothing happens to Kinsey," Jonah butts in, "but we need to know what we're up against. Time is of the essence. I wish we could've been introduced under better circumstances, but please, we need to know everything you know now."

"Lydia Greystone will have a fight on her hands if she dares step on this property," my mom snarls, her sharp teeth elongating.

My eyes round. Damn. My mom is kind of badass. I've been wondering where I got my spunk from, and apparently, she's been hiding this side of herself.

My dad grips her shoulders. "Kinsey, honey. You're mine in all the ways that matter. If I ever had to tell you this, I was hoping it would be under different circumstances. I'm sterile, Kinsey."

My heart drops. A sterile shifter? The truth kicks me upside the head. Of course. A mated pair has to bear shifters. If they don't, they're more than scrutinized. "You used someone else."

Mom nods slowly. She clenches her chest and then reaches up to grab my father's hands. "I couldn't let anything happen to him. Your dad and I are true mates, but when we figured out I couldn't conceive, we had to do something. We were desperate."

"Who's her father?" Jonah asks.

"I am," my father growls.

"Biological," Jonah mutters, grimacing. "Who's her biological father?"

Tears track down my mother's face. "He was your

father's best friend. We knew we could trust him. It's just—" she breaks off.

My father rubs her shoulders. "It's Shane Greystone."

This revelation knocks me back a few steps, and I stumble into Jonah. "The alpha's brother?"

Mom nods. "It took a few times; we didn't know if it was your father or me. Then, we were blessed with you. If I'd been the sterile one, there was no helping us. It killed your father, but we knew we had to do it to save ourselves."

"Lydia suspected something," Dad growls. "That's where the rumors started. We tried to be careful. Shane never would've said anything, but after the rude whispers, we had to stop seeing him altogether. We couldn't keep perpetuating the idea that he and your mother were together. It put all of us in danger, including him. He hadn't mated yet, of course, and then when he did in his second year post-graduation, he jumped at the chance to move to Daybreak. He couldn't stand to see what the gossip did to our family, but at least we were alive."

Jonah tucks me into his side. "Lydia can't know she's putting the Greystone name at risk."

My father scowls. "There were already some whispers about the lateness of us having a pup. Then, when we suddenly got pregnant, everything spiraled. Jacqueline's name was linked with several unmated males at the time. Shane came to see Kinsey when she was a baby, but he couldn't stay. He felt the pull to her. He was relieved to leave after he mated." Dad peers at me, lips turning down. "I want you to know I've always loved you as if you came from me. There was never any doubt that you were mine."

I know we don't have time for this—that I need to separate the imminent threat from right now—but I can't let my father keep looking at me like that. I shrug away from Jonah and move toward him, throwing my arms around his shoulders. "You did what you had to do, Dad. If you hadn't, you would both be dead. I get it. You couldn't let that happen."

"I wanted you," Dad says, voice cracking. "I wanted you so badly, Kinsey. I wanted to do everything in my power to have a pup, and you haven't disappointed. I would do anything for you." He squeezes me tighter, and I press into his chest like it's my last time. Everything is so uncertain right now.

Peeling myself away from him, I try to get myself under control. "What can we do to stop her? She'll ruin us if she makes this public."

"If she hasn't already," Jonah snaps. "We have to hope she won't want to tarnish the Greystone name."

My father's face falls. "I hate bringing Shane into this. He's so happy at Daybreak, and he already helped us once. If you have sexual relations with another person's mate, you're as much in the wrong as they are. This could—" He breaks off, his body tensing. "There's a car coming up the road. You two go."

I shake my head. "No. What will that serve? We need to stick together. We'll tell them what happened."

"Kinsey, you have the most at stake right now. Go," my dad growls. He looks at Jonah who nods.

"No."

Jonah takes my wrist. "Kinsey, they're trying to keep you alive."

"Run!" my mother urges.

The four of us sniff the air. Wolves are coming. Several by the different smells.

Jonah yanks me forward, pushing me in front of him. "Shift. Don't look back."

My heart careens in my chest. My wolf senses the danger and shifts before I even fall to my knees. Her paws sink into the grass. How many times did I fantasize about being a wolf, sunbathing in my backyard? Running with my parents.

My heart cracks in two as she takes off through the forest. Jonah nudges her backside, and she keeps running, doing as he wanted and not looking back. It feels as if I'm going to come apart.

Focus, Jonah's wolf says. *Run.*

Shoulder-to-shoulder, they sprint through the woods. He leads, zigzagging a path through the brush and trees. His beautiful brown fur matted to his body with his speed.

When we're miles away, a howl rips through the air, and my wolf stumbles until Jonah rights her again, pushing her further.

For the first time, my wolf shuts me out as I spiral. She takes the reins, and before I know it, I'm curled up in a ball inside her while she rescues us.

*W*hen I come to, Jonah's wolf is standing above my own, and I'm being thrust into human form. He shifts at the same time, gains his footing, and cradles me in his arms. "We have to go back," I keep telling him as he runs his fingers through my hair. I tighten my grip around him as the memory of that howl hits me with full force. It was one of my parents. I know it. They could be injured, or worse.

"We're not going back without a plan. Let's just think."

He rubs his thumbs under my eyes until I peer up at him. His distraught face curdles my stomach. He lowers his gaze, traveling down the very naked length of me, and I finally peer around to find we're in a huge family room in a somewhat swanky house. I cower next to him as unfamiliarity hits me with full force. My fingers sink into his biceps. He's brought me to the alpha. Or someone else higher up in the pack. Just before I can really lose my mind, he soothes my worries. "It's okay. You're safe. My family owns a bunch of safe houses around Lunar in case we need them for the alpha. We're in one. They're top secret. No one but my father and his higher-ups know their location."

I relax into him, my frazzled brain sighing in relief. It feels as if two coarse pieces of sandpaper are being ground against each other in my head. I retreated so far into my wolf that it's hard to wake up.

"There's food and water. Showers. A nice place to lay our heads. All the security we could want. I also have easy access to my father so he can keep us updated." He's talking more to himself than me, as if he's reassuring his own doubts that this was the best place to hide. He squeezes me again. "I knew I didn't want to leave you for a reason. I felt it. I should've listened to my wolf."

His behavior yesterday makes so much more sense now. His wolf was going nuts as if he could sense the danger that lie ahead. I don't even know if that's possible, but it makes me not want to second-guess him again.

"I wasn't going to let them get to you," he murmurs, staring straight into my eyes.

Of course he wouldn't. My brief moment of doubt about us was just the past coming back to bite me. I cup his cheek. "Ms. Ebon saved me. She woke me up and told me to run."

He nods. "She cares for you, Kinsey. You're not just a job to her."

I bite the inside of my cheek. Lydia must've been pissed when she got there and I wasn't in my room. "Do you think they hurt her?"

He shakes his head. "As smart as she is, I'm sure she told them you ran off."

That's partially true anyway, so that makes the most sense. "How did you know where to find me anyway?"

He tucks me under his chin and continues to rock me. His fingers comb through my tangled hair as I press into his bare chest. "You were broadcasting on high, Little Mate. I felt your fear, your panic. Then, the alpha called my father to deliver the news."

I suck in a breath. Dread shoots straight through me. If the alpha knows.... "Then it's done," I grind out. "What does it matter? If the alpha knows I'm not—"

Jonah pulls away to glare at me. "He's a Greystone, Kinsey. Not to mention that he and my dad have been friends since they were kids. He won't want this to come out either."

I try to sit up then, more alert now that I see a way out of this. "We have to call them. We have to save my parents."

Jonah clasps my face in his big, meaty hands and makes me look at him. His lips pull tight as he appraises me. "We have safety protocols in place. Trust me. I know what I'm doing. This is in my wheel-house, remember? We can't jump to conclusions. We're going to wait here for information. My father won't let anything happen if it gets to that point, okay?"

I close my eyes, breathing in deep. Panic is clawing at me from all directions, and I don't know where to put it all. It makes my brain feel like it's short circuiting. "I'm sorry. I know I'm not helping but I'm just so scared for them."

He stands and helps me to my feet. "In Lunar, when shifters are under suspicion, they're sent to the Pack Council holding facility. They'll be kept there until the situation can be sorted. There's nothing we can do at the moment. They're under our security team's watch, though, so we'll be the first to know if anything progresses." He tugs on my hand. "Come on. Let's take showers and find some clothes."

Everything he says makes sense, and I relax with the knowledge that Mr. Livestrong is in the thick of things. I walk naked through the sprawling safe house that's more luxurious than I would've imagined a safe house could be. I peek out the blinds, spotting a crystal-clear reflection in the distance through a thicket of trees. "We're at the lake?" I raise my brows. I always imagined a safe house would mean a huge room with no windows, but that's exactly opposite the case with this. It's like any of the other extravagant homes on the lake. It's well decorated, modern, and fancy. I'm not sure where all the security Jonah said the house has is, but evidently, it's hidden away somewhere.

Jonah leads me down the hallway, and we pass several well-appointed bedrooms. I glance inside as my mate gives me more insight into the alpha's security. "We purchase properties under different names so no one can trace it to the Greystone's or my family. To any of the surrounding neighbors, this house appears to be like any other rarely used family vacation home. If the alpha were to come under an attack, he could be moved between several different locations to assure his safety. Some of the safe houses are remote, others are hiding in plain sight. I brought you here because this was the closest location that wouldn't also send us straight into the middle of Lunar."

"But this is posh," I protest, still not believing that this is considered a safe house. The high ceilings are decorated with wood beams that open the space up. I'm so busy admiring the design that Jonah has to take me by the shoulders and herd me to a door on the right. A sprawling bathroom opens up with a walk-in shower that boasts two showerheads.

He smirks at me in the mirror as I glance around with my jaw practically on the floor. "The alpha likes things nice. We did a complete overhaul when we bought it."

He opens the glass door and walks in, turning on both showerheads before beckoning me forward. Despite the dried mud caked on his torso, he's a dream. His chiseled muscles flex. From head to toe, he's a perfectly cut, shifter god. I step in after him, waiting for the water to heat. "I've never seen a double shower-head before."

"Rumor has it, the alpha and his wife shower together *all* the time."

I raise my brows at him. As soon as I get lost in his brown eyes, tension crackles in the air between us. His very being calls to me, and with everything going on, I seek his warmth. His comfort that only he can provide.

He tips his head back and the shower spray rains down over his neck and shoulders, glistening down his taut muscles. "It's something I could get used to," he murmurs, watching me with a heated gaze while I step under the showerhead. My eyes close as the hot water soothes the kinks out of my muscles. I dip my head, letting the water run through my hair. It's like a balm to my soul.

"I thought I lost you," he growls. "You didn't stop when I called."

His harsh words make me jump, and I turn toward him, blinking. Rivulets stream down the sides of my face, droplets clinging to my lashes and distorting my view.

His mouth parts, and his eyes widen. "Of course. You could resist me."

I recoil. "I didn't. You brought me to my knees."

He shakes his head, a small smile coming to his lips. "You're a Greystone, Kinsey. Alpha blood."

He reaches for me, and I swat his hand away. Anger seeps through my limbs. "I'm not a Greystone." Hurt fills his eyes at my rebuff, and I groan in frustration. "I'm not one of them, okay?"

"I just meant that you have Greystone blood in you which is why you were able to partially resist my command when I was chasing you through the woods.

I thought it was because you'd distanced yourself so much that you had no allegiance to pack dynamics whatsoever. Honestly, this makes so much more sense."

If distancing myself from the pack was possible, I'd have already done it. Hell, I might even do it now. The freaking alpha's sister—who's technically my aunt—is trying to take me out. "All I wanted to do was make sure my parents were okay." Bitterness laps at me as my words settle in the air around us. Jonah purses his lips. He's right about my alpha blood, and I know he is, but I can't handle the idea of being a Greystone. The concept that people I share DNA with are trying to kill me or make me go Feral is devastating. They'll never be my true family. My parents did everything to have me. They broke the law, and most likely damn near broke each other in the process.

What my father must have gone through when my mother was with Shane Greystone.... It chills me to my core.

I've seen Jonah jealous. I've felt my own jealousy rise up. Fated mates are as primal as you can get, and my parents had to do the unthinkable to make sure they stayed alive.

"Your parents are strong," Jonah reassures me. I peek over, watching water flow down his cut body. Dirt and grime pool at his feet, slowly spiraling toward the drain.

"They did what they had to."

"And we'll do what we have to." He opens his arms, and I walk to him. He wraps me up in one of his humongous hugs—a true mate safety blanket. I settle for real because though everything feels like it's up in the air, this right here—my fated pairing—is the end and the beginning. It's what everything will start and come back to, and as long as I have Jonah, I'll be okay.

He kisses my temple before reaching behind him to grab the shampoo and squirts some in his palm before working it through my long tresses. When he finishes, he tilts my head into the spray to rinse the soap from my hair. While I stay there, he shampoos his own mane, and then we switch positions until we've both rinsed the muck of the day from us. If only I could find something that would erase the worry, too.

Plush towels sit on shelves under the sink. Jonah pulls two out and wraps me in one. The soft material feels like silk on my skin as I dry off. Afterward, he leads me out of the bathroom and down the length of the hallway. At the very end sits a master bedroom. A gigantic four-poster bed sits in the center with enough room around the sides that I could do cartwheels. Immediately, he goes to the closet and brings out two sets of clothes. "We have hundreds of these kinds of outfits lying around," he tells me, passing me a stack. "We call them shift-safe outfits. If you ruin them, it doesn't matter."

My parents had a few of those too, but nothing as nice as this. Their shift-safe outfits were paint splattered, and the kind of clothes you worked in the garden with. These are brand new.

I tug them on, frowning at the fit before I realize these were likely meant for the alpha's wife because what Jonah pulls on also fits him perfectly.

"Come here," Jonah says, beckoning me toward him. He sits on the edge of the bed, looking every bit the alpha right now with his stern, hard jaw and serious face. I walk to him, and he yanks me between his legs, pinning me there with a hard grip on my hips. "You're my family, and my family's family. We'll do everything we can, but I meant what I said yesterday. We'll leave here if we have to. I'm not letting Lydia get her hands on you."

"We can't go Feral, Jonah. We'll die."

"I'll take my chances."

"They won't kill you," I protest. "They're only after me."

The low growl that starts in his chest curls my toes.

"If they touch you, it'll kill me. When are you going to learn that?" His bite into my hips increases.

I place a steady hand on his. "I do get it. But if they hurt you, it's the same for me. If one of us can come out of this, it's you."

Before I know it, I'm flat on the mattress, and Jonah's wolf eyes lock me in place. He's still mostly in his human form, but sharp teeth have elongated past his lips, showing off his fierceness.

I don't care what he says about me being a Greystone, he's obviously the alpha in this family, and I'm just fine with that.

"Don't make me punish you, Kinsey."

I smile at that, but this is so not the place. My hand finds his chest, resting just above his heart. "Fine. I'll stop trying to save you."

He gives me a cocksure smile. "You don't have to worry about me."

He can say that, but it's not going to change my mind. Dread pools in my stomach. I feel so damn helpless. "I'm scared."

Pulling away, he moves us side-by-side and cradles me to his chest again. "Let me take care of you, Little Mate. You don't have to worry when I'm here."

He threads his fingers through my hair. Before long, the day catches up with me, and I start to doze.

I'm not used to running in my wolf form. Hell, I'm not even used to shifting yet.

In his arms, I don't have to worry about what my true lineage means for my mom and dad. Or for me. I know we'll handle it together. And with the Livestrongs completely on our side, I have more family than I've ever had.

*T*he sun's rays warm my face. For a moment, I think I'm lying in the garden, soaking up nature's energy source. But everything comes crashing down on me again when I move my arm and find the bed empty next to me.

I sit straight up, heart pounding, sniffing the air, but my surroundings are so unfamiliar that I can't sort through the different scents to find Jonah. He was so adamant about saving me yesterday that I wouldn't put it past him to run out, leave me here, and do just that. I hop out of bed, and lunge for the door. When the knob turns freely in my hand, I breathe a sigh of relief. At least he hasn't tried to lock me in here.

Stepping out into the long hallway, I pause to search for any sign of him. The house is calm; quiet.

My wolf comes to attention since she knows we're searching for Jonah, and it's the first time I've felt her since she gave up control yesterday. I let her lead the way, picking up his delicious aroma as we make our way through the foreign house. In the kitchen, I find a closed door. I turn the knob and reveal a set of steps that lead down to the basement. His scent is potent here, so I follow the footsteps and begin to relax when I hear his low murmur.

The basement is nothing like the upstairs. Instead of boasting a washer and dryer or a dank, mildewy smell like most houses, this downstairs is set up like a high-tech detective's office. Several TV monitors run footage of the house's surroundings. A locker filled with guns sits along the opposite wall, and on a corkboard to the right of that, a map of Lunar and the other pack territories is pinned down.

Jonah turns toward me, brow furrowing as I make myself known. He motions me to him, and I come closer. He places his arm around my hips while he leans against a counter, a landline phone in his hand. "When is this going to be?" he questions, staring at me but talking into the receiver.

His tone makes my wolf scratch to the surface. It's as if she's reacting to Jonah's wolf on some other level. "What's going on?" I whisper.

He squeezes my hip but ignores my question. Instead, he says, "Yeah, it's Kinsey. She just woke up." He pauses for a moment. "She's okay."

I rest my head on his chest. Being close to him helps soothe me, and I need a whole lot of that.

"We'll stay here and wait this out," Jonah remarks. My shoulders straighten. Whatever he's referencing, I don't think I'm going to like it. He grips the phone tighter. "Talk soon," he says before hanging up.

I pull away. "What's going on?"

He sits on a stool, tugging me into his embrace. "It's Lydia. She's putting your parents on trial."

I breathe out through my nose as trepidation sings through my veins. It's what we expected, but it doesn't make it any easier to hear.

"She has the DNA results in hand, so she can punish them for their transgressions."

I stare at him straight in the eye. "We can't let her do that, Jonah."

"My dad believes she's trying to draw you out of hiding. Your existence is what she's fighting against. Lydia Greystone has always been a purist. Now that she has evidence you're not from a fated pair, she'll do everything she can to stop you from mating with me and force you out of Lunar. We can't play into her hands."

I shake my head. "Jonah, their punishment won't be just a slap on the wrist. She'll cast them out of the pack. Even if by some small chance that doesn't happen, the truth will be out there for everyone. It will completely ruin them. Especially my mother. They'll make her out to be nothing. Less than nothing. If you thought the bullying at the party was bad for me, it'll be worse for her because now they have proof. She'll be ostracized more than she ever was."

Jonah presses his lips together. His eyes soften, but determination still hangs there. He won't break. His only focus is me. All he cares is that his mate is in trouble. It's his nature to protect me at all costs.

"Jonah, I love you," I tell him, reaching out to cup his cheek. "But my parents are my parents. I can't let them go down for this. There's still a chance that we can change Lydia's mind. We have to do it before she tells the whole pack. It'll devastate my parents."

"Kinsey...."

"Jonah," I snap. I'm not budging on this, and thanks to the Greystone blood, he can't make me stay. "I'm going. And if your big, brooding ass wants to protect me, you're going to have to follow."

He drops his gaze to the ground. "You're a pain in my ass."

I place my hands on his shoulders. "Well, according to your parents, that's to be expected."

He half shakes his head. "We don't know how far she's willing to go. If you show up, she might order you killed right there. She's a Greystone. She can pretty much do whatever she wants and no one will question it."

"You won't let her. *I* won't let her. I'm not going to sit back and sacrifice my parents when they've already sacrificed so much. If Lydia doesn't want the Greystone name tainted, she'll shut her mouth. It won't impact me at all to throw them under the bus."

Jonah slams a shaking hand onto the counter, and a crack splits the wood. "Fuck," he roars. After gazing at me for a long time, he picks the phone back up with a frown. "Change of plans," he states when his dad answers. "We're headed into Lunar." Jonah closes his eyes, listening to whatever his father is saying on the other end of the line.

My stomach flips. I know this is killing him. He's going against his very nature to do this for me, but this is the only way.

"Meet you there," Jonah finally says, then hangs up.

I blink at him. "Your parents are coming?"

"My father is. My mother will be home, protected,"

he emphasizes, zeroing his eyes on me. When I don't back down, he continues with a sigh. "He's hoping Lydia will see that we have support and she'll stop. It's a big if, Kinsey. We're going but you're to stay behind me at all times. No buts. I'll be in complete territorial, possessive mode, and if you don't do what I say, there's a chance I'll be the next one in trouble. Murdering a member of the alpha's family is generally frowned upon."

I touch his chest, trying to calm his wolf. "How long until we leave?"

He stands, moving me with him. "We have to hurry if we're going to catch her before the Council meeting."

Jonah sidesteps me and goes into alpha security mode. He grabs an already filled tactical bag from a shelf in the gun locker, and we make our way through the house and outside. Once there, he tells me to strip and then shoves the clothes I was wearing into the bag. "Stay in your wolf form," he orders me. "She'll protect you."

"I'm not supposed to be in my wolf form."

"That's the least of our worries, babe."

He double checks the bag as I stand there waiting for him. The sky rumbles with thunder. Over the lake, the sun still streams down as if the day is going to be beautiful, but behind Jonah, the sky grows dark and threatening, matching the tension in my body. Hopefully, the storm will blow over, the dark clouds will break apart and lose momentum, and we'll once again feel the bright sun shining down on us.

Jonah tugs me forward to kiss my forehead. "Ready?"

I nod into him, and then he steps back and shifts. He paws at the bag, and I bring it around his shoulders before shifting myself. Our wolves take off through the dense forest. Since we're at the lake, it won't take long to return to Lunar proper, but Jonah's wolf presses the pace anyway, making sure we don't miss our opportunity. He skirts the perimeter of Lunar, and when he starts running along the main road that enters the town, a black SUV pulls up alongside him. He shifts, maneuvers the bag off his shoulders and dresses inside the tree line. "Stay a wolf," he reminds me with a glare. "I'll do the talking."

My wolf pulls her lips into a snarl. He knows how I feel about this, but I also know Jonah is in that territorial part of mating, and he won't be able to stop himself if he feels I'm being threatened.

Well, he can thank the Greystones for making our introductory mating period even rockier than it would have been. I can't believe I ever used to fantasize that I was one of them. Now that it's true, it's the last thing I want.

The rear door of the SUV opens. Jonah hops in first, and my wolf follows, settling next to him. Johnathan Livestrong sits in the driver's seat. He meets my wolf's gaze in the rearview mirror and nods. His sharp jaw feathers, and like his son, he's in complete security mode. My wolf howls at the feeling of warmth and family surrounding us. I've gone from believing everyone is against me to having a select few put themselves on the line for me. I mistakenly thought the whole pack was rotten just because of a few, but I was wrong.

"We'll have to be careful," Mr. Livestrong states, locking eyes with his son.

Jonah tangles his hands in my wolf's fur. "I can't let anything happen to her."

"Understood. I'm behind you both one hundred percent. Lydia isn't dumb. She won't want to ruin the Greystone name."

My wolf growls, and Jonah scratches behind her ear. Both of us need this to be over with soon.

Mr. Livestrong smiles. "We have to get her to listen. Like the rest of that family, she's stubborn as hell." He slows the SUV as we approach the Council building. Stopping by the side of the road, he puts the car in park.

His walkie-talkie chirps, and a crackling voice comes over the line. "Lydia arriving now."

My wolf stands, tail swishing. Lydia Greystone is threatening my family, me, and my mate. My animal instinct wants retaliation. Now.

Johnathan picks up the walkie-talkie and presses a side button. "Lead her to the meeting room and watch from the outside."

Jonah lowers his voice and leans toward my wolf. "Since we run security for her as well, Dad's getting her alone so we can talk privately. None of our team knows what we're about to do."

Well, that's useful. I was envisioning us running in and having to take the guards out, but I forgot that I'm literally paired with a member of alpha security. The less people who get hurt, the better. Hope starts to build inside me, and my wolf's tongue lolls out of her mouth in anticipation.

Mr. Livestrong pops the rear door open. "Five minutes," he says to Jonah.

My mate nods, then hops out. My wolf follows after him, and they make their way into the tree line. Instead of shifting like I assumed he would, he leads her further into the woods. He jumps down an embankment, moves some branches, and uncovers a steel door hidden in a rock wall. He grins over his shoulder. "Emergency exit for the alpha. It leads straight to a secret door in the meeting room."

Holy shit. Did he and his father figure all this out when they were on the phone earlier? I'm impressed.

The tunnel has a dank, dirt floor with concrete walls and ceilings. Jonah jogs down it, and my wolf is on his heels. They get to a wooden door, and Jonah holds his ear to it. With my sensitive wolf hearing, I can tell it's quiet on the other side until hinges creak and voices rise up. One of them is most definitely Johnathan Livestrong's while the other has to be Lydia.

Jonah peers down with a strained face. His muscles ripple as if he's one step away from turning. "Please," he begs, "stay behind me."

My wolf nods, stomach in knots, and he pushes the secret door open. She slips out after him, sticking to his side like he said.

Lydia turns, jumping at our intrusion. When she sees Jonah and then finds my wolf at his hip, she growls, fur rippling down her arms. "What is this?"

Jonah's dad reaches his arms out in a placating gesture. "Calm yourself, Lydia. We're here to talk."

She sneers, backing into the desk. Her gaze darts

around at the three intruders until she focuses on my wolf. "You are a shame to our race."

A snarl rips from my wolf's throat.

Jonah moves in front of her. "You will speak to my mate with respect."

"She threatens your line, and yet you would stick up for her?" She turns from Jonah to Johnathan. "And you're backing him? Johnathan, you must show your son that this isn't the way. Her family tricked fate. She needs to leave, if not more. That will be for the Council to decide."

Jonah snaps, his fingers tightening into my wolf's nape. Fur ripples over his arms; his teeth elongate. I can smell how close his wolf is to the surface, and my wolf practically paws at the floor in anticipation, ready to take this bitch out. If it weren't for Jonah's steady hand on her nape, she would've already lunged.

"Calm yourself, Lydia," Johnathan barks. "He's full territorial, and you're bound to get yourself killed. We came here to talk. Not to fight."

"There's nothing to discuss. All you've done is further ruined your family's reputation. How dare you confront someone in the alpha's bloodline like this?"

I nudge Jonah to get him to talk. He studies me, his eyes a wolfy yellow before he peers back at her. "How dare you threaten one of your own?"

Lydia glowers. Her breathing deepens. A sickening feeling in my stomach tells me there's about to be a fight. Jonah won't be able to hold back if I'm threatened. I'm muzzled in my wolf form, and if I shift, Jonah will go apeshit, and we'll have even more to deal with.

"She's a Greystone, Lydia," Johnathan finally announces. "You have the proof that she's not from a mated pair, but how easy will it be to prove she's a Greystone? Think about what this scandal will do to your family."

Her wolf retreats, and she throws her head back, her musical laugher threading through the room. The hair on my wolf's nape stands. I can't believe I'm related to this woman. We couldn't be more different.

"You laugh," Jonah warns, "but we know it to be true. We'll get the necessary tests to prove it."

"I don't need to know who she belongs to. All I need to know is that she shouldn't exist."

"Think about it," Johnathan commands. "She paired with my son. They're true mates. If Kinsey was from a family lower in the pack, by all accounts of what we think we know about pairings, that shouldn't have happened."

I growl at that, but it does work in my favor so there's not much I can really say. Mating with Jonah proves more than one of my pack's theories wrong. Since I didn't come from a fated pairing, I shouldn't have been able to mate with anyone. I knew that everything we were ever told is wrong. Whether the pack knows it's wrong is yet to be seen. They could be perpetuating the lie for their own purposes. Even Jonah said that Lydia was a purist. Maybe their family wants to keep the blood lines pure by all means necessary?

"What I know," Lydia hisses, "is that her mother went outside her bond. She'll be punished to the fullest extent, and this mutt will be cast out where she should've been all along."

"You will not touch her," Jonah growls.

The door bursts open, and my wolf springs to attention. Time slows. A man wearing the Livestrong family crest enters the room, surveying it, and when his gaze settles on me, he raises his weapon and fires.

The bullet hits my left flank, and my wolf howls, falling to the ground in a blitz of pain. Jonah shifts in the blink of an eye and lunges for the man. His father intercepts, tackling his son's wolf to the ground in a bear hug and then wraps his strong legs around its torso, locking him in place.

A swarm of men enter the room and surround us. My wolf attempts to scramble to her feet, but the pain in her side flares, and she ends up sprawling out with a whimper.

Lydia sneers. "Get her."

Jonah and I catch one another's gazes, and in that few seconds, I feel the power of losing him. A howl bursts from his russet muzzle. It echoes around the room, slides through me, and sits in my chest as it cracks.

29

*J*onah struggles against his father's grip, clawing and pawing. He's crazed, maniacal, begging to be released. A careening cry crawls up my wolf's throat that makes him howl in response.

Blood seeps through gashes in his father's shirt and shoulders, but Jonah doesn't stop fighting. Johnathan's face is filled with agony and love as he holds his son down, and the only thing me or my wolf can feel is relief. If he'd lunged and taken out anyone in this room, it would be over for him. Murder is murder, no matter if it's over your fated mate or not.

The same man who shot my wolf walks forward, and she shimmies out of his way, but her injured leg won't move. The pain is bearable, though—most likely due to the adrenaline coursing through her. "Take her to the cell!" Lydia orders. "Johnathan, get your son out of here, and I expect you to deal with this before I get really angry."

My wolf growls. The man closest to her bends down to grab her by the nape, but she snaps at him, taking the tip of his finger off. His eyes turn wolf, and a rumble starts in his chest, but she snarls right back, yapping with a ferocity that scares even me. The man backs away, head bowing.

Holy fuck. He's submitting.

She does it again until he withdraws all the way. Chaos ensues, and she again tries to get to her feet. Lydia barks more orders, telling more of Johnathan's men who've entered to shoot me, but my wolf scrambles to all fours and lunges at Lydia, propelling off the table between them, aiming right for her shoulder. More weapons fire, and another ripping agony hits the same flank but my wolf bears down, growling in her face.

Internally, I'm screaming at her. I'm telling her the whole story. Everything that my wolf can't voice, I'm telling her in my head. *I am a Greystone. My mother did what she did to save her mate. Shane is my biological father.*

Lydia's eyes bulge out of her head as I snap at

her jaw.

Gripping my front legs to steady my wolf, she stares deep into her gaze. Lydia's lips curl. True fear settles over her. "Leave the room! Everyone!" she calls out before shifting underneath me.

Lydia rolls my wolf to her back, and wrestles with her, each of them trying to gain the upper hand until they break apart and face each other, snapping and growling.

Her pure black wolf circles mine, and my wolf stays alert. The meeting room door closes, leaving Jonah and his dad, who are still locked in a battle, the only other two people left in the room.

She snarls. *I am a Greystone.*

Her voice sounds in my head. I'm taken aback at first but fuck, it makes sense. We're *both* Greystones, so we can communicate in our shifter forms. I growl right back at her. Her wolf's look and demeanor—everything —appears as if she's trying to make me submit but I muster all the power I have inside me and resist the urge to bow to her.

I am Greystone.

Lydia's wolf's ears shift straight up, straining. Right away, her stature changes. Her squinty wolf eyes loom closer. My wolf backs up, not trusting the sudden dip of aggression in the air.

Pain still emanates from our two wounds, but she's already feeling better. Stories I've been told all my life are starting to make sense. I haven't been injured while a wolf since this form is new to me, but it's well known that shifters heal better when we're our animal selves. Even so, this healing is impressively fast.

You can hear me.

My wolf growls again. Lydia has backed her into the wall, and she gets antsy, searching for a way to get around her or move through her.

As she comes closer, my wolf starts to pant, effectively freaking out. The blue of Lydia's wolf eyes darken before her whole gaze widens in surprise as she peers into my wolf's. It's such a human gesture in a wolf that it throws me off guard.

Shane? her voice asks in my head.

My wolf starts forward, walking her back. *He was my father's best friend. He and my mother saved my father because he's sterile. Your brother offered to procreate with my mother so they could have me. I* am *a Greystone. You already know it's true.*

She sits, lifting her muzzle in the air, her proud wolf features as aloof as her human side is.

341

You will not hurt my family, I continue. *It won't be hard to prove to everyone else that I'm a Greystone. Jonah already has the DNA samples. If you move forward with your plan, you will regret it.*

Her lip lifts in a snarl. *Shane is stupid.*

That doesn't make him any less my biological father.

Our silent conversation works. She's backing down just as Johnathan thought she would.

"We can forget this all right now," Johnathan negotiates, voice strained. "No one will know what happened. Keeping this secret is in the interest of both parties, Lydia. All you have to do is tell the Council that the DNA test was wrong. This won't have been the first time that the Greystones have done something to save each other."

A warning hum emanates from Lydia's chest. I can hear the threat in her tone, but I also understand her because the same blood runs through our veins. My stomach flips over in disgust, but in essence, that fact may have just saved me. She knows who I am. She can't deny me because she feels it as I do. We may both resent it, but it doesn't make it any less true.

She shifts, her wolf's back arching before landing on all fours, and I see way more of Lydia Greystone than I ever wanted. "To be clear, you are no family of mine. You're an abomination."

The once subdued Jonah growls, and his father returns the sentiment.

"However," she says, speaking over them. "Keeping this secret does seem to be in everyone's best interest. During my meeting with the Council, I will be telling them that the initial tests were wrong. As long as you keep your story to yourself, I will keep mine."

I want to shift and talk to her but being completely naked in front of my mate's father is not on my list of things to do today. She shifted on purpose so she could get the last word. Thankfully, Johnathan speaks up. "You have their word as long as you keep yours. Nothing will happen to the Walkers, and they will be cleared of all charges. Nothing will happen to them in the future either. Put this to bed for good, Lydia."

She nods once. "And Kinsey will never try to gain any sort of importance from the Greystone line."

My wolf growls, the sound ripping from her throat. *I don't want anything to do with the fucking Greystones!*

Johnathan speaks for me. "I assure you, she has no interest in becoming a member of your family."

Lydia narrows her gaze as if she doesn't believe him. Let her believe what she wants. Through my eyes, her family is what's wrong with wolf society. I have no desire to be family with someone who thinks there should be a pack hierarchy, who keeps wolves locked away in the Rejected Mates Academy every day because they believe they know better than fate.

No, despite what I fantasized when I was little, I have no intention of becoming a Greystone.

"Kinsey," Johnathan calls for me.

My wolf peers over at him, zeroing in on his torn shirt and bloody scratches.

"Come to Jonah so he will calm down. Please."

She moves toward him, giving Lydia a wide berth as if she still might try to take us out.

Johnathan strokes his son's fur. "See that, she's not even limping." Interestingly enough, he's correct. Johnathan smiles at my wolf as she gets closer. "Must be the Greystone blood."

Lydia scoffs, but fuck her. I don't like the idea either.

When my wolf is within reach of Jonah's, he nuzzles her. She returns the sentiment, and Johnathan whispers for us to leave. He keeps a secure hold on his son as he opens the secret door and then nudges us both out. Jonah turns around once we're in the tunnel, and Johnathan, standing there in a ripped shirt with healing injuries, nods.

Jonah whines. The light in the tunnel fades as his father closes the door on us. My wolf's superior vision kicks in, allowing me to see. He places his paw over my wolf's shoulder, sniffing her. He nudges the leg she got shot twice in, but she barely feels anything except a numb sort of pain. It's a nuisance more than anything else.

We amble toward the exit. Slowly but surely, light from the entrance comes into view. My wolf follows his out, and he shifts into his human form so he can close the door, locking away the Council and Lydia Greystone.

Finally, I can breathe easier.

I MAKE JONAH WAIT WITH ME BY THE COUNCIL building until my parents are released. Once we physically see them leave with Johnathan Livestrong, I truly let reality sink in. Everything actually turned out the way it should have. My parents will no longer be targeted as the "evidence" came back in their favor, the Council now has no reason to stop me from leaving Greystone Academy, and Jonah and I can finally start our lives together.

Jonah nuzzles me, and we start toward my parents'

house, following the black SUV carrying them inside. The weight lifted off my shoulders practically makes me fly all the way there. Jonah is hot on my heels, nipping and swatting at me playfully.

Maybe it isn't so bad being a Lunar Pack shifter.

30

The echoing footsteps of Ms. Ebon's heels off the academy's floor reminds me of my first night here. Suddenly, I wish I'd allowed Jonah to come in with me, but when she stepped out of the front doors when we arrived, lifting an arched brow as we sat in his idling car, I knew this was something I had to do alone.

Also, I can't complain since he's pretending to go home, but he's actually going to meet me in my room. He can't bring himself to leave me right now.

The academy halls are empty, and even though everything is settled on the Lydia Greystone front, my stomach twists just walking back in here. In front of me, Ms. Ebon swings open her office door and strides inside. She's been quiet the entire trip down the hallway, and I suddenly feel like I'm in so much trouble. I follow her, the office more stifling than I remember it. The huge door closes, and Ms. Ebon spins on her heels to face me.

Except, this isn't the Ms. Ebon I'm used to. Her eyes are glassy. Dark circles sit heavy under her lashes as she studies me. I'm a little banged up, limping slightly from the injuries but since I was shot with a freaking gun and am somehow still able to move, I call that a win.

"What happened?"

Her voice is full of so much emotion that I almost collapse. It's been hours of crying and talking with my parents. Then, Jonah's mother showed up, and it was more crying and talking. I thought I was rid of every single tear in me, but my eyes heat again.

I can trust Ms. Ebon, but in order to keep my promise to Lydia Greystone, I can't tell her the truth. "The paternity test was wrong," I state, voice cracking a little with the lie.

She tilts her head to the side. "So I heard. Your parents are free."

I nod slowly. "My parents are free, and since there's no longer any objection to my lineage, I'll be able to leave with Jonah as soon as the Council meets about my release. You have another satisfactory case."

I smile, and she returns it, wiping at her eyes. "Somehow, I believe you're the one who fixed everything. Well, you and your mate, of course."

She has no idea who was all involved. Even as I think about it, I can hardly believe it. Jonah's parents really rallied behind us. I'm not sure what will happen to the security guy who shot me, but he didn't know any better. If it weren't for the fact that we were trying to keep it quiet from everyone, his team would've been behind us, too. At least that's what Johnathan was trying to get through to Jonah so he wouldn't find the guy and rip his head off.

A shiver runs up my spine.

"I'm glad it's over with," I tell her, hoping that's enough to satisfy her.

She narrows her gaze, nodding. I make a silent wish that she won't push the issue. I owe Ms. Ebon a lot. Lying to her seems wrong.

"I've never seen Lydia Greystone so furious."

I clear my throat. "She was...unhappy," I tell her, keeping up my vague pretense.

"You know, it's odd," Ms. Ebon says, moving to her desk and tapping my file that's still sitting on top. "I always knew you were strong. The first day you were here, you were able to disobey a direct order." She studies me, stare slicing through my outer walls as if she can read straight through to my DNA. "I bet Lydia didn't like how strong you are."

I swallow the thickness in my throat. Ms. Ebon's absolutely correct. She ordered me to stop shifting right here in this office, and I didn't. I fret over my lip. She either knows or has an inkling of who I really am. "She really didn't like it," I confirm. "I'm glad it's over with so Jonah and I can move past this." Before she can question me further, I ask, "Do you know how long it might take to get me out of here?"

My advisor throws her head back and laughs. The sound is so light compared to her usual severe expressions. "I'll push for the Council to review the paperwork tomorrow. I'm sure with the correct paternity information and Jonah's write-up, they will have no qualms about you leaving Greystone." She gives me a smile. "What will you do?"

Honestly, I just want to go to Jonah's house for a good, solid month and acquaint myself with my wolf, my mate, and my new family. We might *have* to do that while Jonah goes through his territorial state, but then, I don't know. I guess I can do whatever I want. "I'm not sure, but I love that I actually have a choice." I approach her desk, letting my fingertips skate along the edge. "What do you really think about Greystone Academy, Ms. Ebon?"

It's my advisor's turn to look as if she's trying to skirt around the truth. Her brow furrows, and her lips thin. "Miss Walker, I'm in the business of returning mates to each other. It seems barbaric, but when societal norms can't be dismantled, we all have to do the best we can."

My heart clenches. The shifters at Greystone Academy are lucky to have someone like her because every single person here doesn't deserve it. What happened to free will? What happened to fate? "I wish I could do something about that," I muse.

"We all find our role in things," Ms. Ebon states. "When you're ready, you'll find yours." She nods toward the door. "Now, you better get to your room before your mate destroys it."

My mouth drops, and then a slow smile curves my lips as she winks at me. I reach the door and stop with my hand on the knob before turning around. "Thank you, Ms. Ebon. I may think this place is a bunch of bullshit, but you helped bring Jonah and me together, and I'll never forget that." Her eyes glass over again, and she nods. I start to leave but remember one more thing. "My friend from Daybreak? Mia? She could really use some help with her mate. He's a bit of an asshole."

She frets over her lip. "I'm aware of her situation. She's one of our students who's been here the longest."

My heart pangs painfully. "She's a good person. I hate to leave her. It's not right that she can't get out of here because he's wrapped up in someone else."

She glances at me apologetically. "Our society demands—"

"I know, I know."

"Maybe you've found your calling after all, Kinsey. Why don't you use your newfound *power* to try to make a difference?"

I rub the back of my neck with my free hand. I'd love to use this Greystone DNA to change things, but unfortunately, I've muzzled myself for the foreseeable future. No one will listen to me as Kinsey Walker, and I can't come out as a relation to the alpha's bloodline because that will out my mother. "Maybe one day," I tell her, wishing it could be now, half cursing myself that I entered into that agreement in the first place. But when I close my eyes and see how my parents hugged while we were standing in the house, I know I did the right thing.

"I'm sure you'll figure it out," Ms. Ebon hedges. "Goodbye, Kinsey. I'll make sure you're the first to know as soon as you're able to leave."

"Bye, Ms. Ebon."

Finally, I tug the heavy door open and slip out into the hallway. My mind is freer than when I first found myself here. I had my misgivings about Ms. Ebon, but she's actually one of the good ones.

I take the stone steps up to the Daybreak and Lunar floor two at a time. When I come around the corner, Mia pushes off the wall, staring at me in wonder. "There's a very naked mate in your room."

I laugh at her grimaced expression, walking up to her and throwing my arms around her shoulders, squeezing. At nineteen years old, she was my first friend, and she's a damn good one, too. "Thank you for being so nice to me."

She sighs. "I guess this means you're leaving, huh? There were a bunch of rumors about why Lydia Greystone showed up at the academy yesterday."

I pull away from her, shaking my head. "Shit got scary for a bit."

"But you're okay now? Do you need chocolate?"

I grin. "I'm okay now. I'll be leaving as soon as my Pack Council meets and allows me to."

She glances toward my door. "And your mate is in your room because?"

I stifle a laugh. "Because he's full-blown territorial right now."

"So, that's the reason he snapped at Nathan, then?"

I gasp. "He didn't!"

Mia makes her eyes round and nods. "He did. Jumped right into your room in his wolf form and went ballistic. He shifted and apologized, but I'm pretty sure Nathan has PTSD."

My head falls to the side as I regard her. "You guys were waiting for me?"

"We were worried."

I wrap my arms around her again. "Is there a way we can keep in touch when I go? Phone? Visits?"

She tightens her grip around me, too. "You better keep in touch. Think how bad it would look for you if you lost your first and only friend."

I chuckle. "Yeah, this is all for show. Nothing else."

"Naturally," she says, pulling way. She stares at the floor. "I'll let you get back to your mate. You'll let me know before you leave?"

"Of course."

She takes off, shoulders rigid. I watch her all the way down the hall until she turns into her room. She doesn't look back once, and I can't blame her. She's one of the longest running students here, and I'm sure it doesn't matter that she likes me, she probably hates me a little right now, too.

I hate the whole system for what it's done to her.

With a deep breath, I open the door. Jonah pulls the sheets over his naked torso as he sits on the edge of the bed. When he sees it's me, he stands, and the fabric falls to the floor. "I just wanted to make sure it was you."

"Yeah, Mia left, and I heard Nathan left before that?" I raise a brow, waiting for his excuse.

He shrugs. "There was an altercation, but it ended quickly." His smirking face tells me he's actually pretty proud of himself for whatever went down.

I shake my head. "You're something else."

"No, *you* are something else, Little Mate." He closes his arms around me and drags me toward him, pressing me against his hard ridges. I'm liking being up close and personal with Jonah's nakedness whenever I want. I can't see ever tiring of it.

I jump, closing my legs around his hips and sliding my arms across his shoulders. Threading my fingers through his hair, I smile. His eyes glaze over as he stares at me with so much love that my heart might actually burst from it. "How much time do you think we have before they let me out?"

"At least until tomorrow." He rocks into me, the full length of his erection sliding between my legs.

"And if I don't go to class, they can't kick me out, right?"

He turns and lowers us to the bed. "You don't have to go to class here ever again," he growls.

My thighs clench at his promise. So far, he's fulfilled every single one he's made me. He kept me safe. I'm leaving the Academy. And when we do escape this place, we'll be going to his cottage in the woods.

He places his lips on mine, kissing me slowly, taking his time exploring my mouth when I open for him. Fate knew what she was doing when she mated Jonah and me. Right now, she's probably looking down on us and thinking *It's about fucking time*.

I couldn't agree more.

EPILOGUE

The sun shines on my dirty hands, warming them through my worn gardening gloves. I use the spade to free some posies from the dirt and repot them in white ceramic.

A shadow falls over me, and I lean backward, peering up at my hulking mate who's blocking out all my sun. "Hey."

He grins down at me. "You need help moving these out front?"

"Yeah, the posies bloomed, and I know people have been asking for them. Your mom's going to go nuts." I smile at the thought of my most enthusiastic client. She single-handedly helped me get my little business off the ground.

He runs his fingers through my hair and kneels next to me. "She's so proud of you."

Cindy has become like a second mother. With all the rumors squashed, my parents are welcome at parties again, which the Livestrong's orchestrated. By their acceptance, the other Lunar couples were happy to see them return.

"Wasn't Lee's wife also wanting posies for her front yard? I'll have to take some to work tomorrow."

I stand, brushing my hands on my gardening pants. "We'll set one aside." Reaching in, I pick a white pot up and carry it in my arms as Jonah steers the wheelbarrow toward the road. His parents sold us half their property a month ago, and we plan on reinvesting the profits of my roadside stand into building greenhouses off the path that leads to our little cottage.

I watch Jonah as he steers, his bulky muscles poking out from under his short-sleeved, black shirt that boasts the Livestrong Security logo. "You'll get dirty," I warn.

"When has that ever stopped me?"

I bump into his shoulder, and he beams at me again, his brown hair reflecting the sun's strong rays. Despite our rocky start, Jonah is the perfect mate. Bonding to another shifter so completely is everything they've ever told me and more. I cringe about all those times I wished I wouldn't bond with anyone because I can't imagine never having *this* in my life. Someone who loves fully and openly, and who accepts me and my flaws like they're his own. Our love comes as easy as breathing; as easy as the flowers that blossom in the sun.

I don't pretend to believe it's all fate, though. Jonah and I are so wonderfully matched that it can't possibly be all nature. It took some nurture, too.

"Dad thinks it's time that I start at the security business full time."

"Yeah?" I grin. Jonah's been waiting for this. Brixton isn't his thing. "That's great."

He sets the wheelbarrow down, and we line the flower pots up in the spot I cleared earlier. A car pulls over while we're working, and I sell a whole flat of petunias before turning to Jonah. He's sitting on the table, feet dangling over the ground, and watching me with a soft expression.

I stride toward him and pop up on my toes to brush my lips over his. "I'm so proud of you."

He cups my head, deepening the kiss in the way only my possessive mate can. It turns out, he never really got past that territorial phase, but that's fine by me. In my mind, I feel all his emotions. They ricochet through me, and I send them straight back to him.

He's so proud to be able to provide for us. Full-time work at Livestrong Security means full-time pay, and with my growing side business, we'll be doing just fine. He purrs in the back of his throat. "We'll be able to get those greenhouses up by next summer."

I bite my lip, toes curling in my shoes. Before, I never allowed myself to actually think about what I wanted. I was just trying to avoid people and going Feral. Once I opened myself up, the answer became clear. I haven't set foot in an academy since I left Greystone. I never even attempted to go to Brixton. It's not what I want.

What I want is this right here. My mate. My flowers. And one day, maybe some pups running around. But dear lord, I still have to have a talk with Jonah's mom about birthing shifters the size of the Livestrong's breed out of me. That might change my mind.

Jonah squeezes my hips and yanks me to him. His face is flushed, eyes drilling into me. He must have picked up on my thoughts. "Yes," he growls, scanning my length. "All of it. The life. The babies. *You.*" He jumps from the table and throws me over his shoulder. I squeal in mock protest, but in actuality, this might be my favorite thing about Jonah. Molten heat pools in my core, and my thighs shake in anticipation.

With one strong arm around me, he runs back to the house so we can start working on our happily ever after.

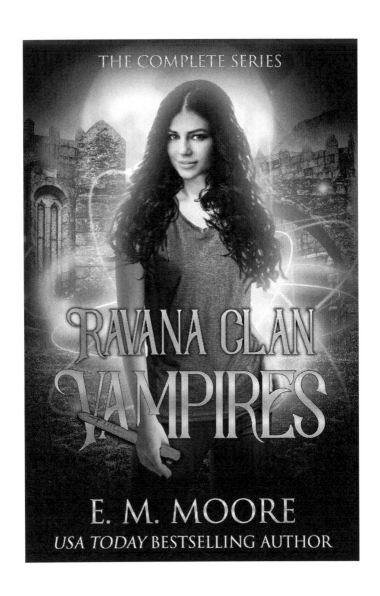

THE COMPLETE SERIES

RAVANA CLAN
VAMPIRES

E. M. MOORE
USA TODAY BESTSELLING AUTHOR

ORDER OF THE AKASHA | BOOK 1

SUMMONED BY MAGIC

E. M. MOORE

USA TODAY BESTSELLING AUTHOR

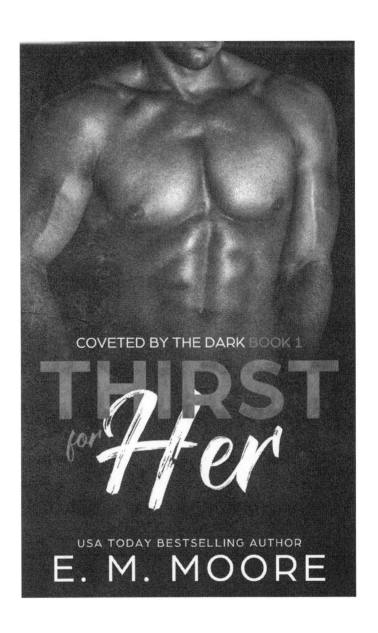

COVETED BY THE DARK BOOK 1

THIRST
for Her

USA TODAY BESTSELLING AUTHOR
E. M. MOORE

About the Author

E. M. Moore is a USA Today Bestselling author of Contemporary and Paranormal Romance. She's drawn to write within the teen and college-aged years where her characters get knocked on their asses, torn inside out, and put back together again by their first loves. Whether it's in a fantastical setting where human guards protect the creatures of the night or a realistic high school backdrop where social cliques rule the halls, the emotions are the same. Dark. Twisty. Angsty. Raw.

When Erin's not writing, you can find her dreaming up vacations for her family, watching murder mystery shows, or dancing in her kitchen while she pretends to cook.

Printed in Great Britain
by Amazon